"Husband and wife con artists mus scheme goes spectacularly wrong in this criminally good debut by King.... Surrounding them is a cast of superbly sketched characters whose competing motives constantly trip up their plans.... With a story every bit as intricate and entertaining as the personalities who fill it, King's uncommonly solid debut is a must-read." —*Kirkus Reviews*

"Loved the story, loved the characters, loved the con, loved the feel of the crime. *The Traveling Man* is a great first novel. Michael P. King is a writer to watch."—Charles L. P. Silet (author of *Talking Murder*)

Married con artists, using the aliases Tom and Patty Brown, arrive in the small city of Seanboro with their partner, Buddy Ray, masquerading as land speculators. Their plan is to falsify the environmental reports on a contaminated tract of lakefront property and sell the land to a local gangster who is involved in real estate development. But as their plan progresses, and the double-crosses pile up, they find themselves pursued by their now ex-partner Buddy, seeking revenge, and by an old enemy plotting their murder. *The Traveling Man* is a dark crime thriller that will take you for a roller coaster ride.

THE TRAVELING MAN

THE TRAVELERS: BOOK ONE

MICHAEL P. KING

BLURRED LINES PRESS

Blurred Lines Press

The Traveling Man

Michael P. King

ISBN 978-0-9861796-2-4

The Traveling Man is a work of fiction. The names, characters, places, and events are products of the author's imagination or are used fictitiously. Any similarity to real persons or places is entirely coincidental.

For Sarah, who makes the life I live possible, all my love.

PART I

THE LAND GRAB

1

SETTING THE SCAM

The Traveling Man, a con man currently going by the name Tom Brown, turned off the highway west of Seanboro onto the limestone gravel driveway marked by the bright red mailbox. At the end of the driveway sat a peeling, brown and white ranch-style house under a half-dead elm tree. He parked in front of the garage and got out of his black Cadillac Escalade, his leather briefcase tucked under his arm. For this job, he wore neatly barbered gray-black hair with a closely trimmed beard, fake horn-rimmed glasses, and a charcoal pinstripe suit. He stood by the car for a moment to collect himself. The morning sun was hot for September, and the air felt thick with pollen, but he took a deep breath anyway and exhaled slowly, falling into his role of land speculator, getting ready to play his part, before he walked across the gravel to the front door and rang the bell. An old man with red-gray hair thatched over a white, jowly face answered the door.

"Mr. Yost?" Tom asked.

The old fat man nodded his head. He had one hand on the door-jamb and the other hand on the doorknob.

"I'm Tom Brown. I spoke with you on the phone. Me and my

associates are interested in the property you own on White Bear Lake."

The old man laughed. "I thought it was some kind of prank call."

Tom shook his head. "I assure you, Mr. Yost, that we are very serious."

Yost turned his head back into the room. "Mary," he yelled. "That fella is here about the property."

"Really?" she called back. "Well, the house is a mess. Go out to the picnic table."

Yost turned back to Tom. "Meet me at the garage."

The garage door went up. Inside, the garage was decorated like a porch. The room was paneled with vertical knotty pine boards. White curtains hung in the windows. In the middle of the room was a green wood picnic table that could have come from a city park. Two metal-framed folding chairs with a small white table between them sat to the left near the front opening. Yost hobbled down the steps from the house and indicted the picnic table with a wave of his arm. Tom sat down on one side. Yost eased himself down on the other side, gripping the table and grunting as he lowered himself. Mary Yost, stoop shouldered and white haired, shuffled out of the house. The screen door slammed behind her. She wore a button-up housedress with matching slippers and was carrying two glasses of ice tea. She set the glasses on the picnic table and sat down next to her husband. "Tea?"

Tom smiled. "Thank you, ma'am."

She nodded. "Garage is still cool."

Tom could feel the sweat at the back of his neck. "Yes, ma'am."

Yost took the other glass in both hands, took a sip, and set it down. "So what is this nonsense about the lake property?"

"As I said on the phone, I believe we can broker that property for you."

"Young fella, let me review the facts for you. My grandpa farmed that land, did well, but he and my pa didn't get along—"

"Too much alike," Mrs. Yost said.

"Too much alike. So when Grandpa retired, he leased it to the Air Force. That was in about 1950. They used it for Cold War training—

you know, secret hush-hush stuff. Congress put it on a decommission list about ten year back. After the Air Force left, we lost our income. Developers had big plans, especially for the lakefront. We put all our money in. Then some environmental folks said the land was contaminated, so we went after the Air Force for a cleanup."

Mrs. Yost cut in. "Air Force said the land was fine."

Yost nodded. "Judge ruled with them. So we should have had a happy ending, right?"

Tom nodded. "I know all this."

Yost continued. "But the county said, 'No, the paper says it's contaminated, dangerous to people, you cannot build.'"

Mrs. Yost continued. "We borrowed to fight the county, but it didn't do any good. Had to sell the big house to pay off the loans."

Yost looked Tom in the eyes, a big frown on his face. "So you're wasting your time."

Tom took a sip of tea. "Mr. and Mrs. Yost, me and my partners know your situation intimately. We studied everything in the public record. We believe we can overturn the county's previous ruling and get your property developed."

"We don't have any money."

"You don't need any money. Right now you've got nothing."

"Worse than nothing." Mrs. Yost chimed in. "We've got tax liability."

"Exactly," Tom continued. "We'll do whatever it takes: overturn the county, find a developer, get the legal paperwork done. In exchange, we take fifty percent on the sale of the land."

"Fifty percent?"

"We do all the work and pay all our expenses out of our half. All you have to do is sign this paper." Tom took a contract out of his briefcase. "It says that we have the sole right to act on your behalf in the sale of the lake property, that we pay all expenses—all of them—and that we receive fifty percent of the sale."

"Fifty percent is mighty high."

"We're taking all the risk. This is an expensive proposition."

Mrs. Yost glanced at her husband. "Right now we've got nothing."

Yost ground his teeth. "We should run this by our lawyer."

Tom shook his head. "This only works if it's all kept secret. Word gets out and enviro nuts start harping. I'll be honest with you: I can't guarantee you'll actually get what the land should be worth. I can just guarantee that you'll get as much as it's possible to get."

"As much as it's possible to get." The Yosts held hands.

"Give us a minute to read this contract." Yost took a pair of wire-rimmed glasses out of his shirt pocket, slipped them on, and started reading the contract, his finger moving along under the text while his lips moved. Mrs. Yost followed along over his shoulder, squinting while she read.

Tom sat back and sipped his tea. The sun was slanting into the garage and he could feel the sweat running down from his armpits. He got out his handkerchief to mop his brow. He hoped he hadn't sold them too hard.

The Yosts looked up almost at the same time and turned to each other. Mrs. Yost nodded her head slightly. Yost turned to Tom. "Okay, we'll sign. I'm just warning you that you're throwing your money away."

Tom handed him a pen. "We'll take that chance."

By LUNCHTIME, Tom was sitting in a booth at the Superior Diner with his wife, currently going by the name of Patty, and their partner Buddy Ray. Patty was forty-two, but even carnies misguessed her to be five years younger. She was thin and willowy, with her dark hair cut short in a way that made her eyes and mouth seem more childlike. Today she was wearing a black skirt suit with a triple-strand gold necklace. Buddy, who sat across from them, was thirty years old. He was blond, heavily muscled, and wore a black crewneck shirt with a pair of khaki pants. Tom cut off a piece of his meatloaf, pushed some mashed potatoes on top of it, forked it into his mouth, and washed it down with a sip of iced tea. "So, the first step is taken care of. We are the sole representatives of Mary and Phillip Yost."

Patty picked at her salad. "And now we assemble the pieces of the puzzle."

Buddy set his half-eaten hamburger down on his plate and picked up a French fry. "I still can't believe we're going with the fifty-fifty split."

"There's plenty of money on this job. We'll take two hundred and fifty thousand, if it all goes to plan," Tom said.

"That's beside the point. We shouldn't leave any money on the table. We should always scrape up everything we can. You taught me that."

"Yeah. I also taught you not to get caught. The idea is to make this score look legit. It doesn't pass the smell test if we cheat the Yosts."

Buddy dabbed his French fry in the ketchup on the edge of his plate. Patty looked from Tom to Buddy. "It's time to move on, guys. We all know what you both think. It was Tom's call. End of discussion."

"Thank you," Tom said.

Patty continued. "So now we can take the soil cores, deal with the county environmental officer, find our local real estate agent, and work our magic on a developer."

"Yes, indeed," Tom said. He glanced at Buddy. "You got the coring equipment, the GPS locator, and the property maps?"

"Good to go."

"Then get started on the cores while we keep developing our cover. Lay a grid, get a sample from every square, document it all like a science project. This has to look convincing."

"Come on, Tom, that's a big-ass piece of property. It'll take days. It's all bullshit anyway. Can't we just make it up?"

Tom shook his head. "Want boxes of samples tied to locations. Want a thick wad of analysis. That's the amount of material that will enable the environmental officer to create a convincing story."

"If we get him on board."

Patty smiled. "*When* we get him on board. He's a divorced guy with two kids in college. He'll be jumping when I snap my fingers."

"So get the cores done," Tom said. "And then, for fun, you can find and corrupt our real estate agent. Sound fair?"

Buddy picked up his burger. "Anyone I want?"

"As long as she'll play ball."

Buddy bit into his burger. With his mouth full, he said, "I'll hold you to that."

TEN DAYS LATER, Buddy was sitting in a dark back booth at the Home Run Bar and Grill, a sports bar in a strip mall on the west side of town that was a favorite hangout of real estate agents for Friday afternoon happy hour. He had a fresh haircut and shave, and his shoulders bulged out of his blue golf shirt and navy blue sports coat. The waitress who brought him his tap beer had eyed him over approvingly. He'd made a mental note to check up on her later. As he'd been sitting there, cross-checking the patrons against a computer listing of local real estate agents on his smartphone, the scene had become progressively more crowded and loud. After his second beer, with happy hour winding down, he noticed Marcie Tolliver standing by herself at the bar. She was as tall as a basketball player, busty, with auburn dyed hair and legs like an athlete. Her navy blue sports coat was a little loose and her khaki skirt was a little tight. He slipped up beside her, smiled when she glanced at him, and ordered another beer from the bartender. When he'd gotten his beer, he looked at her like he was seeing her for the first time. "How's it going?"

Marcie was sipping at a tall mixed drink. "Long day."

"Me, too." He looked her up and down. "Looks like we have the same taste in clothes."

She had a look on her face like she was going to blow him off, but after she saw his blazer and khaki pants, she said, "You're not wearing high heels."

He nodded. "The added height makes me too intimidating, so I have to stick to flats."

"I'm taller than you."

"Only in those heels, girlfriend."

She smiled. "You got your repartee going on." She shook the ice in her glass. "I haven't seen you around here before."

"I'm just in town with my partners working on a land deal."

"Really? You know this is the real estate agent hangout?"

"You're kidding. I thought agents were too competitive to hang out."

"You can't keep score if you don't hang out."

"Ouch. Now you're sounding a little bitter."

She drank off the bottom of her drink. "Like I said, long day. I've got to go."

Buddy stuck out his hand. "I'm Buddy, by the way."

She shook his hand. "I'm Marcie."

"Good to meet you, Marcie. Maybe I'll bump into you again."

She shrugged. "Maybe." She started to leave, but then turned back. "You really working on a land deal?"

"Marcie. So cynical. You must be having a bad week. Yeah, like I said, I'm here with my partners working on a land deal."

"What's that about?"

He shook his head. "We have to keep things quiet, or you local wheeler-dealers will cut us out. See, you're not the only person who knows what a bad week is."

She took out a business card and handed it him. "Well, if you need any local info, call me and I'll give you the skinny."

"Thank you, Marcie. I appreciate that. You have a good evening."

He watched her walk away. She was already hooked; she just didn't know it. Her career wasn't going very well and she was sitting by herself in a bar where she should have friends or be making friends. Probably wasn't cut out to be a real estate agent. But she did have an agent's license. And in the very near future, she was going to have some new friends and opportunities she'd never dreamed of.

ON MONDAY AFTERNOON, Patty drove up to the Boford County Office Annex, a tan sheet-metal building located next to the county water works and the industrial park. She was driving Buddy's blue Ford

Explorer. In the back were forty-eight core samples taken from random locations in each of forty-eight grid squares marked out on the Yost property. Each core was marked with its GPS location. She was dressed for a business meeting: black skirt suit, black flats, white collared shirt tastefully unbuttoned to show some cleavage if she bent over a report, white lacy underwear. She had an appointment with Bernie Revere, the county environmental officer, who was, by all accounts, a drinking, gambling good old boy, recently divorced with two daughters in college. She parked the Explorer on the side of the building next to the loading dock and walked around to the front entrance. Bernie was expecting her. He stood up out of his chair and extended his hand over his desk when she was ushered into the room. He was about the same height as her, five feet ten, with thinning black hair combed over the top of his head and chest hair sprouting out of the open collar of his short-sleeve oxford shirt. His shirt had a dirty spot on the front from where his beer belly rubbed up against his desk drawer. As she leaned forward to shake his hand, he didn't bother to hide the fact that he was looking down her blouse.

"Have a seat, Ms. Brown."

"Call me Patty."

He grunted his approval. "What can I do for you?"

"As I said when I called, I've got a batch of core samples from the Yost property that I'd like to get tested for environmental contamination."

"That property is well known to be contaminated."

"So I've heard. But those tests were done a long time ago. Testing standards have changed."

"So you think that more accurate tests will show the property is safe to develop? That's a pretty far reach."

"If the old tests, the ones done twenty years ago, were lost, and you did a thorough analysis, who knows what you might find."

"Maybe."

She took an envelope from her briefcase and set it on the desk. "Of course, we expect to pay to have the cores processed, and for the final report, all on an expedited schedule."

"That could run into a few dollars, what with the overtime and all." He set a hand on the desk. She pushed the envelope toward him. He took the envelope, glanced at the money inside, and put it in a drawer.

"Especially when you'll have to take care of it yourself." She reached into her briefcase and took out a file folder. "Let me show you what we have in mind."

She came around the desk, put her left hand on his shoulder, leaned down, and opened the file folder in front of him with her right. "The top memo tells what we're hoping you will find."

"Hoping I'll find?"

"Everybody's got a right to hope, don't they, Bernie?" She massaged his shoulder with her left hand. "The other papers are the records that go with the cores."

He turned his head to look up at her and found that he was speaking into her cleavage. "Where are the cores?"

"In my truck out by the loading dock."

"Let's go have a look."

They walked out through reception at the front of the building, where a thin, middle-aged woman with a no-nonsense look on her face sat behind an oak office desk. "I'll be back in a few, Nancy," Bernie said.

At the Explorer, Bernie opened the hatchback and looked over the cores. "You know, honey, you're asking an awful lot for the money I'm going to make."

Patty stood up close to him. "Since you're not actually going to do any of the work, other than writing the report, I'd say the money's pretty generous."

"Yeah, but if any people get sick . . ."

"We're not out to hurt anyone." She reached over and rubbed the front of his pants. "In fact, we're just trying to make people happy. The Yosts, a developer, people who want to live on the lake, and you. What could be wrong with that?"

He moved her hand away. "That's the first time anyone tried to give me a lap dance with their hand."

"Bernie, don't tell me you're shy. Why don't we sit in the front of this truck, and I'll see if I can't convince you of how happy we want you to be?"

Bernie shut the hatchback. There was no one in sight. "I know a spot close by here that's a little more private."

"Sounds good. Let's roll over there."

He nodded. "I'm just telling you now that I haven't made my mind up, and I might not make it up today."

"No problem. Just relax. I'm sure you'll end up making the right decision."

They got into the Explorer and drove down a dirt road at the back of the county office annex, Bernie giving directions as they went, until they came to an old wooden shed with a large padlock on the door. "Drive around the back."

Behind the shed was a shady spot enclosed by bushes. Patty put the car in park, and slipped out of her jacket and skirt. When she lay them up on the dash, she positioned her briefcase so that the mini-camera in the clasp would film the interior of the vehicle. In the meantime, Bernie had pulled down his pants. She straddled him in the passenger's seat. "We always take care of our friends, Bernie; we always take care of our friends."

"Hush up, honey. You can talk in a minute." He unbuttoned her blouse and shoved his face into her breasts. She gripped his shoulders and rode him hard, rocking the car. A few minutes later, his head came up. "Oh, Jesus," he said, "oh, Jesus."

She smiled. Her work here was done. All she had to do was make a copy of the digital recording of his office, the loading dock, and the payoff, and he was in their pocket for the duration.

At 6:00 P.M., Buddy pushed through the doors into the Home Run Bar and Grill. He was looking for Marcie. Tom had checked her out. She'd been in real estate two years, she'd had a falling out with her mentor, she was underperforming, and her husband was currently unemployed. So Buddy's intuition about her had panned out. She was the perfect local wrapper for their program. All he needed to do was close the deal. He peered through the crowd over at the place at the bar where she had been standing on Friday, and there she was, a creature of habit, beaten down by another unsuccessful day and in no hurry to go back home to her disappointing husband. He circled the bar so that he could approach from her blind side and squeezed up to the bar between her back and the back of a fat guy in a gray suit who was part of a threesome. Beer sloshed on the fat guy's hand, he gave Buddy a dirty look for pushing him over, Buddy replied with a quick consolatory smile, and then ignored the guy and stuck his hand up for the bartender. "Tap beer, please."

The bartender brought him a pint and placed a piece of cash register tape in a shot glass in front of him. Buddy nodded. "Thanks."

Marcie looked over her shoulder. "You again?"

"I could say the same thing."

She turned toward him, noting his black golf shirt, jeans, and hiking boots. "Your outfit's different today."

"I was out in the field marking lot lines. Not a jacket and tie sort of day." He sipped his beer. "How about you. I see you're dressed for success. Have any luck?"

"You know how it goes—hot and cold. I worked some prospects, but they can't quite make up their minds."

"You'll get there."

"Yeah." She lifted her highball glass, saw that her drink was nothing but ice, and set it on the bar. "Well, I should get going."

"So soon? Have one more. That's all I'm going to have. Then we'll leave at the same time and free up the bar."

"You just got that one."

He picked up his beer and drank it down. "It's gone now. Come on, you wouldn't make a stranger in town drink by himself, would you? One more and out into the sunshine we go."

"Okay."

He flagged down the bartender and indicated he wanted a round. The bartender brought them a beer, a clear cocktail of some sort, and a new bar tab receipt. "What you drinking?" Buddy asked.

"Vodka tonic." She stirred the drink with the thin straw and then set the straw on the bar. "You just didn't happen to end up standing next to me, did you?"

"No," he smiled. "Had fun talking to you on Friday. Thought I'd repeat the experience."

"And if I come in here tomorrow?"

"We'll probably talk some more. Could be I'll know all about you by the time I leave town."

"That depends on what I want to tell you. Maybe I don't want you in my life. Maybe I like you being the handsome stranger."

"Handsome stranger? Okay, I can go with that." He stood up on his toes and turned his profile to her. "This what you had in mind?"

She smiled. "You are the devil." She pointed to her wedding band. "You know I'm married, right? Or is that part of the attraction?"

He held his hands up. "Hey now. I'm not trying to complicate your life. We're just standing here having some laughs. Everybody needs to wind down at the end of the day, make a successful transition to home life. You're lots of fun. You're a pretty girl. Why would I want to talk with anyone else?" He patted her shoulder and drank some of his beer.

"But you don't have any home life to go to."

"Empty apartment. My partners are married to each other. They want to include me, but I hate being the third wheel all the time, know what I mean?"

"So your life isn't all sweetness and light?"

"Don't get me wrong. I make a good living, but we're on the road most of the year, hunting for deals or closing deals, adding the synergy that makes things happen. So sometimes things can get lonely." He smiled. "But that's not a problem for you, is it? Your husband is at home. Going to ask about your day. Give you the sympathetic ear. Make you feel like it's all worthwhile. You got kids?"

"No, not yet."

"But you're wanting them, aren't you?" He sipped his beer. "Of course you are. Family life. The complete package. You don't know how lucky you are."

The color drained from her face. His free hand was on the edge of the bar. She put her hand on top of his. "Your apartment near here?"

He nodded. "Just on the other side of the strip mall. That's one of the reasons I came in here to begin with."

"Furnished?"

"Yeah."

"Bed any good?"

He turned his head and studied her eyes. "No morning backache."

She drank down her vodka tonic. "Let's go find out. But I've got to hurry. Can't get home too late."

The sun was bright in the parking lot. Buddy got into Tom's black Escalade. Marcie followed in her red Taurus. They drove across the strip mall parking lot, past the Save-A-Lot grocery store, and into the apartment complex's access street from the strip mall. Buddy pulled around the first building and parked in the end spot at the left corner of the second building. Marcie pulled in beside him. He got out and waited for her on the sidewalk in front of his car, watching her glance around nervously before she shut her car door and stepped up to the curb. He didn't say anything; he just smiled his most winning smile, took her hand, and led her through the wooden gate to the door to his studio apartment. He got out his key and opened the door without letting go of her hand, as if the lack of physical contact would cause her to change her mind and bolt. He pulled her through the door, locked it behind them. There was a kitchenette to the left, a leather sofa and flat-screen TV in the middle of the room, and a queen-sized bed to the right. She looked the room over, but she didn't move, she didn't speak. She turned toward him and closed her eyes, her lips slightly parted. He pushed her up against the door. He kissed her lips, her face, her neck. He grabbed her sports coat and pulled it down from her shoulders so that she couldn't move her arms. He scooped her up and carried her to the bed.

"Don't—" she said.

He put her down. "You aren't going to ask me to be gentle, are you?"

"Careful with the clothes. They have to pass the sniff test." She pushed him away, stood up, turned her back to him and stripped naked, laying her clothes carefully over the back of the sofa. He pulled off his clothes as he watched her from behind. Then she turned back to him, moving to accentuate her curves, put her arms around his neck, lifted herself up onto him, and wrapped her legs around his waist. They fell onto the bed. She laughed.

"What's so funny?" he asked.

"I was just wondering who was fucking who?"

"I guess we're going to find out."

Afterward, Marcie got up immediately and went into the bathroom, where she wet his washcloth in cold water and began wiping herself off. Buddy followed her and stood in the doorway, naked, watching her. "You weren't kidding about your timeline."

"My husband has a temper on him. He's never hit me, but I don't want the evening to be ugly."

"Well, maybe you can call this business."

She stopped wiping off her leg and looked at him quizzically. "How's that?"

"My partners and I have a deal lined up, but we need a local real estate agent to close it for us. It's a sensitive deal, so we want someone we can count on."

"Sensitive?"

"Not illegal. Just subject to misinterpretation. And we don't want any misinterpretation. I'm thinking maybe you could be our agent."

She went back to wiping herself off. "What's it pay?"

"The agent takes a percentage, not a standard commission, so it's the gravy train."

"I'd have to hear the details."

"I'd have to talk with my partners. Then they would have to meet you, but if you're interested in the job, and you have the time to put us first, it could work out."

She rinsed the washcloth out in the sink. "Sounds good." She hung the washcloth over the shower curtain rod and turned to leave. Buddy was standing in the way.

"Can we talk some more tomorrow?"

"Talk?" She smiled. "Maybe. Can you meet earlier?"

He stepped out of the way.

She went to the sofa, put on her underwear and bra, and then turned back to him, patted his cheek and kissed him. "You aren't going to turn into a puppy dog, are you?" She pulled on the rest of her clothes. Before she opened the front door, she got a business card out of her jacket pocket. "Call me after two o'clock, but not too late. My husband's not working right now, so he's got plenty of time to think."

"Two o'clock it is."

She was gone. Buddy got down on his knees and reached under the bed to pull out the laptop computer that was wirelessly connected to the camera hidden in the clock radio on the night table to the left side of the bed. He forwarded through the recording at double speed. Excellent. He wondered how Patty's recording looked compared to his. In the Explorer, God knows what the lighting was like; the values were probably shit. Oh, well. That was her problem. He slipped the computer back under the bed and headed for the shower.

IN THE MEANTIME, Tom was meeting with Big Jim Rollins, a local mobster whose tax cover and money laundry were real estate development. Big Jim's offices were located in Sunny Grove Professional Office Park, a new complex he'd completed two years ago on land reclaimed from a private landfill. His tenants—accountants, dentists, lawyers, and chiropractors—were already complaining about water damage, ill-fitting doors and windows, and poor soundproofing, but by the time they could break their leases, he'd have the contract with county health and human services, a contract that had cost him very little in bribes to obtain, so he was going to be happy to get rid of the whiners, who would mainly be moving to one of his more expensive properties. Big Jim was not tall, but he was big around, with short legs and thin blond hair combed back on his large round head. He always wore golf clothes and he always had a fat cigar stuck in the corner of his mouth. He was sitting in a high-back, black leather chair behind a hand-built teakwood desk. Tom, dressed in his usual suit and tie, sat on the other side of the desk in a low-back leather chair.

"Coffee?" Big Jim asked.

Tom nodded. "Please."

"Eddie." Big Jim waved at his assistant, a nondescript young man wearing khakis and a golf shirt, who disappeared into a hallway and came back with two mugs of coffee. Big Jim set his cigar in an ashtray, sipped his coffee, and looked at Tom over his cup. "So why are you here?"

"You develop land, my partners and I represent the Yosts, who have land they want to sell."

"Everyone knows their land can't be developed."

"Smart investors make money everyday doing things that everyone says can't be done."

"Is that right?"

"You know it's right. You've done it many times yourself."

"But this deal will have to get by the county environmental office."

"And that's why the price is less than the value of the land. Even though the land can be proven safe for development, there is extra risk because of public perception, so that risk is compensated by a price reduction."

"This deal still seems too good to be true."

"The Yosts know they can't get full value for the land. They want what they can get. Right now, the property is a liability. They've got taxes. They've got trespassers—vagrants, meth labs, teenage parties. They've got the sheriff on the phone wanting them to increase security. And they need money."

"So why me? Why you trying to help me out?"

"Even with a clean bill of health, banks are going to be squeamish. So we need a developer with deep pockets."

"So what's the discount?"

"If the Air Force had never been out there, the land would be worth over a million."

"In somebody's dreams."

"You can get it for six hundred and fifty thousand. All that premium lakefront property, a beautiful woodland setting, heavy utilities already in place, near to the main road and only a few minutes from town."

"Still have to demolish the old hangars and runway."

"Good place to store equipment while you develop the prime land."

Big Jim put his cigar back in his mouth and lit it with a large, carved-stone lighter. "How many of these cold calls have you made?"

Tom smiled softly. "Enough."

"I bet." Big Jim knocked the ash off his cigar. "Tell you what I'm going to do. I'm going to give your proposition some serious thought."

"Don't think too long. When the land comes back clean, word will get out and the price will go up."

"How does that hurt you?"

"Time is money. The longer the process is drawn out, the longer we stay here, and the less money we make this year. We want it quick and easy."

"I'll be in touch."

"Thanks for your time."

Tom left the office. Big Jim picked up his desk phone. "Lou? This is Jim. Listen, a guy named Tom Brown just pitched me a deal on the Yost property. Find out everything you can about him and his associates. And tell our mutual acquaintance to stop using the old runway until further notice. It may start getting busy out there."

Big Jim set his cigar down and sipped some more coffee. There had to be a way to get that property for nothing or next to nothing and make it look like he paid for it. It'd be a quick way to hide the bookie money and bury some of the tavern profits.

Eddie stuck his head in the door. "Danny on the other line, sir."

"Tell him not to call here anymore. He deals with Frankie now. Tell him Frankie will meet him at Walmart at five o'clock. Then call

Frankie. Tell him to smarten up that idiot. I don't want him using phones."

"Got you." Eddie disappeared. Big Jim sat back in his chair and looked out the window into the half-empty parking lot. *Time is money.* Yeah. This Tom Brown had to be working some sort of angle. And if he were working an angle, he wouldn't want police involvement, which meant he was vulnerable to all sorts of plays. Big Jim rubbed his chin. He just had to think of one that would work after he had the deed to the land.

Two WEEKS LATER, Patty was standing under a streetlight in the twilight beside Tom's Escalade, in the parking lot of the city park that was situated directly across White Bear Lake from the Yosts' property. The sun had just disappeared below the trees, which cast long shadows across the picnic area. In the distance, Patty could hear happy voices coming from the barbecue pit and picnic tables on the other side of a stand of yew bushes. She looked at her watch. 7:30 p.m. A rusty gray pickup truck came over the hill and drove down into the lot to park beside her. Bernie Revere, the county environmental officer, got out. "Hey, girl," he said.

Patty stayed where she was. He got out a cigarette and lit it, then joined her under the streetlight. "Have you got the report?"

"I do."

"Good news?"

He nodded. "You'll be pleased."

"So why are we meeting here?"

He took a drag off of his cigarette. "'Cause I need some more money."

Patty reached into her shoulder bag and took out a DVD. "Have you got something that will show this?"

"What is it?"

"A movie of you taking a bribe and fucking me to seal the deal."

He threw his cigarette down, grabbed her by the shoulders, and shook her. "You're not going to ruin my life."

Tom stepped out of the Escalade with a nine-millimeter pistol down at his side. "Don't be overdramatic, Bernie. Nobody's life is going to be ruined. Unless you don't let go of her."

Bernie dropped his arms. His comb-over had fallen down in his face. He raked it back into place. "You're a despicable bastard."

"But I keep my word. We paid you to perform a service. You stick to your end, you'll come out okay." He turned to Patty. "You all right?"

"He didn't hurt me." Patty put the DVD back in her shoulder bag. "It's not personal, Bernie. We've got no reason to hurt you if you don't hurt us."

"I deserve more money."

Tom put the pistol into the waistband at the back of his pants. "I get it. You thought you'd get some more cash and another fuck or two before everything was done. Now you found out you've been outnegotiated and your feelings are hurt." He shrugged. "You're just going to have to get over it."

"The DVD?"

"When we leave town, we'll erase the original and smash the copies. We sure don't want to attract any attention to this deal."

"Goddamn bullshit."

"Give us the copy of the report and file the original. We'll do everything we can to get out of town as soon as possible."

Bernie went back to his truck. When he opened the door, the light came on inside. Tom and Patty watched him reach down into the floor.

Tom pulled the pistol back out of his waistband. "You come out of that truck with anything other than the report, you're going in the lake."

Bernie turned toward them with a fat file folder in his hand. "You're crazy, you know that? Point that gun away. I'm a family man. I don't want to get in no gunfight."

Tom held the gun down along his leg. Patty took the file from Bernie. "I just don't believe in taking chances," Tom said. "That's the most important thing you want to remember about me."

. . .

A FEW DAYS LATER, Tom, Patty, and Buddy were sitting in an office at Ace Real Estate across the desk from Marcie Tolliver. The office was snapshot typical: wood-trimmed Formica-topped desk, large window, framed licenses and diplomas with words too small to read, a large framed poster of a bucolic scene of homeowner bliss. Tom studied Marcie over the top of his fake horn-rimmed glasses. Her blue sports coat hung over the back of her chair. Her white blouse was unbuttoned to reveal some cleavage. She was as easy to read as the comics. She was a dyed redhead with an easy smile who thought her flattery and manipulation always sounded sincere. Tom set a fat file folder on the desk, sat back down, and then leaned forward, his elbows on his knees, the picture of authority with his banker-length haircut and tightly-trimmed beard. Marcie glanced at Buddy with her flirty eyes; Buddy replied with a wolfish can't-get-enough-of-what-you-got. He'd been working her for the last two weeks while they'd been waiting for Bernie Revere to create his phony analysis and write his report, but now it was up to Tom to sell her on the details.

"I understand that Buddy's told you about the deal."

She nodded, crossed her legs, and sat back in her office chair. "Generalities."

"Let's be very clear with each other. That file folder contains the analysis that proves that the old Yost property isn't contaminated in any way; it's perfectly safe to build there, regardless of rumor or any previous finding."

"Then why don't you just put it on the market?"

"Because these reports are very difficult for the layperson to understand. And once the experts start arguing—well, you know how that ends. The Yosts have nothing right now. They were going to die with nothing. So we made a deal. The Yosts get half of what we take in; we split the rest. They're happy. Big Jim Rollins buys the property for less than market price, develops it, he's happy. The difference is what we keep. You get an equal share, instead of your real estate commission, so you do even better the more you drive up the price."

Her heels clicked on the floor as she leaned forward and set her hands on the edge of her desk. "Why Big Jim? I can think of four developers off the top of my head who'd jump at the chance to get the Yost property. Do you know who you're dealing with here?"

"We've heard of his reputation."

"It's more than reputation. Try to find someone around here who's crossed him. Not someone who's crossed him and wants to talk about it, just someone who's crossed him."

"We've checked around, Marcie. We know who runs the big kids' table in Seanboro."

"Really?"

"Big Jim is going to get well on this deal. He's going to thank us. And he's going to thank the agent who brokered this deal. Trust me. He's the only one around here with the deep pockets and influence with the county to carry this project through. This is a win-win for everyone who gets on the train."

"So why me? Sounds like all you need is a real estate license. Why cut me in for a share?"

"We like everyone highly motivated to overcome any possible problems that might arise. That's worth paying for. As the old saw goes, nobody washes a rental car. So we like everyone bought in. Sure, we could have gone with anyone. It's a sweet deal. But you're a friend of Buddy's. So it's up to you." He smiled as his voice trailed off.

Marcie's tongue glided back and forth along the inner edge of her upper lip like it was pressing keys on a calculator. Their story didn't quite make sense, but they weren't asking her to do anything illegal, she really needed the money, and she figured her share should be about twice her usual commission.

"We're on a tight schedule. We need your answer or we need to push along."

She glanced at Buddy and nodded. "I'm in."

Tom stood up and extended his hand over the desk. When she took it, he put his left hand on top. "You're just doing your usual job. We've already primed Big Jim. Just push him to the deal."

Patty flashed a toothy smile. "Congratulations."

As Tom and Patty turned to leave, Buddy put his hand on Marcie's shoulder. "Call me when you get off."

Tom and Patty and Buddy walked down the hall and through the outer office where three office assistants were processing paperwork. Out in the parking lot, a soft breeze fluttered the leaves on the saplings in the median strips, but the sun reflected hot off of the new concrete. Tom switched to black wraparound sunglasses. "You did good, kid. She is definitely the one."

"Thanks, old-timer."

Patty smoothed down Buddy's lapels. "Keep her close."

Buddy smiled. "Not a problem."

"I bet it's not."

Tom jingled his car keys in his hand. "So now it's 'all good things come to those who wait.' See you later, kid."

Tom and Patty started across the parking lot. The lunch crowd at the Burrito Palace next door in the strip mall had filled up the parking lot while they were in the real estate office, putting their Escalade in a tight spot. Buddy turned toward his Ford Explorer; then changed his mind and jogged a few steps to catch up to his partners. "How about a little side project to help pass the time until Marcie squares up her end?"

Patty squeezed Tom's hand. "What you got in mind?" she said.

"A lot of cocaine ships through this town. I know a guy who sells bricks that have fallen off the truck—steep discount—and I know a guy from Pittsburgh who'll be passing through on the way home from Florida. We could double our money just passing a bag between folks who don't know each other."

"What's the timeline?"

"The next couple of days."

Tom pulled off his sunglasses and squinted at Buddy. "We've got two rules. Remember rule number one? No complications. That's why we're wearing street clothes and walking around on the outside. We make a plan; we stick to it. This gig you're talking about—it might be great. I don't know. I do know it has to wait until this job is done."

"Look, I could understand if we were actually working. But this little project will be all done before the next step in your plan. It's not going to interfere."

"It's ripples in the pond, kid, ripples in the pond. Once you toss the pebble in, the ripples start. They can't be stopped. You got time on your hands—bang your new best friend, do a crossword, catch up on your sleep. If she's any good, we'll be pushing up the timeline anyway."

Buddy frowned, but he nodded his head. "Okay, okay. It was just a suggestion. I'll see you later."

Buddy cut back across the lot toward his car. Tom put his sunglasses back on. "Why are you encouraging him?"

Patty smiled.

"You were just doing that to fuck with me."

"He's just trying to be productive. How does it hurt us? If you think he'd flip, you wouldn't be working with him."

"One job at a time."

Tom looked from his wife to Buddy, watching her watch him walking across the parking lot. When did they start needing a partner? When did he become too old to hustle the girls himself? They'd pulled Buddy in four years ago as muscle on a gun job, but when they were done, they kept him on. Then he got the research out of the bank secretary—well, she was even younger than him—and he'd taken over that role ever since. Tom looked at his wife's smile, but he couldn't tell what she was thinking. Did he quit hustling the girls to prove his loyalty to her, because he was in love with her? And was that the same reason he didn't stop her from hustling Buddy?

They got into the Escalade. Patty smoothed down her skirt before she fastened her seat belt. "Hey, you think Marcie will actually read that file?"

"You kidding? We're talking IQ small numbers. She might call the Yosts, but they won't tell her anything."

AN HOUR LATER, Tom sat beside Big Jim as he drove his golf cart down the path, navigating the distance from the middle fairway to the fifth hole green, the steering wheel rubbing the belly of his golf shirt, their clubs clanking behind them over the bumps. Big Jim yapped incessantly, bragging about developing the course, pointing out a local judge, waving at some poker buddies, hollering some vague flattery at a foursome of middle-aged women off in the distance, all the while gesturing with a heavily ringed hand. When he finally took a breath, Tom said, "We've got the real estate agent roped in now, a girl named Marcie Tolliver. You just play it like she's actually convincing you—fat chance—and you'll be marking lots in a month."

Big Jim nodded, stopped the cart, and took out his putter. "So she's not on the inside?"

Tom shook his head. "She's just part of the window dressing. Making it all look fair and square."

Big Jim walked onto the green, examined the lay of his ball, and then turned, smiling, and pointed his club at Tom. "You're a sneaky bastard."

"Just trying to make a living."

Big Jim pulled off his cap and mopped the sweat trickling down his forehead. "The con job you pulled on the Yosts, getting them to believe they need you: It's a thing of beauty."

"Ninety-nine percent truth, one percent fiction."

"That simple?"

"No. It's got to be the right one percent. That's why you're going to pay me. You get plausible deniability and the only large-acre undeveloped lakefront property in three counties, all wrapped up in a bow."

"So how do I know that you're not screwing me?"

"You've seen the soil and water reports. They're all certified. But that won't budge a banker. You're the only one who can actually develop the land, so you're the only person in this deal that I can't con." Tom examined the lay of his ball. He was three feet farther back and down the slope than Big Jim. "Besides, the most important part of my plan is leaving this town alive."

Big Jim smiled. "Sounds like you've got your priorities straight."

Tom held up a twenty-dollar bill. "Bet I make the hole in fewer shots than you."

Big Jim squared up his cap. "You're on."

.   .   .

BUDDY, still in his gym clothes, opened the door to his studio apartment. Patty was standing there—long, loose skirt, tank top, dangly silver earrings, looking as sexy as a well-toned fortyish woman could look—cradling a six-pack in a paper sack. "Where's the boss?"

"I don't have a boss, Buddy. Tommy's buttering the mark. Are you going to ask me in?"

He stepped out of the way. She sauntered in, took a beer from the bag, and passed the bag to him. "I catch you on your way out?"

He shook his head. "Just got back."

"So you're all warmed up." She made a circle around the room: a gym bag sat on the coffee table, the blinds were drawn, khakis and a golf shirt were laid out on the bed. "This isn't a bad-looking place."

He took an icy-cold beer out of the bag and set the bag on the counter at the kitchenette. "I don't mean to be rude, but why are you here?"

She sat down on the arm of the rented leather sofa and crossed her legs. "I'd like to get in on your baggage handling project."

He drank from his beer. The liquid felt good going down. "Tom change his mind?"

"No. This is just me and you."

"How does he feel about that?"

"He won't feel anything if you don't tell him."

Buddy grinned and took another drink.

"So was it all bullshit, or are we going to make some money?"

"No, we're definitely going to make some money. I just got to make two phone calls."

"Great." She stood up, set her beer on the counter, and unhooked a catch on her skirt, which slipped to the floor at her feet. She wasn't wearing underwear. "Do you want some of this?"

He set his beer on the counter next to hers. "Are you playing with me?"

"No, sugar, I'm not playing with you. The question is: are you going to play with me."

"How do you know Marcie isn't on her way over here?"

"You telling me you're in love with her, or that you can't handle two women at once?"

"Tom is going to be pissed."

She laughed. "You going to tell him?"

He leaned in close to her. "I'm going to wear you out."

"Then you better get your clothes off, baby." She gave him a push; then she pulled her tank top off over her head and unhooked her bra.

MARCIE'S HUSBAND Kenny was lying on the sofa in the living room, watching ESPN, when she came through the back door into the kitchen. The day's dishes were scattered across the counters and the morning newspaper was still open to the comics' page on the kitchen table. She set her handbag down on a kitchen chair and poured herself a glass of white wine.

"Hey, Marcie," Kenny hollered over the back of the sofa, "where you been? How come you haven't made supper?"

She walked over to where she could see him if he looked back toward her. "You work today?"

His head popped up over the sofa. "I told you that job didn't start until next Monday."

Marcie walked back into the kitchen, hung her navy blazer on the back of a kitchen chair, and kicked her high heels under the table. Kenny followed her in. Barefoot, he was just taller than she was. His brown hair was pulled back into a ponytail. He had military tattoos on his chest. His arms and shoulders were hard muscle, but his belly hung over his belt. He crowded an empty beer bottle onto the counter by the sink.

"Did you ever put on a shirt today?"

"Where you been?"

"I've been working on something to make us some real money."

"Is that right?" He got another beer from the refrigerator. "Like what?"

She shooed him toward the table. "You get out from underfoot." She turned on the oven and took a pizza from the freezer.

"Aw, how about some real food?"

"I been at work all day. I'm tired. This is the best you're going to get unless you fix it."

He sipped his beer. "Then I guess it's the best I'm going to get."

She slid the pizza onto a pan and set it on the top of the stove until the oven preheated.

"So tell me about this deal."

She opened the refrigerator, peered around, and then started pulling salad ingredients out onto the counter. "It's a real estate thing with some big players new to town. They've got something going with Big Jim Rollins, but they need a real estate license." She turned and curtsied.

"Uh-huh."

She rinsed some lettuce and tore it into a bowl. He came up behind her. "How much money?"

She shrugged. "More than usual. And this is no 'sell it first,' this is definite cash."

He grabbed her by the hips and rubbed up against her. "That sounds real good."

She smacked his hand. "You quit sniffing around. Supper will be ready soon." The oven beeped. She slid out from between him and the counter and put the pizza into the oven.

PATTY STOOD at the sink in the kitchenette of their one-bedroom apartment, rinsing leaf lettuce under the tap. Two previously cooked chicken breasts sat on a cutting board on the counter behind her, next to the dinner plates where she was going to assemble their salads. After she had come home from Buddy's apartment, she'd changed back into the business wear she'd been wearing earlier in the day, so she'd put on an apron. Her high heels lay on the carpet under the coffee table in the living room. Tom sat on the gray leather sofa in the living room, his feet up on the coffee table, his laptop computer in his lap, checking their expenses on the credit cards and at their bank. He was still dressed from the golf course. Patty shook the excess water off of the lettuce and divided it onto the two plates. "So Big Jim is good to go?"

Tom glanced up from his computer. "Yeah. He's suspicious, but not too suspicious. He knows we're up to something, thinks we're screwing the Yosts, doesn't think he can cut us out of the equation."

"Yet." Patty started slicing the chicken into strips to lay onto the lettuce.

Tom smiled. "Yet. That's why we need to move fast. No screwing around." His phone rang. "Hello?"

"Tom? This is Bernie. I tried to get a hold of you earlier."

"I was in meetings all day. What's up?"

"Lou Turnbolt—Big Jim's lawyer—called me. He had a lot of questions about my report and what I knew about you guys."

"I'm sure you handled it."

"This is getting all crazy. Big Jim could ruin me, get me fired."

"Nobody forced you in. You made your choice and we've got it recorded."

"Mister, blackmail only goes so far. I lose my job, I'm screwed. I've got to have some more money."

"I hear you, Bernie, and I want to be fair, I really do. I'll get you two hundred dollars more. But that's it."

"Only two hundred? What I did is worth a lot more than that."

"A deal is a deal. We've got the recording."

"But you can't use it without blowing up your game. You expose me, you expose yourselves."

"Bernie, Bernie, Bernie, you think we're amateurs? You've got family to worry about. I understand your younger daughter is at the state college in Portersville. I hear they have a terrible assault rate there, especially for freshmen."

"You stay away from my daughter."

"Keep your word and keep your mouth shut. Everything will be fine." He ended the call.

Patty looked up from chopping some black olives. "Bernie getting cold feet?"

"Yeah. The usual."

"You want me to put some 'good cop' on him?"

"I don't think fucking him is going to make him more cooperative." Tom closed his computer. "He just overreacted because he got a
call from Big Jim's lawyer. After he's had time to settle down, I'm sure
he's going to see things our way." He walked over to the counter that
separated the living room from the kitchenette. "I'm really more
worried about Buddy. I've got a feeling he might do something
stupid."

Patty looked up from putting the olives on the salads. "Why?
Buddy's been with us a long time. He's always been reliable."

"He's getting too argumentative. Thinks he knows best."

"You're like his dad. He just wants to feel like you're listening to
him."

"He's getting too big for his britches. Maybe it's time for him to go
his own way."

Patty shrugged. "Let's get through with this score. Then you can
evaluate how valuable he's been." She set the salads on the counter in
front of Tom. "No reason to be in a hurry, right?"

Tom nodded. "So you don't care if we move on without him after
we're done here?"

"I'm good with whatever keeps us earning and out of jail, you
know that."

He looked over his salad, the tomato slices, olives, and herbs
fanned out over the chicken slices on the bed of lettuce. "This is
beautiful, honey."

"Thanks." She passed him a fork and a knife.

2

COMPLICATIONS

A t 8:00 a.m., Tom walked into the High Five tavern carrying a briefcase. He'd made the drive to Pikesville in record time, just over an hour and a half. It was dark and quiet inside, the long walnut bar running all down the left side. A silent jukebox sat in the back corner. Some recently wiped Formica tables filled the floor. The bartender, an older black man with a graying Afro and a toothpick hanging from his lips, looked up from his newspaper. Tom waved, "Hey, Gary."

"Traveling Man, when did you get back in town?"

"Just driving through. Stella here?"

"She's expecting you." Gary motioned with his head toward the employee-only door.

In the backroom, a dark-haired, middle-aged woman wearing a man's button-down collar shirt, tail out over a pair of tight jeans, sat in an easy chair watching the *Today* Show.

"Hey, Stella."

"Hey." She turned off the TV. Cases of dry goods were stacked up the back wall. To the right was a small desk with a schoolteacher calendar blotter on it. "Keeping busy?"

"Can't complain."

"It'll cost you twenty for the hundred."

Tom set the briefcase on the desk and opened it. Inside were two banded bundles of hundred-dollar bills. "Count it."

She rolled her eyes. "Please." She dragged a stepladder over to the wall of boxes. "Give me a hand here." She moved boxes between piles until she found the right one. "Here."

He took the box from her. She pushed some more boxes around until the wall looked like it did originally. Then she hopped down. "Set that box on the desk."

She tore the tape off the top, opened the cardboard flaps, and pulled out her own banded stack of hundred-dollar bills. "See? These bills are just like the last ones you got. Twenties, fifties, and old-style hundreds run through a washer so they look well used. They won't stand up to a light show, but for regular use, no one can tell the difference."

"Why use real cash for expenses?"

"There you go. Just don't dump too many in one neighborhood." She returned the stack of bills to the box.

He closed the cardboard flaps and picked up the box. "Always a pleasure, Stella."

"Don't be a stranger."

BUDDY SAT IN A STOLEN, cream-colored Volvo sedan on a side street in the downtown shopping area. In the trunk was a duffel bag containing the five kilos of cocaine he was going to trade for $100,000. He'd picked up the bag in the early morning from a biker friend named Jimmy Dale, paid $50,000 for it, half of that Patty's, so he was going to double their money in one day. Easy money. The worst part was the waiting. Craft fair today. Lots of cars, lots of pedestrians, lots of out-of-towners to mix things up, make the usually unusual into the usual. A black Lincoln with tinted windows drove up. The driver's window lowered. A bearded man in a black T-shirt spoke with a Dominican accent.

"You Buddy Ray? I'm Ruben. Freddy's waiting on you. Follow me."

He followed the Lincoln out to Evert's Motor Lodge by the freeway interchange. He'd thought this place was out of business. The parking lot was mostly empty. Two rooms had their windows boarded up. Weeds were growing through the cracks in the sidewalk and flat blue paint was peeling off the side of the building in strips like birch bark. He couldn't see anyone in the office. As he parked the Volvo, he was trying to remember if Freddy was the kind of guy who would rob an old friend. Ruben waited at a motel room door while Buddy pulled the black duffel bag from the trunk. Inside the motel room, Freddy greeted him with a bear hug. "Hey, man, you're looking good."

"So are you."

Freddy was wearing chinos and a yellow and red Hawaiian shirt. He had a tall man's slouch, his long, dark, gray-streaked hair hanging around his face. "I was surprised to hear from you. How long you been down here?"

"Just passing through."

"I bet. You still running with that guy and his old lady? What's his name? Tom Brown?"

Buddy nodded. "You know how it is."

"I do. Well, let's get this done. I've got a lot of driving to do today."

Buddy swung the duffel bag onto the rumpled bed. Freddy looked inside before he passed it to Ruben, who pulled a Ziploc bag at random and carried it over to the banged up desk where he'd set up his kit to test the cocaine for purity.

"How's your brother?" Buddy said.

"Died last year."

"No shit? Sorry to hear it. We had some good times. He was younger than you, wasn't he?"

Freddy shrugged. "He got that bad cancer. Took him out in a matter of months. So much for clean living."

"Bad break."

"You got that right. His wife and kids are looking to me, and I can't afford to take care of my own."

Ruben looked up from his test kit. "This is some good dope."

"Of course it's good." Buddy glanced around the room. "Where's the money?"

The motel room door swung open. Buddy spun on his heels. Two men with guns in their hands and police badges hanging from chains around their necks stood in the doorway.

Freddy shrugged. "Sorry, Bud."

Buddy shook his head. "You couldn't warn me somehow? I thought we were friends."

"I don't have friends anymore, Buddy. I've got a wife, a mortgage, and kids in school. I've got obligations. It's not like the old days. I can't go to prison."

The cop on the right, a fat, bald man wearing a blue blazer over a red golf shirt, chuckled. "Freddy, you and Ruben can get out of here. Sit down, Mr. Ray."

Buddy sat on the edge of the bed. The other cop, the younger of the two, decked out in worn jeans and a brown leather jacket, closed the door behind Freddy and Ruben.

The bald cop shook his head. "Why do they make you punks so stupid?"

The young cop walked over to the bathroom and glanced in. "I don't know if stupid is the right word, Rusty. I was thinking greedy, maybe."

"Yeah, stupid's the right word. Just for once I'd like to get involved in a case like on TV, where the mopes actually have a plan and two or three cops actually have to work their brains."

"Please, Rusty, can we hurry this up? I can't be late for supper any more this week. I'm already in the doghouse for missing the PTA."

"Okay, Malcolm, okay. Mr. Ray, I'm Detective Fadiman and this is Detective Bigalow. We've got you selling drugs to a confidential informant. We have warrants; we have a recording. But it's your lucky day. Stupid counts in your favor today."

"That's right," Bigalow continued. "Because the crew you're involved with is somehow connected to a person we're interested in."

"I don't know what you're talking about."

"Five kilos is an awful lot of time," Fadiman said.

"I'm serious. I just do what the old-timer tells me."

"Uh-huh."

"Really. Do you think I'd be doing risky drug deals if I was all connected up on something big?"

Fadiman pulled over the desk chair and sat facing Buddy. "Look, Buddy, we know you're partnered up with Tom and Patty Brown. We know you've got something going on with Big Jim Rollins. The only way you're getting out of this is if we get the dirt on Big Jim and your partners. Are you following what I'm saying?"

Buddy nodded.

"Then you better start filling in the blanks."

MARCIE AND BIG Jim were riding on a dirt track through the brambles and scrub trees surrounding the old airfield on the Yost property, Big Jim bouncing his Suburban through the potholes, thinking more about his 4:00 p.m. tee time than the saplings he was mowing down. Marcie, dressed in her best navy skirt-blazer combo, was pointing out the window and talking fast. "This section butts up against White Bear Lake. That's the most valuable home-building land. This whole place used to be one of the most productive farms in the state, until Yost's grandpa, Johnny Billings, decided to retire in 1950 and leased it to the Air Force. So really, this land would be great for all kinds of uses." She took a deep breath, cued up the next paragraph of sales information in her mind, and then stopped. "I don't know why I'm talking, Mr. Rollins. You're a lot more familiar with the history of this property than I am. Is there a specific question you have that I can answer?"

Big Jim glanced at her. "Just keep filling me in, Missy; you might tell me something I don't know."

Marcie looked straight ahead through the windshield. Her hands trembled. This was her big opportunity and he couldn't even get her name right. But it was the only chance she would have. She couldn't count on being alone with him some other time, and it wasn't the kind of proposition she could make over the phone. "Well, Mr.

Rollins, it seems to me that there's a lot at stake in this deal. A lot of upside and a lot of downside."

"Go on."

"What's the real condition of the land, for example? Whether or not Tom Brown and his associates are straight shooters. See what I mean? If you had a friend on the inside to keep an eye on them and keep you informed of what was really going on . . . well, it seems to me that you'd have an advantage."

Big Jim smiled. "And you'd like to be that friend?"

"Yes, sir."

"Call me Big Jim, darling." He reached over and patted her hand. "I like to see initiative. You've heard, no doubt, that I'm the kind of boss who expects results?"

She was too afraid to look at his face. His fat, hairy fingers gripped the wheel at ten and two. "Yes, sir."

"And you still want the job?"

She nodded like a grade-school girl.

"So what can you tell me?"

"You're their only prospect. They think you've got the county commission in your pocket. They think a person without connections won't be able to see this project through."

"And what does that tell you?"

"That you should lowball them."

He pulled a cigar from his shirt pocket. "You're off to a good start. You remind me of my daughter at your age. What they paying you?"

"My agent's fee plus a bonus based on the sales price."

"You be my eyes and ears with these folks, you keep me up on anything they get up to, no matter how trivial, and I'll make sure you come out of this feeling good."

She settled back into the truck seat. Her fear of a few minutes ago seemed silly now. No matter what happened she was going to get paid. She glanced at his profile. "I'll take care of it."

He lit the cigar with the dash lighter and lowered his window. "See that you do. Remember, I want to know about anything. No matter how trivial."

. . .

PATTY AND BUDDY were standing close together in the parking lot of
Seanboro Park, which was situated downtown on the shore of White
Bear Lake. A light breeze cast ripples across the blue-green water.
The nearby tables were filled with families picnicking their supper,
little kids in swimsuits, moms in beach cover-ups and dads in shorts
and T-shirts. Patty adjusted the collar of Buddy's shirt and then
patted his cheek. "You got my money?"

Buddy smiled. "No 'good to see you. How did it go?' None of that,
huh?"

"You're here. I'm here. I just want to get my money and get home
so that Tom will never know."

"'Cause if Tom found out, that would mess up your program."

"You got that right."

"But you're going behind his back to earn more."

She shrugged.

He leered at her. "You like money better than sex."

"Better than sex? Do I have to choose?"

"Well, you're with Tom for the sex, but now you're with me for the
money. Admit it. You don't think he has the juice anymore."

"He brought me this far."

"Diminishing returns. Getting old and fearful. Unwilling to take
the money off the table."

"You got my money?"

"I ran into a little problem."

"Ran into a little problem." She stepped back. "What kind of
problem?"

"The kind that's going to work for us."

"Really? Okay, now that you've tried to spin it, give it to me
straight."

"My buyer narced me out."

Patty knew she should run, call Tommy, pitch the phone out the
window, dump the car. Instead, she very slowly took a second scan of
the parked cars and the picnickers. Then she put her arms around

Buddy and kissed him like a long-lost lover while her hands ran over his back, his buttocks and his groin, feeling for wires or listening devices. She stepped away and folded her arms across her chest. "So you're clean. I thought you were a smart guy, but now you're back on probation. How are you going to get out from under? And how are you going to get my money back?"

"I'm going to feed Tom to the cops."

"Are you insane?" She felt the adrenaline pumping through her body. The picture in her mind was of Tommy pressing the barrel of a pistol up against Buddy's head.

"The cops are after Big Jim. They think we're working with him to cheat the Yosts. I know; they're completely clueless. I told them Tom was behind the drug deal. I'm supposed to tell them when we're closing the deal on the Yosts so that they can swoop in, arrest everyone, and flip Tom on Big Jim. So all we have to do is separate Tom from the money. We give them Tom; we give them Big Jim; we keep the money; I pay you back out of my end. Everyone else gets burned, including the Yosts. Instead of a quarter of half the take, we split the pot fifty-fifty."

"And we leave at a hard run. This isn't what I agreed to."

He shrugged. "Yeah, I know you agreed to have your cake and eat it, too. But now it's shit or get off the pot. I'm the future. You come with me and you've got one. You stay with the old-timer—best case, you're down at the prison on visitors' day 'cause he's holding the bag for the dope and the con."

"What's to stop me from telling Tommy?"

"You want to blow this deal and go on the run broke? You think Tom can outgun me? We're all waiting for the money train. You want to go all O.K. Corral with the money in the middle? You think Tom can man up for that? He's old, girl. That's why you came to me behind his back."

Patty nodded her head. Why was Tommy always right? Buddy was a loose cannon, liable to do any stupid thing. But she hadn't listened, and here she was. She didn't want to tell Tommy about the dope deal. She could see him capping Buddy, Marcie just to tie up loose ends, her, pouring the gasoline, tossing the match, driving away while the apartment burned. He loved her. There was no doubt about that. She just didn't think love would keep him from killing her if that's what it took to stay out of prison. Especially if it were her own fault. He'd feel bad about it, he might even cry about it, but he'd get it done. She looked at Buddy, standing there with the look of certainty on his face that indicated stupidity. She'd been a fool to partner up with him, to think that someday he might replace Tommy, but she was stuck now. She had to look out for herself. So Buddy was right. He was the future. He just didn't know how short that future was going to be, because while he was in the driver's seat, she was going to find a way to cheat him out of his end of the score and get away clean. She sighed. "You're right, Tommy can't beat you, but that doesn't make it easy. Me and Tommy have got a lot of history. I want him to have a fair chance to get away."

"I can go with that."

"So the Yosts get paid, which makes the scam look legitimate. We leave Big Jim on his own, so he has less reason to come after us. We take Marcie and Tommy's cut—so we split half the pot fifty-fifty—and you slip out from under the cops. Tommy finds his own way or he flips on Big Jim."

"That's a lot of money to leave behind."

"That's the way it's got to be if you want my help. Otherwise"— she pointed over her shoulder—"I'll just get in that car and drive away. No amount of money is worth getting killed for, or going to prison."

"Okay, Patty, we'll do it your way. Just to cement our new relationship. But I'll deal with the details, just in case you get cold feet."

A FEW DAYS LATER, Tom drove down a dirt track on the Yost property, windshield wipers slapping slowly back and forth against the soft rain, the Escalade bouncing and jolting though the deep potholes, saplings and tall weeds brushing against its sides. Up ahead, out in a clearing on the lakefront, was Big Jim's Suburban. Tom pulled up beside it, ran out of his car, and climbed into the passenger's seat.

Big Jim sat behind the wheel, smoking a cigar with the air-conditioning on and his window halfway down. "Glad you could meet. Have any trouble finding your way?"

Tom shook his head. "No, it was a straight shot."

"I've been coming out here for a long time to watch the lake, enjoy the solitude. All that would be over if someone else bought it."

"This looks more like a place to deal with troublemakers than a place for reflection."

"Yeah, well"—Big Jim shrugged—"there's some of that, too." He puffed on his cigar. The rain picked up, and they listened to it dance on the roof and watched it bounce off the water among the little whitecaps. Tom didn't say anything. Big Jim had called this meeting, and he was waiting to hear what he had to say.

"My guys have studied the paperwork," Big Jim continued. "You know as well as I do that if Bernie Revere hadn't signed it, nobody would accept it."

"But he did sign it."

"And he's not going to change his mind?"

"Not in this lifetime."

"You sound pretty sure of yourself."

"I'm paid to be."

"So if some bad boys strong-armed him, his story wouldn't change?"

"A man who's afraid will say whatever he thinks will save him."

Big Jim's mouth gaped open as if he were smiling. "But that doesn't mean he wasn't lying to begin with."

"Look, I've already told you that we're willing to discount the price of the property. It ought to be worth a million dollars."

"So you want six hundred and fifty thousand." Big Jim shook his head. "Still too high. Too much risk."

"What you got in mind?"

"Four hundred thousand."

Tom laughed. "I guess this isn't your first negotiation. That number is absurd. We've got expenses. The Yosts have got to be paid."

"Everybody's got expenses. All the contractors will want combat pay just in case they're being poisoned working out here."

"If that's your best offer, I'll have to take my chances and open it up to bidding."

"You don't want to do that. Publicity, public scrutiny, the phone will be ringing off the hook at the county annex."

"We came to you because you're the guy who can get things done around here. Your expenses aren't going to be as high as somebody else's."

"Call it a half million, then. But that's my best offer."

Tom took a deep breath. "You're killing me here. Make it five-fifty and it's a deal." He stuck out his hand. Big Jim paused for a moment, watching Tom's face, and then shook his hand.

"You won't be sorry," Tom said.

"I better not be."

"Marcie Tolliver will be in touch about the paperwork."

"Have her call my lawyer, Lou Turnbolt." Big Jim threw his cigar out into the rain. "We done here?"

"Good doing business with you." Tom rushed through the rain back to his car, turned around, and started back down the muddy track.

Big Jim pressed the button to raise his window and then sat for a few minutes, listening to the rain on the roof of his truck and admiring the view of the park across the lake. He picked up a throwaway phone and called Frankie Steele, the lieutenant who ran his bookie operation.

"Yeah, boss."

"Closed the deal with Tom Brown."

"Get the price you wanted?"

"Paid more than I wanted to, but I don't think I was too easy."

"So he's expecting to get paid, not double-crossed."

"You got it. Now you're going to make sure I get my money back after I've got the deed."

"They won't cross the county line with your cash."

"I don't need to know the details, just take care of it."

"Consider it done."

AT 10:00 A.M. on the day before the closing, Tom and Patty were in their bedroom getting dressed for the day. CNN played softly on the bedroom TV. The coffeemaker in the kitchenette buzzed that the coffee was made. Tom tucked in his shirt and adjusted his belt. Patty stepped into her dress. Someone knocked at the door to the apartment.

"Zip me up."

Tom zipped up her dress, fastened the hook and eye at the top, and then caught her in his arms before she could step away. More knocking. Just as he cupped her breasts, she wriggled around, pecked him on the lips, and pushed him away. She gestured toward the living room with her head. "The door."

Tom glanced at his watch. "It's Buddy." He picked up the .38 revolver from the nightstand on his way out of the bedroom. He held the pistol down along his right leg and opened the door with his left hand. "Hey, kid."

"Hey, old-timer."

"Come on in."

Tom slipped the pistol into the back of his waistband. Patty looked over the counter that separated the kitchenette from the living room. "Hey, Buddy. Want coffee?"

"Yeah, sure. You two about ready?"

Tom looked at the mirror on the wall over the sofa to tie his necktie. Patty set coffee for Tom and Buddy on the countertop. "Where's your girlfriend?"

"I let her go."

Tom stopped in the middle of tying his tie and turned his head. "Who said you could get rid of her? She's part of our cover."

"We don't need her anymore. There's no reason to cut her in. I told her that her commission was plenty and that if she didn't want her sex pictures on the Internet, she'd keep quiet. She cried into her pillow, called me a bastard, but I was giving her the comfort before she left."

Tom looked at Buddy like he was on day release from the psychiatric unit. "Giving her the comfort. What makes you think she'll hold up?"

"She'll hold up. What's she going to do?"

Patty nodded. "She's getting her commission."

"Commission? That's not the point," Tom said.

Patty put her hand on his shoulder. "It's not personal, baby. Money's too hard to come by to give away to people who haven't earned it."

Buddy slurped out of his cup. "That's right. Look at the old folks —they get half the cash for doing nothing. How does that make sense?"

Tom pointed his finger at Buddy. "We're not stiffing the Yosts. Them sitting on their hands with their mouths hanging open like clueless yokels is what gives us our cover. We stiff them, Big Jim knows the deal's bad, plus we got the cops on us. We pay them, the cops get no cooperation, and we're long gone before Big Jim can start looking. End of story."

"Baby," Patty said, "we're just talking. There's no harm in talk. We could give them a taste. That's more than they have now. They probably wouldn't know the difference."

"We don't scam civilians. Rule number two. We use them, we pay them, we stay out of jail." Tom tapped his chest with his hand. "I put this job together. I call the shots. We're paying the Yosts. You put a job together, you call the shots; I decide if I'm in or out." Tom looked from Patty to Buddy. He felt a flash in his mind. It couldn't be true, but it was. Patty and Buddy were tag-teaming him. Yeah, now that he was inside the game, it was obvious. Buddy just didn't quite have the chops to slip it past him. But Patty? It was her bread and butter. So when did they get started? Before this job? Or was the first attempt when Buddy offered up the drug deal? And what did it mean? Had Patty switched allegiances, or was she just getting greedy? He tried to see through their body language, but nothing was clear. "So why are you so interested in switching everything up now? We all agreed on the plan before we started."

Buddy held his hands up in surrender mode. "It just didn't seem fair after I got to thinking about it. But I can understand your point of view. Let's just leave everything the way it is. I can live with that."

"Okay, then." Tom turned back to the mirror and finished tying his tie. He could feel Buddy's confidence. Buddy was up to something, no doubt about it. Tom snugged the knot and smoothed out his tie. They almost had Big Jim's money. It was the worst time for change-ups. But he couldn't risk a double-cross. He was going to have to shake things up until he found out where Buddy and Patty stood.

THAT AFTERNOON, Tom went to Ace Real Estate. The outer office where the assistants worked was empty. He walked down the hallway of agents' offices until he came to Marcie's. Her door was open. She was sitting at her desk working at her laptop. He knocked on her open door. "Marcie, I just heard what Buddy did. I am so sorry."

She sat back in her chair, crossed her legs, and started slowly rocking, but she didn't say anything.

"I'm just here to say that we made a deal with you, and we're going to stand by it. That's what I told Buddy."

"So you're in charge?"

He came into the room and sat on the corner of her desk. "That's right."

She looked up at him. "I appreciate you sticking up for me."

"A deal's a deal."

"But Patty and Buddy would have cheated me."

He waved it away. "Forget about it. You did your part; you're going to get paid."

She stood up close, almost between his legs, her cinnamon-scented breath in his nostrils. "What about the video he made?"

He shook his head. "As soon as we're done here, it'll be erased."

She put her hands on his knees. "You're a good friend, Tom. I know how to be grateful."

It was clear from her approach that she really didn't know how to seal the deal. She expected him to fuck her just because he was a man and she was willing. All he wanted to do was get out of her office without hurting her feelings. He put his hands on the desk in back of him and leaned away from her. "I said forget about it."

She took a step back. "You sure? You think Patty wouldn't cheat on you?"

He shrugged. "Patty's got nothing to do with it. I won't cheat on me."

"You won't cheat on you? What the hell does that mean?"

"And I won't break a deal with a partner. You should be happy. You get paid tomorrow with the rest of us."

AN HOUR LATER, Tom stood in the sun in the half-empty parking lot of Friendly's Coffee in a strip mall six blocks from Marcie's office, leaning in at the passenger-side window of the Ford Explorer, talking across his wife to Buddy in the driver's seat.

Buddy slammed his hands against the steering wheel. "Jesus Christ, what right do you have to spend my money?"

"It's done now. Marcie's back in."

Patty looked at Tom's face. "Buddy's right. We're supposed to make decisions together. Could you take off those sunglasses?"

"It should come out of your end," Buddy said.

Tom pulled off his sunglasses and held them by the legs in his right fist. He was getting the reaction he had hoped for. "Just how does that work?"

Patty looked from one to the other. "Would you two settle down? Damn it, honey, why're you so squirrelly? We have to get on the same page."

"I told you this was my job. I told you we weren't changing the rules in the middle of the game."

Buddy pointed his finger. "No more going behind my back."

Patty nodded. "You have to pull us in, baby. We all want the same thing. Let's finish this deal and move on. We'll all feel better when we have the cash."

Tom stood up and slipped his black glasses back on. More and more she couldn't help taking the kid's side. Time to see if they'd take the bait. He leaned back in. "Tell you what. I want to be reasonable. I've been thinking about what you said this morning. When the time comes, I'll see if I can't get the Yosts to settle for a third instead of a half."

Patty and Buddy glanced at each other. "A third," Buddy said. "The difference is what? Three times Marcie's cut after the commission? Now you're talking." He turned back to Tom. "Hey, I'm sorry about losing my temper."

Tom smiled. For a moment the kid had been looking at Patty and talking as if he weren't there. "Forget about it. I got a little heated myself." He turned to Patty. "I'm going to the gym. You riding with me?"

Patty shifted in her seat. "It's my off day. Buddy will run me home. Come and get me when you're done."

Tom walked away. He half expected Buddy to betray him. He was belligerent, argumentative, thought he knew best. But he couldn't believe that Patty would betray him. She was his only one. They'd been partners forever and ever, almost twenty years; she'd always backed his play, but she and Buddy definitely had some sort of side arrangement. But about what? Was it this job or was it something else? And with Patty in the mix did he really have anything to be worried about? Just the thought that maybe he couldn't trust her anymore gave him the willies. Still, he couldn't take any chances. He needed to find a way to stay one step ahead of them until he could figure out what they were really up to.

MARCIE DROVE up the gravel driveway to her house. The wraparound porch, the clean trim lines, the oaks overhead—it was picture perfect. The bushes she had planted along the front of the porch three years ago had finally come into their own, the tiny yellow flowers just beginning to pop. A pickup truck that she didn't know was parked at the side of the house. Some friend of Kenny's, she guessed. Three to one he hadn't gotten off the couch today. Men. She parked at the end of the drive so that the truck could back out. Buddy and Big Jim—they were easy to figure—but Tom, he was a trip. She knew he wanted to have sex with her; she could see the bulge in his pants. And he wasn't trying to hustle her out of her end of the deal. So what was driving him? It wasn't that bullshit about not cheating on himself, whatever that meant. She got out her phone and called Big Jim. "Mr. Rollins? This is Marcie Tolliver."

"Missy. What you got for me?"

"This may not be important, but remember I told you that last night Buddy told me that they didn't need me anymore, that I'd only get my agent's fee."

"Sure."

"But today, Tom came to my office, apologized, and promised me I'd get my bonus."

"I see."

"Weird, right? Could have knocked me over with a feather. It's like they can't agree on what they're doing."

"You did the right thing, calling me. You stay on this until we get the papers signed."

"Yes, sir."

She pushed the car door shut with her hip and went up the porch steps and through the front door. Kenny, bare-chested and wearing worn-out jeans, was lying on the couch watching ESPN, just like he had been when she left for the office this morning.

"You're late, honey."

"Late showing across town. Whose truck is that?"

Kenny sat up, but he kept looking at the game highlights. "Mine, baby, I bought it today."

She shook her head dismissively and kept walking toward the kitchen. "Yeah, right." She set her handbag on the kitchen table. "And what did you buy it with?"

"Aren't you getting paid tomorrow?"

"Are you serious?"

"I needed a ride, honey."

"That's my money. Money I already had plans for. You're going to have to take that truck back."

He looked at her over the sofa. "Make new plans. I'm keeping the truck."

She picked up a dirty glass from the kitchen table and threw it at him. He ducked, even though her throw was wild. The glass shattered against the living room wall.

"You're just making work."

She picked up an egg-smeared plate, thought better of it, and took it to the sink. "Fuck you."

"Maybe you should try that. Go back in the bedroom, put on some gift wrap and see if you can get me whipped. Then maybe I'll follow you around and do what you want. Take you for a drive in my new truck."

She leaned over the sink and held her face in her hands. "Bastard," she muttered, "fucking bastard." She took a deep breath, stood up, wiped the tears from her cheeks with her index fingers. She walked back over to the kitchen table where she could see Kenny on the sofa in the living room. "Kenny, I'm sorry I've been so busy."

He turned his head to look at her.

"I know it's been tough on you being out of work, feeling all the pressure about our bills. But this deal with the out-of-town players I was telling you about, this is our big chance."

"Is that right? Is that why you been fucking the young one?"

"What are you talking about?"

"Think I didn't know?"

"You've been following me?"

"Just from one shack-up to the next."

"It's not what you think. They're all a bunch of crooks."

"I bet."

"They tried to cheat me out of my cut today, but I got back in.

Tomorrow is payday. All I have to do is keep after them tomorrow and we're in the clear."

She walked over to the sofa, leaned down to put her head next to his and her arms around his neck, but he pushed her away. "You're such a liar."

"I'm telling you the truth. After tomorrow, I'll make everything up to you. After tomorrow—"

Kenny grabbed her wrists. "Right now. You're going to tell me the truth right now. You're going to tell me everything."

BUDDY AND PATTY were lying together in the backseat of Buddy's Ford Explorer, under the shady black maples on a secluded lane in a city park, still breathing hard, still in the moment before they each started thinking of their own timelines, their own to-do lists, their own manipulative needs and desires, when Buddy's phone rang.

Buddy reached for his pants in the front seat, fumbled around in his front pocket, found the phone, looked at the number. It was Detective Fadiman. "Shit."

Patty lifted her head from the seat. "Who is it?"

"It's nothing. Relax." Buddy took the call. "Yeah?"

"Hey, Buddy, you got anything for me yet?"

"I'm working on it."

"I can see you're working on it."

Buddy sprang up in the backseat and looked out the car windows. "You following me?"

"Of course I'm following you. You're a crooked bastard. You'd lie to me in a heartbeat. Look up the hill."

Buddy saw an arm waving out the window of a silver Ford Taurus. "Are you trying to get me killed?"

"A biker was murdered last night; task force guys say he went by Jimmy Dale. Looked like a cartel killing. Somebody you know?"

"Christ."

"Maybe management is dealing with product shrinkage. Your

time is short, Buddy. Ticktock. Get the job done." Fadiman ended the call.

Buddy tossed his phone into the front seat. "Damn it."

Patty pulled her dress on over her head. "Who was that?"

"Cops."

"Thought you had them under control."

"I do. They're just dogging me."

"Following you around town? You were looking up the hill."

Buddy pulled on his pants. "I don't need a lecture. I'm taking care of it." He buttoned his shirt. "Won't matter after tomorrow anyway."

"We'll see. If the cops are stuck to you, you won't even see me leave."

"So what else is new? Don't you have somewhere you need to be?"

She looked at her watch. "Take me home. Tom will be done at the gym in thirty minutes."

Buddy smirked. "Have you got your mind around giving him up? Tomorrow is the day. It's a hard thing to quit a partner you've been with so long."

Patty slipped on her shoes. "'Quit a partner you've been with so long'? How about double-crossing the love of your life? Don't you worry about me. I know how to do what I got to do."

"Don't be so melodramatic. It's just business. After Tom settles down, he'll understand."

"I'm not going to jail, and I'm not going to be around when Tom starts hatching his plan to get even. No matter how hard he tries, I won't be findable." She got out of the backseat and into the front. "Let's get out of here."

3

THE DAY OF THE CLOSING

T om, trying his best to hum along with "A Night in Tunisia" on the jazz station, pulled into the cracked-up parking lot of the Super 8 Motel and drove along the row of rooms until he saw Patty's white Honda Accord. Something wasn't right. He felt it before he saw it: the cracked windshield, the car door swung out, the bullet casings on the sidewalk, the trail of blood still red from the car to the open room door. He screeched to a halt, swung out of his Toyota Avalon, and ran into the room, pulling the .38 revolver from the back of the waistband of his suit pants. Too late. All that was left was the whir of the air conditioner. The air smelled of blood and gunpowder. His wife lay crossways on the near bed, her head hanging off the side toward him, her eyes open, blood trickling from the hole in her forehead. He turned with a jerk and vomited on the carpet, splattering his highly shined shoes. He must have seen wrong. It couldn't be her. He turned back, and she was still there, her slim, boyish figure flopped across the bed like a rag doll, her short dark hair hanging like yarn strands. He gripped his wrist to steady his gun hand as he inched toward the bathroom. No one between the beds. The second bed pristine, never even been sat on. Their clothes strewn around in the doorway to the bathroom, her panties and his white dress shirts. The money gone. In the bathtub their partner, the kid, was pumped full of holes, his blood leaking down the drain, his blue eyes looking at the shower head, his hand still gripping the automatic that wasn't big enough to handle the gunfighters who'd tailed them here. Sirens screamed from far away.

Tom woke with a start, breathing fast, his heart racing. Light filtered through the curtains of the bedroom from the streetlight in the parking lot. Tears welled up in his eyes. He took a deep breath and turned his head, expecting the worst. But there she was beside him, turned away with her head lying over his outstretched arm. He shifted, threw his other arm over her and pulled her close, breathing in her scent. She snuggled back against him, smiling. His tears dripped onto her shoulder. She wriggled around in his arms. "Tommy? What's wrong, baby?"

"You were dead, Patty. You were dead. Murdered with Buddy at the rendezvous."

"Baby, I'm right here. Right here." She took his face in her hands and kissed him hard. "Everything's fine. We're on schedule. It's all good."

"God, it was so real." He ran his hands over her, assuring himself of the reality of her, not wanting to wake up in the motel room with her dead body and the cops standing over him. His hands came to rest on her ass.

She reached down between his legs and squeezed him gently. "That real enough for you?"

He let go of her and rolled onto his back. He wiped his eyes with a corner of the sheet. She laid her head on his shoulder. "That must have been some dream."

"It was. It was the craziest, realest dream I've ever had."

"Well, it's all over now." She walked her fingers up his soft belly.

"We've got to get rid of the kid."

"We can't do that, baby."

"He's always stirring up the pot. Can't leave well enough alone. Has to shit where he eats."

"You're just fussing now. Let go of that dream. We're too far along. We have to follow the plan."

"You're right. You're right. We've just got to be careful. I'm not going to get shot or end up in prison over some stupid change-up." He kissed her forehead. She tilted her head back, and the next kiss met her lips. "What time is it?"

She squirmed up against him, put her arm around him, and kissed him again. "We've got plenty of time, baby. Plenty of time."

Later, Tom and Patty lay snuggled together; he spooned around her. A car started up in the apartment complex parking lot. Tom shifted his weight and pulled the sheet up over his arm. "You awake?"

"Uh-huh."

He kissed her shoulder. "What do you think about the endgame?"

Patty flipped onto her back and turned her head to see his face in the thin early light. "Baby, why are you so worried? You haven't settled down at all since we started on this gig." She adjusted the covers up under her arms.

"I know I'm sounding like a broken record, but Buddy and Marcie are trouble. He always has to complicate things—every job he gets worse until now it's been nothing but bullshit every step of the way—and she's in so far over her head and doesn't know it that she thinks she's a player. The fact that he found her makes her even more suspect."

Patty sighed. "Yeah, well, I wanted to get rid of Marcie, remember? But Buddy has proven himself plenty of times. Why are you so down on him now?"

Tom sat up. "Why are you taking his side?"

"I'm not on his side. Don't take this the wrong way, okay? It's just that Buddy reminds me of the way you used to be when you were his age."

"Faster, stronger, willing to take a risk—"

She punched his shoulder. "I didn't say that. You think I want to fuck him? Come on, he's just a kid."

"That's right." He tried to keep his face neutral. So now he knew. She was fucking Buddy.

She knelt on the bed facing him, her hair mussed, her shoulders shrugged, her hands palm up. "I'm with you, baby. It's always been the two of us. Whatever you decide, I'll back your play. You just tell me what you want to do."

"I don't know." He looked down at her knees. The tone of her voice, her beautiful body that he never tired of holding, every gesture she made, the subtle expression of her face—all said nothing was wrong. But a twinge of intuition told him this score was swirling in the toilet, and he was afraid she'd read it in his eyes.

"Walk away? Pack our shit and get out now?" she asked.

"Too much invested; too sweet."

"Well, if you're worried about the endgame, we can't just play it out. We have to change something."

"I know, I know."

"You're not talking about killing them when their part is done?"

His head shot up to find her face. Was he completely wrong? "That's way too messy. We could change our getaway plans. Give them their end after we're sure we're clear."

"We could change the plans and tell them."

"Then they'd just screw up the new plan."

"They're going to be pissed. Think we double-crossed them. Buddy will come out gunning."

"That depends on how it plays out. He'll chill out after he's paid. Then we're done with him, okay?"

"Okay."

"I mean it."

"I mean it, too."

"I love you." He got up on his knees, put his arms around her, and kissed her tenderly on the eyes and then on the lips.

When his lips moved away from hers, her eyes still closed, she said, "I love you." And right then, the complete conviction in her voice told him that he shouldn't trust her anymore.

AT 10:00 A.M. Tom pulled into a parking space in front of Ace Real

Estate. The day seemed just like any other: a few clouds in the sky, the promise of a warm afternoon. But the day wasn't like any other. If anything could go dangerously wrong with their plan, today was the day. Tom felt a sense of hypervigilance. Everything he did today had to be done in the correct order and in the correct amount of time. The longer he kept trouble at bay, the better his chances of making good his escape and going on a well-deserved vacation. The clock started now. Two female assistants, dressed for success in black and white outfits and business-wear makeup, sat at computers in the front office behind the counter. The one nearest the door looked up at him over her computer glasses as he walked in. Had he seen her when he was here before? He smiled and waved at her as he passed down the hallway to Marcie's office. Marcie stood up from her desk and smiled when she saw him, but her eyes were puffy and her face seemed pale.

"Everything okay?"

"Yeah, everything's fine. Didn't sleep well last night."

"Pregame jitters?"

"Yeah, pregame jitters. Here's the cashier's check, made out just as you requested."

"How did Big Jim seem?"

"Happy as a clam. His lawyer looked over the paperwork, gave his okay, and Big Jim was grinning that big grin of his as he handed me the check."

Tom glanced out the window into the parking lot and then around Marcie's office, enjoying the momentary surreal feeling that always came at the point of no return. "Then it's all good. I'll be out to your place later with your cut." He slipped the check into the inside pocket of his suit coat.

"You remember how to get out there? Highway Nineteen to the right after you drive out of town on Douglas Avenue."

"No problem."

"I'll be looking for you."

He pointed at her. "This is the fun part, Marcie. So just relax. I won't forget you. Story and a half with a front porch. Pick up your champagne before you head home."

Tom left the real estate office. Timing was everything now. Get people paid and get away before they could spring their trap, whoever "they" were. Buddy, certainly—he had the most to gain from a double cross. His wife, maybe; more than maybe if she really was sleeping with the kid. Marcie—he'd inoculated her by pulling her back in, unless that was all just part of Buddy's bullshit plan. And Big Jim? There was nothing to stop him from trying to get his money back now that he had the deed. Though as long as he thought the land was good, he'd probably try to avoid a scandal. Tom climbed into the Escalade. He ought to just run. Zigzag across a couple of states like a bat out of hell. He could contact Patty in a few days. But then he would never know if she'd betrayed him. Maybe there wasn't a scam at all. Maybe she'd just been letting the kid dip his wick. He'd never really know. And if he didn't know, he'd never be able to trust her. He'd always have to be afraid that the hammer was about to fall. It didn't matter that he loved her, that there was no one in his life but her, that she was the only person who mattered to him. If he couldn't trust her—there couldn't be any space between them. They had to be skin on skin. He had to know for sure. And she was too important to leave behind if his intuition were wrong.

At the First National Bank, the teller, a very helpful young woman with braces on her lower teeth, converted Big Jim's cashier's check into several smaller cashier's checks. Then Tom drove out into the country to the Yosts' house. When he pulled into their gravel drive-way, the garage door went up and they came out of the garage, Mr. Yost leading the way with his walker, Mrs. Yost shuffling along beside him in her cloth slippers. He got out of the Escalade with a folder containing a copy of the real estate transaction papers.

"Is it finally done?" Yost asked.

"The deal is done." He opened the folder and showed them the net proceeds. "Five hundred thousand dollars. It might not be as much as we hoped for, but it's the best we could get." He took out their check and handed it to Yost.

Yost held one side of the certified check while his wife held the other. $250,000. They stood there chuckling with tears trickling out of their eyes.

"I never thought we'd see anything but trouble from that land ever since the Air Force lease ran out."

Mrs. Yost nodded her head. "I never did, either. The cleanup hanging over our heads. You can't imagine the relief."

Yost slapped him on the back. "We can finally get this place fixed up. Come in the house. Have some coffee."

"I'm sorry, I don't have time to stay. This is a busy day for me."

Mrs. Yost grabbed him by the arm. "Are you sure? I've got some homemade coffee cake."

Tom nodded. "You should get in the car right away and go deposit this check before you do anything else."

Yost shook his head. "I still can't believe you did it. I don't know why anyone would buy that land. But it's Mr. Rollins's problem now."

"It'll seem more real when the money is in your bank account. Good-bye. It was great doing business with you."

Tom tapped the horn twice as he pulled out of the driveway. It was a beautiful afternoon—the trees in full leaf, the sun dappling the road, the pieces of the puzzle falling into place. As he reached the outskirts of town, Patty called.

"I'm with Buddy at the apartment. How's it going?"

"It's all gravy. The Yosts were more than happy with a third. I've just got to give Marcie her cut and then all we have to do is get rid of the kid."

"When will you get here?"

"Listen, honey, I don't want to come back to the apartment. Clear out of there and go to the cabin out in the woods. Nobody's been there so it should be clean for at least a couple of days."

"Are you sure you don't need help?"

"I'll be right behind you. If I need anything, I'll be in touch. Just make sure you aren't being tailed."

Tom drove to the downtown Greyhound bus station, a grimy building set in a corner at a busy intersection. He walked in through the front double doors, past the customers in line with their bags, past the people waiting in the bolted-down chairs or playing the noisy arcade games or snacking on nachos with cheese, and out the loading zone and across the street to a mailbox rental store. "I need to rent a second box."

"No problem, Mr. Brown. Sign here. I'll copy your info from your first rental."

"Great." He had $100,000 counterfeit in his first mailbox. The kid's end—a three-way split if Tom had given the Yosts $167,000—was $90,278. If he could unload the counterfeit on the kid, it would only be justice. He put Marcie's check—one quarter of $250,000 equaled $62,500—into a separate pocket, put the remaining checks into an envelope, licked the flap, and put the envelope into his new mailbox. Then he walked back through the bus station and got into his SUV. On his way to Marcie's, he stopped for gas and put the mailbox key into the car jack compartment.

It was midafternoon by the time that Tom drove up the bumpy gravel to Marcie's story-and-a-half, white clapboard house. The house sat up a slight hill, under a grove of large-trunked oaks. Except for a rusty junk car sitting in the side yard, the property was a model of careful maintenance. Marcie's red Taurus was parked next to the side of the house. Bushes of yellow flowers ran along the front of the wraparound porch. Tom honked his horn before he got out of the car, but no one came out on the porch. He rang the bell. Marcie, barefoot, dressed in jeans and a T-shirt, opened the door.

"Hey, come on in."

"Surprised to see me?"

She laughed. "No. Come on through to the kitchen." She started walking. "You want some tea?"

"I don't really have time."

"Always about the business."

"That's right."

Once they were in the kitchen, she picked up a glass of iced tea from the kitchen table. "Sure you won't change your mind?"

Tom reached into his suit coat pocket for the check. When he looked up, check in hand, Marcie had an automatic pistol pointed at him. He almost laughed. She really was the youngest babe in these woods, thinking force would work. She didn't have the first clue about how quickly all her hopes and dreams could turn to mud.

"Are you kidding?"

"I'm not kidding."

"'Cause if you're kidding, it's not funny."

She gestured toward a kitchen chair. "Sit down."

He sat down in the chair and put her check on the table. "It's just as we agreed."

"So you say." She yelled over her shoulder. "Kenny!"

Kenny came out of the pantry carrying a length of rope. He had the goofed-up look on his unshaven face of the wannabe who's been practicing his tough guy in the mirror too long.

"So this is how it's going to be."

"Shut up." He tied Tom's wrists to the chair behind his back. Marcie glanced at the check before she folded it into her front pants' pocket.

Kenny frisked Tom, laying his .38 revolver on the table along with his wallet, his car keys, and his phone. "That's all he's got."

She pointed with the automatic. "Where's the rest of the money?"

"I don't have it."

"Look, I'm not trying to rob you; I'm just wanting to see for myself that the cut is fair." She turned to her husband. "Check his car."

Kenny picked up the car keys and went out the back door.

She slipped the automatic into her waistband and picked up Tom's .38. "You could end up as a suicide."

"But that won't help you."

She drank the rest of her iced tea, and then swirled the ice around in the glass.

"I treated you fair," he said.

"Maybe. I know what the sale price was. But I don't know what you gave the Yosts."

"You got what you were promised. That's all you're getting. Get used to it."

The porch door slammed. Kenny came through from the living room. "There's nothing there."

Tom shrugged. "I told you."

Kenny took a pair of leather work gloves from a kitchen drawer. "So now we beat it out of him."

"I don't have any more money."

"We'll see."

Tom watched Kenny pull on the tan gloves. He was fairly certain he knew what Marcie's limits were, but he had no idea of how stupid her husband was, or if his stupidity was contagious. Kenny cocked his arm back and hit Tom in the eye, knocking him and the chair over. Tom's head bounced off the wood floor. He saw stars. Then Kenny kicked him in the stomach as he lay tangled with the chair.

"Hold up," Marcie said. "I don't know if this will get us anything."

"Shut up. You said he'd have the money."

"But I don't know now—"

"You stupid slut. Were you fucking him as well as the young guy? Now we're going to get that money. All of it. He'll tell us everything before I'm through." He kicked Tom again. Tom vomited, choked, and sputtered.

"Stop it." She grabbed Kenny's arm. He jerked free and back-handed her across the face. She stumbled; spat blood. Tom's .38 in her right hand fired once, twice, three times, the noise bouncing around the room as loud as a ship's cannon. Her husband fell in a heap.

Tom looked up at her through his good eye. "It's okay. It's okay. Take a deep breath. Sit down and take a deep breath."

She sat on the floor, gasping. He thought she might cry, but she didn't. Finally, when her breathing slowed, she stood up and tried to drink the melted ice out of her tea glass. He watched her, lying on his side tied to the chair, the smell of his vomit in his nose, her dead husband bleeding a few feet in front of him. She shook the ice, sucking the wet into her mouth, then turned her head and looked at the sink faucet as if she had never seen one before. She set the .38 on the counter, filled the glass, drank it down, and filled it again. She laughed. "You still here?"

"Yeah."

"Smart money would have run."

"I guess I'm not so smart."

"Will you come with me?"

"Would you believe me no matter what I told you?"

"You've got rules like no one I've ever known." She set the full glass on the kitchen counter, wiped the counter around it dry with a dish towel, picked up the .38 and left through the kitchen door. Tom heard a car start and then roll away down the gravel. He felt very lucky that he hadn't been shot. He started rocking the chair, trying to find a way to work his hands free. Even money said she would be at the police station confessing within two hours. He intended to be long gone with his prints wiped clean before the police arrived.

EDDIE, Big Jim's assistant, sat low in a beige Honda on the shoulder of the road in the shade of a scrub maple just below Marcie's driveway. He'd followed Marcie home from the real estate office. It was his assignment to keep her under surveillance until Big Jim told him otherwise. He was bored, smoking a cigarette, wanting to go to the bathroom. He'd parked in the shade up against the bushes to make the car more inconspicuous, but now the mosquitoes had found him, buzzing around just enough to be an aggravation. He wanted to turn on the radio, but he knew he had to listen for what he couldn't see. When he heard the gunshots, he felt more relief than excitement. He called Big Jim.

"Have you seen anyone leave?"

"No, sir. Tom Brown drove up there a little while ago, but nobody's left."

"Stay in the car. Follow whoever leaves. Call me when you know who it is."

When Marcie screeched out onto the highway, Eddie pulled out behind her and pressed the speed dial on his phone. "Sir? Marcie Tolliver's on the move."

"She by herself?"

"She's the only one I can see."

"Call Frankie. Tell him to go to her place and clear up whatever mess he finds. You stay on her. I want to know everyone she meets with."

TOM DROVE to the convenience store he'd passed on his way out to Marcie's. There were no cars parked in front of the store. He pulled his SUV around to the side and parked on the patched asphalt facing away from the building. The cows in the neighboring pasture were grouped in the mud hole by a shallow creek. Tom took off his suit coat, rolled up his sleeves, and put on a ball cap. He kept his head down as he pushed into the store. The teenaged clerk gave him a glance. He gave a polite nod in return. He bought a bag of ice, a bag of mixed nuts, and a soda. When he got back to the Escalade, he turned on the radio to the classical station. He lay back in the seat with an ice pack on his eye for fifteen minutes and then rinsed his wrists in the bag of ice. He drank the soda and ate the nuts. He was thinking about all the deep unknown in a person, the unknown that was surprising and unaccountable, the unknown that only good luck could protect you against. Then he found himself thinking about Marcie's house again—the living room and the kitchen, the surfaces he touched and the surfaces he wiped off, Marcie's husband transformed from belligerent asshole to passive meat sack at the squeeze of a trigger. He reached along his side, feeling his ribs.

When he woke up, over an hour had passed. The bag of ice was melting into his passenger-side floor mat. He reached into the icy water and then patted his face with his cold, wet hand. Time to go. He popped open the passenger's door, sloshed the ice bag out onto the asphalt, and started the SUV. Marcie had made their closing scenario more complicated, but she hadn't made it worse. Now all he had to do was deal with Buddy. He drove back toward town, still a little dazed but feeling the need to keep moving, when his phone rang.

"Baby, I've been worried about you."

"I'm okay."

"I'm glad. I'm glad you're safe. When I hadn't heard from you, I didn't know what to think."

"The plan went to crazy town, but everything is all right now. I'll explain it when I see you."

"Don't hang up, baby. Don't hang up. We have a problem here."

He pulled up at a red light. He could feel the plan beginning to shudder and bounce like a fast car with two wheels off the shoulder and onto the grass. "What problem?"

"Marcie showed up here. She and Buddy are in cahoots. They want the whole score. They say they'll kill me if you don't give it to them."

"Did you tell them I'd just walk away?"

"I told them."

The light turned green. He drove through the intersection and then pulled over on the shoulder. "Let me speak to Buddy."

He heard the phone being passed. "Yeah?" Buddy asked.

"Your girlfriend tell you what happened at her house?"

"Yeah."

"Then you know all you're getting is your part."

"Old-timer, you love this woman. She's all you got and she's real pretty right now. But she won't stay real pretty for long. Me, I'm just a businessman like you; I'd have a hard time fucking up your lady. But you've seen Marcie; she's riding the roller coaster. She's already paid the fare, and she means to take the whole ride. Where are you at?"

"I'm at the north end of town."

"Patty's got one hour. You can take all the time you want, but she's got one hour."

Tom held the steering wheel with both hands. He still had three checks, plus the check to cover the overhead, safely sitting in the mailbox. Everything about this situation told him that he should just walk away. But Buddy was right. They had him by the short hairs. He couldn't leave town without Patty. And he really, really, really didn't want to rush in there guns blazing. He'd leased the cabin. The landlord could identify him. Besides, there wasn't enough time to disappear the bodies and get out of town well ahead of any possible problem. More importantly, he still didn't know whose side Patty was on. Whenever he looked at her, he still saw that naïve seventeen-year-old girl walking up the dusty shoulder of that blacktop highway with her soon-to-be ex-boyfriend, a tough guy she had so whipped he couldn't have remembered his own name if she hadn't told him. She hadn't realized her own power, but even driving by them in his sky-blue Cadillac, Tom had. He knew that day he had to have her, had to make her into everything she could be. So he'd pulled over and pushed open the passenger's door. Then, somewhere along the way, he'd fallen under the spell he'd taught her to create. There was only one way to find out if he could still trust her. He was going to have to put himself and the money at risk. One hour. Barely enough time to get there if he took the beltway and hit all the lights. The highway behind him was clear. He put the car into drive.

THE CABIN WAS LOCATED at a lonely spot at the end of a sandy road. It was a simple, two-bedroom, barn-red cabin with an open floor plan, an attached carport, and state forest trail access from the back, but it was far enough from the public access that few people walked the trail behind the cabin and no one ever carried their picnic this far. Tom pulled up beside the blue Explorer and the red Taurus that were already parked under the pines in front of the house and went inside without knocking. He was expecting the worst. This was the most obvious of setups. He just wasn't quite sure if he could play his part. Patty, dressed in a blue golf shirt and a tan skirt, was sitting in a kitchen chair. Marcie stood behind her, holding an automatic pistol to Patty's neck. She had an empty look in her eyes.

Buddy was holding Tom's .38 revolver. He gestured at Tom's eye with the barrel. "Looks like you've been having a rough day, old-timer. Turn around." Buddy put the barrel of the .38 up against Tom's spine and frisked him. "Sit down."

"Why bother? We're not going to be here that long."

"So where are the checks?"

"You okay, Patty?"

"I'm good, baby."

"Let her come to me."

Buddy nodded to Marcie. Patty crossed over to Tom. He hugged her tight and kissed her cheek. "I'm glad I came for you."

"The checks," Buddy said.

Tom squatted, dug around in his left shoe, and brought out a key. He handed it to Buddy, who examined it. "Mailbox?"

"That's right."

"That's where it is?"

"That's all there is. Mailbox place near the downtown bus station."

Buddy motioned with the gun. "Get out of here."

Tom took Patty's hand. "Let's go."

She pulled away from him. "I'm not going with you, Tommy. You've gotten too soft, too willing to leave money on the table. The old you never would have come here without a plan to get me and keep the money."

Tom looked from his wife to Buddy to his wife again, wondering how much working room he had if he didn't want to get killed.

Buddy pointed the .38 at Tom's chest. "He's got to go," Buddy said.

"Don't worry." Patty said. "He'll leave. He wants to live. Don't you, baby? That's just the kind of guy he is."

Buddy shook his head. "He's got too much pride. He's used to having his own way."

Marcie sniggered. "And he's in love with you, Patty. I offered him a taste and he wouldn't even take a look."

"Is that right, baby? You wouldn't fuck her because of me? I'm touched. That's flowers on my birthday."

Tom looked down at the faded carpet between them, concentrating, hoping to choose the right words without appearing to have chosen them. "Okay, you won. You've screwed me. Just give me enough money to cover the expenses and I'm gone."

Buddy laughed. "You don't listen at all, do you? Get out while you can."

Tom turned to Patty and held his hands out. "Honey, come on, come with me, you don't want to do this. Please, please, for old times' sake. Think it through, Patty; you know you belong with me."

Buddy laughed. "Christ, old-timer, now you're just embarrassing yourself. Try to take it like a man."

Patty stuck her hand out to Buddy. He looked at her puzzled; then, smiling, handed her the .38. "This is for old times' sake." A tear ran down her cheek. She pointed the gun and fired. Marcie jumped.

Tom fell back against the wall and slid down to the floor, still breathing, his eyes closed, blood trickling out of his side. She could have shot Buddy. He would have loved to see the look on his face. They could have talked Marcie out of her pistol. Instead, he knew now he should have tossed the cell phone out the car window, collected the checks, and kept on going after they called him to set him up. He never had a chance. All he'd done by coming here was prove them right.

Marcie leaned in for a closer look. "So that's what it looks like when you see it happen."

Buddy, grinning, shook his head. "I didn't think you'd do it. I really didn't think you'd do it."

Patty knelt down beside Tom, set the gun down, and went through his pockets. There was nothing she wanted to take. She used his handkerchief to wipe her eyes, and then she took his face in her hands and kissed him. "Let's get out of here."

She handed Buddy the gun. He tucked it into his waistband, still grinning. "Don't get mad, Patty. I mean this in the sweetest way, I really do—you are one crazy bitch."

BUDDY, Patty, and Marcie left in the Taurus. The evening was quiet, except for the crickets chirping in the woods and the sound of their car bumping through the potholes. Along the roadside, the lights from the camping spots got brighter as the dark came on, but there was still time to get to the mailbox store before it closed for the day. There was no talk of one person going and everyone meeting later; they were all stuck together until the checks were collected and cashed and the money divided, which meant mailbox, motel room, and bank in the morning on the way out of town. Buddy was driving, trying to figure out how to get the .38, Marcie, and Patty together with the police before the bank opened in the morning. If Tom died, the direct connection to Big Jim would be broken, but giving up Marcie and Patty for the two murders ought to make the drug charge go away. The easiest way to get rid of them would probably be to call Detective Fadiman after they settled in for the night and negotiate a new deal, if he could do it without giving up the mailbox key. He glanced at Patty, who was riding shotgun. Was she already working her plan to separate him from the checks, or had she really thrown in with him? He guessed that he'd find out if he couldn't feed her to the cops. He checked Marcie in the rearview mirror. She was sitting in the middle of the backseat, hunched forward with her hands gripping the tops of the front seats. The other little problem was how to get the check Tom had given her out of her pocket. Maybe Patty could help him with that.

Marcie tapped Patty's shoulder. "Turn the radio on."

"What?"

"The radio. Turn it on."

Buddy started into an S curve. "Fuck no. No music."

"Why not?"

He was in the middle of the S before they saw any other headlights. As he slowed down for the end of the S turn, an old rusty pickup truck flew past them, pulled tight in front of them, and hit the brakes. "Jesus."

He braked, started to pull around, but a black Avalon boxed them in from the side. They all slowed to a stop. "Eyes open, ladies."

"Four guys, shotguns," Patty said.

Buddy jammed the Taurus into reverse and stomped on the gas, skittering back down the S.

"They're turning around," Patty said. Marcie reached back for her seat belt.

"Here goes nothing." Buddy spun the wheel and hit the brakes hard. The Taurus squealed around, but Buddy misjudged the road and the Taurus jumped past one hundred and eighty degrees and into the ditch facing the woods.

"Come on, come on, come on," Patty yelled.

Marcie banged on the driver's seat. "They're almost here."

Buddy floored it. The rear end pushed around and the tires started to smoke.

"We're hung up on something." Buddy flicked off the headlights. "Make a run for the trees." He jumped out of the car with the .38 in his hand.

"On the ground."

Four men wearing dark clothes and holding shotguns at their shoulders had him covered from front and back. He lay on the ground. The closest man came up, stepped on his wrist, and took the .38.

"Out of the car."

Marcie and Patty got out with their hands up. "Who are you?" Marcie asked. "What's going on?" Two of the men pushed them toward the road.

A burly, unshaven man with a pushed-in nose pulled Buddy to his feet. "Keep your mouths shut if you want to live."

The man waved the Avalon down. The trunk popped open. Buddy, Marcie, and Patty were herded to the side of the black sedan, frisked, and loaded into the trunk like so much luggage.

"I got three phones and one more gun," the burly man said.

"Okay," someone said.

"What about their car?" another man asked.

"Bring it."

. . .

TOM WOKE up in the dark, lying on a stretcher being jostled across the yard of the cabin to a waiting ambulance. Voices were talking; red and blue lights were flashing. He really didn't feel as bad as he thought he ought to. He turned his head and saw that his black Escalade was lit up by somebody's headlights. His mind flashed to the key in the car jack compartment. He squinted when the stretcher slid into the bright light in the back of the ambulance. The EMT, a black woman wearing beaded cornrows and a city firefighter's blue uniform, smiled down on him. "There you are. How you feeling?"

He nodded.

"I'm going to hook up an IV."

He felt a prick in his arm and a coolness running up the vein.

"Lucky you dialed 911 before you passed out."

He remembered—what? The gunshot, Patty leaning over him, reality falling away. The EMT patted him on the shoulder. "Just rest easy. You're going to be fine."

BUDDY, Marcie, and Patty were pulled out of the Avalon's trunk inside a pole-built warehouse with a garage-style entry door. They blinked in the fluorescent lights, trying to get their bearings: open space, concrete floor, tan sheet-metal walls, an office with window to the far right, a padlocked storeroom beside it.

A burly, balding man dressed in a black nylon jacket, black crewneck shirt, and black pants pointed to a long, metal office table with folding chairs pushed in around it. "Strip down to your underwear and put your clothes on the table." The three other men, still holding shotguns, pushed them along. "Do it yourself or we'll do it for you."

It was clear that arguing would only lead to pain, so Buddy stripped down to his boxer-briefs and Patty stripped down to a bra and thong set. Marcie kicked off her moccasins and wriggled out of her jeans. She turned to the boss. "I'm not wearing a bra."

He looked her up and down. "You'll do."

One of the men went through the pockets of their clothes, piling keys and wallets on the table. "Found a check in her jeans and a mailbox key is his pants."

The boss read the check. "This is a start." He turned to Buddy. "Where's the box?"

The closest man prodded him in the belly with a shotgun barrel. "Mailbox store by the bus station."

The boss gestured with his thumb toward the storeroom. "Lock them up."

Marcie smiled. "Can we have our clothes?"

The boss shook his head.

There was a bare bulb in the ceiling of the storeroom, dusty metal shelves on three walls, and a small air vent in the back corner closest to the office. The door slammed shut and the bolt ground into place. No one was escaping from here. Buddy leaned back against the side wall and folded his arms, trying to look tough. Patty sat down cross-legged on the cold concrete floor near the back wall. Marcie tried the door handle. A frightened little sound escaped her. Her hands were shaking. Everything had happened so fast that she still hadn't processed her feelings from having murdered her husband. Until a few moments ago, she'd been in a euphoric bubble. She was certain that her luck had finally changed, that she'd proven herself to the others and that in a few months they would all be the best of friends. But now the gravity of her situation hit her harder than Kenny's slap.

"We're all dead."

Patty doodled with her finger on the concrete. "Maybe. Maybe not. Whining won't help. If the plan was to kill us, there was no reason to bring us here."

"Then what do they want?"

"They took the check and the key."

Buddy slid down the wall into a squat. "So who do they work for?"

Patty looked up. "Buddy, use your brain. They're either drug thugs who've caught up with you, or Big Jim's guys out to reclaim his money, or a rip-off crew. Not that it matters until they get a look in that mailbox. The fun starts if they don't find what they want. The real question right now is how they found us." She glared at Marcie.

Marcie's mouth dropped open. "What makes you think it was me?"

"The odds favor you. Your play with your husband went south. Buddy had hoped to screw Tom and, probably, me. He didn't want any partners."

Buddy smiled. "And how do we know this isn't a setup? Tom using you to cheat us out of our part?"

"Cheaper to pay employees than partners? I shot Tommy. You think that was part of his plan?"

Marcie sat down on the floor, pulled her legs up under her T-shirt, and covered her face with her hands. "I wish I still had the gun."

Patty looked from Marcie to Buddy. She was trying hard not to think about Tom, but he kept creeping into her mind. She hadn't had any choice in shooting him—she had to sell Buddy on her loyalty and she didn't want Buddy to kill him. Like Tom always said, it's the ripples that get you. And the damage control from going in on Buddy's drug deal had brought her here. Drug thugs would kill them tomorrow, fast or slow, depending on the money count. Big Jim couldn't know the land was worthless yet, so he might let them go, if the checks were in the box and they added up. A rip-off crew? Maybe she could talk her way out, but they probably would have raped her by now. Tommy was always so good when the pressure was on. He wouldn't have gotten locked in this storeroom. Back in the day, he was the ultimate song-and-dance man. If only he hadn't gotten old, lost the juice. She sighed. Why was she writing his obituary? She was the one who'd probably be dead tomorrow. If not, she'd have plenty of time to enumerate her regrets.

DETECTIVE FADIMAN SIPPED his coffee while he looked over the dessert menu. He didn't need to read the items; he was just refreshing his recollection. The Twelfth Street Diner was mostly empty now. Two other tables were finishing up, a middle-aged couple he saw all the time and a family with a toddler in a high chair. The other waitress, Bobbie he thought her name was, was setting out place settings for the breakfast rush. Janet came over, wiped her hands against her apron, pulled out her order pad and pencil, and smiled. "What's it going to be, Rusty?"

"I don't know. Might skip dessert."

Her eyes laughed. "You never skip dessert."

"I don't like dessert. I just don't want to miss a chance to talk to you."

"You're not much of a detective." She pointed to her wedding ring.

"Oh, well. Make it the banana cream pie."

"More coffee?"

He waved his hand over the top of his cup. "Coffee's fine."

She turned away. He picked up his phone and called Buddy. No answer. Again. He called his partner.

"Hey, Rusty, can I call you back? Reading the bedtime story. Ten minutes."

"Hold on. Buddy's not answering his phone. He might have rabbited."

"Tomorrow. First thing. I'll jump on it early."

Janet slid the pie in front of him. He mouthed a thank-you. "I got a bad feeling about this. If we can't find Buddy, we need to start shaking the tree: Tom Brown, the Yosts, Bernie Revere."

"Tomorrow, Rusty. Right now I'm on dad duty."

Fadiman took a forkful of pie, banana and cream, no crust. He watched the precise way Janet cleaned the last table, the even pressure she put on the rag. He looked at his watch. He made a note on his pocket pad.

4

THE DAY AFTER THE CLOSING

"You are the luckiest man alive." The emergency room doctor —green scrubs, stethoscope, a brown, immigrant face speaking suburban English—smiled down on Tom as he lay on the hospital bed in bay number six. "The bullet went straight through, didn't hit anything but your spare tire, no serious damage. You really didn't even lose that much blood. You're all patched up now."

Tom swam up out of the pain meds and fatigue. "Thanks, Doc."

"We're going to keep you a few more hours; then we'll probably send you home."

"Okay."

"You got someone to look after you today?"

He smiled. "My wife will take care of me."

The doctor patted him on the shoulder. "Press the button if you need anything."

The doctor disappeared. Tom looked at the ceiling. The gun swung around toward him all in a blur. Marcie's house, the cabin in the woods, the images melted into each other. The gunshots reverberated in his head. Marcie's husband, Buddy, the images slowly separated. Marcie shot her husband. Patty shot him. She dumped him for Buddy. Buddy got the counterfeit money and both the girls. So why hadn't he bled to death? Riding in the dark on the stretcher. He took a careful breath. The room was bright and cool. He could hear the machine white noise; the hospital personnel moving around, talking in low voices; the occasional sputter or moan of a patient. It felt so good to be here, so safe and comforting. But he hadn't dialed 911. Patty was kneeling over him, going through his pockets. She must have pocket-dialed his phone. What was she up to? Did she think she was saving his life by shooting him? Or was she just cementing her new relationship, no hard feelings? God, she was a beautiful, crafty bitch. Because her emotions were always real. She could love him and make a play against him. Nobody could learn to defend themselves against that level of guile. Not that it mattered. He'd never taste her lips again. He closed his eyes.

When he opened them, two police detectives were standing over him. They held up their badges and identified themselves as Rusty Fadiman—fat and bald—and Malcolm Bigalow—brown leather jacket and jeans. Fadiman spoke. "We'd like for you to make a statement."

"I was shot."

Fadiman sighed like the long-suffering straight man for a second-rate comedian. "We already know that. Who did it?"

"I don't know."

"A stranger?"

"I can't remember anything about what happened."

"Really?"

Bigalow leaned in toward the bed. "This have anything to do with your real estate business?"

Tom shook his head. "I have no idea what you're talking about."

Bigalow turned to his partner. "We're wasting our time."

Fadiman shrugged. "When your associates find out you're on the street and not in a body bag, you'll wish you had cooperated. We know you're connected to Big Jim Rollins. When you're tired of ducking bullets, give us a call. Just don't wait too long." He set his card on the bedside table.

After the detectives left, Tom picked up the card. These cops had Buddy written all over them. Patty was too savvy to spill information into the wind. Marcie didn't know the illegal part and was wearing her husband's body. All their meetings and discussions had been in places that couldn't be bugged beforehand. So if the cops were sniffing the job, Buddy must have screwed the pooch. Big surprise. Tom set the card back down on the table. Maybe Patty had done him a favor.

THE DOOR to the storeroom groaned open. Three thugs with shotguns, hard men with thick necks and heavy, scarred hands, ordered Buddy, Marcie, and Patty out into the warehouse and prodded them over to the long table, where three metal folding chairs now sat in a row. The boss stood there in a black suit, smiling, rested and ready, his thin hair carefully combed back, his white shirt pressed, his floral print tie knotted. "Have a seat."

The thugs pushed them into the chairs. The boss walked leisurely back and forth in front of them. "We used the key this morning, found a box of cash, thought we'd be giving you your clothes back as a gesture of good faith, but guess what? The cash is bogus. Good looking, crisp engraving, but bogus. So now our feelings are hurt."

One of the thugs smacked Buddy in the side of the head with the butt of his shotgun. Marcie squealed. Buddy rocked sideways and then folded his head down to his knees and rubbed a spot above his ear.

"I bet that hurt," the boss said.

Patty looked down at her lap. When had Tommy bought the counterfeit money?

Marcie blurted out, "We didn't have cash. It was all cashier's checks, like the check in my pants pocket."

"Sure," the boss said, "but where are the checks?"

"Tom had them. He gave me my check. He gave Buddy the key. That's all we know."

"I wish I could believe you. But until I'm sure that you think you've got no choice but to tell me the truth, well"—the boss shrugged—"you can see where we're at."

"I need to go to the bathroom."

"No bathroom. No food. No water. There's nothing but pain until I have the cashier's checks." He nodded toward Buddy. "Take him."

Two of the thugs leaned their shotguns against the chair next to the boss, grabbed Buddy by his arms, and threw him out away from the table. The third man kept his shotgun trained on Buddy.

"Wait a minute. Let's talk about this." Buddy raised his hands to shield his face. One of the men punched him in the side of the head where the shotgun butt had hit him. He staggered back. The other man hit him from the other side. They beat him, each taking his turn, until Buddy couldn't crawl away anymore when he was kicked. Patty and Marcie sat in their underwear on their folding chairs watching: Patty gray and silent, Marcie red and sobbing.

The boss looked at the women. "You can see how serious this is." He pointed to Buddy, hamburger-faced, covered in welts and bruises, barely breathing. "This is what's on the breakfast menu. Either of you have anything you want to say?"

Marcie put her hands together as if she were praying. "We told you . . . we told you everything."

The boss looked at the men standing over Buddy. "Put him to bed." They dragged Buddy back into the storeroom.

The third man grabbed Marcie by the shoulder. She grabbed onto the folding chair with both hands, trying to stay seated. "Please, please." He passed his shotgun to the boss, pulled Marcie and the chair up with one hand, and punched her in the face with his other hand. The chair clattered away. Marcie pissed herself. Blood ran down her chin. She put her hands to her face. When she saw the blood, she screamed and started gasping.

Patty took a deep breath. Marcie didn't have the stones for this. Who did? "You're not going to die. Your nose is broken. You're hyperventilating. Cup your hands over your mouth and try to breathe normally."

The boss turned to Patty. "So you're the tough guy here." He smiled. "Look, I'm not enjoying this. I'd love to give you your clothes and send you on your way."

"You can't kid a kidder. It's garbage bags and shovels as soon as you have the checks."

The boss shrugged. "Maybe. But it could be quick and easy instead of slow and hard. Maybe I change my mind because you're so helpful. Maybe I get a last-minute call. Maybe I don't have to kill you because you can't go to the cops." He looked her up and down appraisingly. "What we do know is that right now you're a honey trap, a sweet little thing that wraps men around her finger. You take every-thing they got, leave them broke, and they're still happy they met you. Am I right?"

Patty felt like she needed to swallow, but her tongue was stuck to the roof of her mouth.

"You want to risk spending the rest of your life with a broken face, missing teeth, and a limp? Over money you're not going to keep anyway? Please, do yourself a solid."

"I wish I had something to tell you. Hell, I wish I could think of a lie that would slow this all down, but there's no turns in this road. She's already told you everything we know. Tommy picked up the check, went to the bank, converted it into smaller checks, paid her off." She motioned toward Marcie with her head. "She tried to rob him but he wasn't carrying the other checks, we got him to give up the key, left him shot, you scooped us up. Have you been to the cabin?"

"There's nothing there but a bloodstain on the rug and police tape. You'll have to do better." He nodded toward his men.

Patty followed the movement of his head. So the 911 call had gone through. Tommy was probably still alive. But why had he pleaded with her? What was his scheme? He couldn't have known about the double cross. One of the thugs reached for her. "You're Big Jim's guys, aren't you?"

The boss waved off his man, but he didn't say anything. He just stood there, watching her with his cat eyes.

"We can make a deal. We can get those checks; we just need some time. We just need to figure out what Tommy did. He's at the hospital."

"You're not leaving here."

She sprang up into her boxing stance before the thug could pull her from the chair, bobbing and weaving and trying to remember what she'd learned in the ring wearing headgear and gloves. The thug laughed as he closed in, but she managed to connect two punches to his chin before a stiff right knocked her across the table.

"Just let me talk to Tommy."

The thug dragged her off the table and football kicked her before she hit the floor. She didn't say anything else. A few minutes later, she was a limp pile on the concrete.

"What a goddamn mess," the boss said to no one in particular. He sat down at the metal folding table and got out his cell phone. "Big Jim? It's Frankie."

FADIMAN AND BIGALOW walked into Bernie Revere's office in the Boford County Office Annex. Bernie was sitting behind his desk, papers spread out on both sides of his laptop computer, a glazed donut and a mug of coffee within easy reach. A pair of mud-covered work boots sat against the wall under the window. "Detectives, can I get you some coffee?"

"Don't have the time," Fadiman said.

"Then how can I help you? When you called you said it was urgent." He motioned toward the office chairs facing his desk. "Have a seat."

They sat down. Fadiman got a pad and pen out of his sports coat. "We understand you examined soil core samples from the old Yost property and wrote a report."

"It's public record, Detective. Want me to send you a copy? Or give me an e-mail and I'll send it to your computer."

"What was your finding?"

"Basically, the land along the lake is only suitable for low-density development, unless it goes on the city sewer, which isn't going to happen in the immediate future."

"No contamination?"

"No widespread contamination of the sort that would bar development."

Bigalow uncrossed his legs and leaned forward in his chair. "Who paid for the analysis?"

"Tom Brown, acting for the Yosts."

He glanced at Fadiman and nodded. "Is the land for sale?"

"I don't know for a fact, but I assume so. Why else go to the expense?"

"Has it been sold?"

"I don't know. Hang on." Bernie opened the browser on his laptop and looked in the county property database. "Nothing here. How recent you wanting to know?"

"Right up to today."

"New transactions wouldn't be in the database."

Fadiman tapped his pen against his pad. "But somebody must know. There's paperwork somewhere, right?"

Bernie shrugged. "Let me call over to the courthouse." He picked up his phone. "Hey, Jerry, I got the police over here wanting to know if the Yost property traded hands in the last few days." He looked up at Fadiman and Bigalow. "It'll be a few minutes. Any other questions for me?"

"Yeah," Fadiman said. "How long ago did Tom Brown request the analysis?"

"Dropped the soil cores off a few weeks back. Why?"

"You always get an analysis done so fast?"

"He paid for expedited. I worked overtime. County Executive expects this kind of service for business people." He turned back to his phone. "Thanks, Jerry." He hung up his phone. "You must be clairvoyant. Jim Rollins just bought the Yost land. The whole property. Paid cash."

"Paid cash?"

"Yes, sir."

Fadiman and Bigalow glanced at each other, and then stood up. "Thanks for your time."

"Glad I could help."

Bernie sat in his chair with his hands together, looking at the closed door as if he could see through it to watch the detectives walk down the hall and out of the building. He took a bite of his donut and washed it down with lukewarm coffee. The land had been sold yesterday and the police were already interested. That couldn't be good. How long would it be before they wanted an expert opinion on his analysis? The data he used couldn't stand close scrutiny. A bad analysis could cost him his job, but made-up data? He'd go to jail. He got out his cell phone and called Tom Brown.

BIG JIM's gold-colored Cadillac rolled through the garage doors into the warehouse and right up to the long metal table. Marcie, Patty, and Buddy, their faces mashed and swollen, were slumped down on the metal folding chairs in their stained underwear as if their skeletons had been replaced with rubber. Big Jim and Eddie got out of the car. "Jesus, Frankie, I told you to solve this problem, not create a bigger one."

Frankie shrugged. "You told me to get the check back. Whatever it took."

"It's really worked out well, hasn't it? What a stench." Big Jim shook his head as he looked down the line of chairs. "Is that Missy? My God, what did you do to her?" He tried to help her up, but she shrieked, put her hands up in front of her face, and cowered in her chair. He knelt down in front of her. "It's okay, honey; it's okay. This was all a mistake. We cleaned your house up. It looks like your husband finally ran off. None of this was supposed to happen."

Marcie started crying.

"We're going to get you fixed up." He turned to Frankie. "Get her clothes." He turned to Eddie. "Take a car from outside. Take her to Dr. Khan at the clinic. Go in through the back. Tell him I want her fixed up like new—like this never happened."

"Yes, sir."

He took a fat envelope from his jacket pocket and pushed it into her hands. "Just as we agreed. And this is just the start. I'm going to look after you, just like I promised." He gestured to Eddie. "Help her up." Eddie walked her across the warehouse to the doors. One of Frankie's men shoved her jeans and moccasins into her arms.

"Christ, Frankie."

"I'm sorry, Mr. Rollins. Looks like Tom Brown had them jammed up before they shot him."

"That bastard. Get these two cleaned up and put some clothes on them. We've got to try something different."

THE TAXI DRIVER dropped Tom off at the cabin. "Keep the change, brother."

He slammed the taxi door, felt a twinge in his side, and tried to stand up straight. He took a deep breath. The pine trees smelled great. The breeze through the trees sounded inviting. He was still alive. The Escalade and the Explorer were in the yard. He limped his way over to the Explorer. The hood felt cold, so nobody was home. The keys to the Escalade were in his pocket. He was already packed. All he had to do was drive away. He could change out of the red T-shirt and worn khakis the nurses had wrangled up for him later. But first he had to have one more look in the house. He shuffled up the steps to the yellow police tape, which had already been torn out of the way and was flapping in the breeze. He pushed his way through the door. The living room had been gone over twice: once in the methodical police-response-to-shooting way and once in the looking-for-something-smaller-than-a-bread-box way. He looked down at his bloodstain. It was larger than he thought it would be. He remembered the night before, where each of them had stood, what they had said. Buddy his usual horse's ass, crowing about having the upper hand. Marcie still processing strange from killing her husband. Her first kill, angry and personal. Patty, what? Completing the con, yet playing harder than she had to, as if she had to prove it to herself as well as the others. That bad dream from the other night really had come true. She was dead to him. Would he have saved his marriage if he'd fucked Marcie, pulled her over to his side, and changed the equation? Or maybe he should have crashed head-on into Buddy early, risked losing the fight, kept Patty's respect? It didn't matter now. The smart play was to get out of town ahead of the cops and Big Jim and Buddy, or whoever else had been nosing around in here after the cops.

His cell phone rang. He fished it out of his pants pocket. "Yeah?"

"Tom? It's me, Bernie."

"What's up?"

"Two cops were just here asking about the Yost property."

"What did you say?"

"I told them the truth."

"Good."

"What if they examine the data?"

"Why? Where's the probable cause? Stick to your story. They aren't interested in the land. They're interested in who bought the land and why. You analyzed the cores. You drove around on the property. You did what you always do, right?"

"Yeah."

"Then don't change your story. You're in the clear. If you made a mistake, it was because you were manipulated. You did due diligence."

"That's right. Due diligence."

"There you go."

Tom put his phone back into his pocket. It was time to get out of town. He went into the largest bedroom. The mattress was pushed up against the wall in front of the windows. The box spring had been slashed. The closet door stood open and the empty dresser drawers all hung out. Wire hangers and bits of trash littered the floor. He knelt down at the dresser, pulled the bottom drawer all the way out and flipped it over. The manila envelope was still taped to the bottom. Inside were forged drivers' licenses for him and Patty, credit cards, $500 cash, and a $10,000 cashier's check. His escape packet. He emptied the envelope into his pockets, humming to himself, glad he hadn't told Patty where he'd hidden the packet. She was against hiding stuff out in the open. Thought it too risky. And she was right. It was too risky until the big flushing sound drowned out the universe. He walked back out into the yard and checked the car jack compartment of the Escalade to make sure that the mailbox key was still there before he sat down in the driver's seat. He had a full tank of gas. He felt dizzy and slightly nauseous, the result of the pain meds and blood loss, but he wouldn't have to drive very far to get into the clear. At least for today. Tomorrow, after he rested, he'd collect the checks from the mailbox. Then he'd disappear. He was supposed to go in to the doctor for a checkup in a week, but he'd do that somewhere else.

His mind wandered as he drove the country roads on the drive back into Seanboro, but once he got into town the stop-and-go rush hour traffic focused his attention. Every time he stepped on the brakes, his side throbbed. One town down the road would certainly be far enough to drive today, but a silver Taurus two cars back seemed to be following him. He pulled onto the beltway entrance ramp. It followed. He pulled off at the next exit. It followed. He turned into an apartment complex. So did the Taurus. It must have picked him up at the cabin. Or maybe it had come with him from the hospital. His phone rang. It was Big Jim. Tom parked in front of someone's apartment, a concrete stoop with evergreen bushes on both sides, a gray steel door with a peephole.

"Yeah?"

"I've got your wife and your partner."

"Why should I care?"

"Talk to your wife."

"Baby"—her voice cracked—"I'm begging. They're going to kill me—"

He could hear the pain in her voice. He blinked away his tears. He'd tried to warn her. She'd chosen badly. Big Jim was probably listening on the phone. "The last time I tried to help you, you shot me." He hung up. He wasn't going to die with her, and he couldn't bear to hear her voice. Why didn't the love end with the betrayal? The phone rang.

"Yeah?"

"She goes in the ground if I don't get my money."

He gave a bored sigh. "She's not really my wife, and somebody's tailing me. It's not you or we wouldn't be talking. My advice is dig the hole deep. A man in your position can't afford complications." He hung up. He felt empty and alone, and he knew the nightmares would come, but there was nothing he could do to help her. Her only chance was if Big Jim didn't believe she was leverage and didn't think he needed to kill her. Either way, Tom hoped she didn't suffer much longer. He pulled out of the parking space and drove back toward the beltway. If the Taurus were the local cops, they wouldn't be able to follow him out of their jurisdiction without cause. He took the ramp onto the beltway and the first cloverleaf onto the interstate. The Taurus seemed to be gone. He felt tired and slow. Pain throbbed from his side. His eyes closed for a second, and when he opened them he found that he was driving with two wheels on the shoulder. He pulled over, put the car in park, yawned and stretched, careful of the pain. How far to the nearest rest stop? He reached for the map in the glove box. Big Jim's voice played in his mind. *I've got your wife and your partner. They're going in the ground.* No mention of Marcie. Why? Was she working for him? He smiled. She would have sold them all out in a heartbeat. He searched his pockets for Detective Fadiman's card and dialed the number.

"Fadiman."

"Find Marcie Tolliver and you'll have a way in." He hung up. That was all he could do. Maybe the cops would get there in time.

MARCIE SAT at her kitchen table in her terry-cloth bathrobe that evening, her eyes black and her nose taped. Dr. Khan assured her she'd look fine in a few weeks. Yesterday's ghosts hovered wherever she looked, replaying the point of no return: the crack, crack, crack of the .38, Kenny's wide-eyed look, mouth slightly open, as he crumpled.

Tom's steady eyes and level voice. She wasn't sorry she killed her husband; she just wished he were there with her now so she wouldn't have to be alone. She looked at the packet of hundred-dollar bills, less money than she would have gotten in commission if the sale had been completely legit, afraid for her life, afraid for her future. She didn't even have any tears left. There were too many people scamming this scam for her to make out. Was it always like that, or was her luck just that bad?

She heard a car on the gravel driveway, wished she had a gun in the pocket of her robe, but went to the front door anyway. Two men were walking up onto the porch. They held out badges, and identified themselves as Detectives Fadiman and Bigalow. "May we come in?"

She shrugged and shuffled back through to the kitchen. She sat back down at the kitchen table. "What do you want?"

Fadiman gestured at her face. "What happened to you, ma'am?"

"Accident."

"Where's your husband?"

"I don't know."

"He didn't go to work today."

She looked off at the wall and noticed a fleck of blood the cleanup crew missed. "Is that supposed to surprise me?"

"Where's your boyfriend?"

She looked up at Fadiman. "What boyfriend?"

"Buddy Ray."

"He's not my boyfriend."

"You can call your relationship with him whatever you want. We know you're seeing him."

"So you say."

"He's missing."

"Are you the Missing Persons Bureau?"

"We know you're involved with Buddy in a real estate rip-off. You can help us or you can lose your real estate license."

"Maybe I don't care."

Bigalow pointed at the packet sitting on the table. "What's in the envelope?"

"Why exactly am I talking to you two?"

Fadiman started again. "You want to go to jail? It looks to me like this little project has gone sideways for you. You think you've seen the worst of it, but I'm telling you, Marcie, the weight of this mess hasn't even begun to bear down. Now's your chance to get out from under. I think somebody killed your husband."

"You're crazy. He's probably out horndogging somewhere."

"I think you know who did it."

Marcie didn't want to look at Fadiman's face. She looked down at the wood plank floor. She could see Kenny lying there, Bigalow's snakeskin cowboy boots right in the middle of his back. "How would I know that?"

"Because I think they put a beating on you to shut you up. And either your boyfriend Buddy is in with that crew, or they're still working him over. Either way, we want him. Just tell us where Buddy is, and we'll forget all about your part in this."

Marcie looked up at Bigalow. She felt a little woozy from the pain pills, but not woozy enough. "There's a bottle of white wine in the fridge and a glass to the left of the sink, cowboy. Why don't you pour a girl a drink?"

Fadiman nodded his consent. Bigalow poured a glass of wine and set it in front of her. She gulped down half the glass. The cold wine shot down her throat and exploded in her belly. She gasped.

"You okay, Marcie?"

She laughed. No, she wasn't okay. She was under Big Jim's thumb. He'd dumped Kenny's body. He had the gun. Any time he wanted her dead all he had to do was snap his fingers and one of his thugs would pay her a call. She remembered her own screaming, saw her own blood, felt her warm urine running down her leg. She'd been humiliated and beaten, but she wasn't dead. All her choices were dangerous bad. Which one scared her least?

She held the wineglass in both hands. "I don't see how either of you big, strong men can help me even the least little bit."

Fadiman snorted. "I think we can do better than you've been doing on your own."

"Still alive." She took a sip. "Still alive."

"How long? You won't be safe until these guys are in prison."

She looked back down at Bigalow's cowboy boots. So much cop bullshit, that was all it was. She took another drink. She was starting to feel the wine in her blood. "If I tell you where Buddy is, you can't tell anyone I told you, and you have to promise me immunity."

"We'll do you one better. You tell us where he is, we'll say we got an anonymous tip. There's no paperwork. We leave here, we forget all about you. It's that simple."

Even though she thought he was probably lying, she could feel the weight begin to lift. No one had seen her shoot Kenny. At least no one who would talk. She hadn't done anything else illegal. "Midafternoon, Buddy was being held at warehouse D in the industrial park. That's all I know."

"You sure?"

"I didn't get this way at a movie matinee."

"Is he alive?"

"He was breathing then, but he looked a lot worse than me."

LATE IN THE NIGHT, the SWAT team had warehouse D surrounded: snipers were positioned on nearby rooftops, the back door was covered, and a city dump truck with a front blade was positioned to drive through the garage door. The police had some of the streetlights turned off to enable them to get in closer without arousing suspicion. They were all set to cut the power to the building. Inside, Big Jim, Frankie, Eddie, and four of Frankie's crew sat around the long metal table with the remnants of a Chinese take-out meal. No one else was visible.

Fadiman, Bigalow, and the SWAT team commander stood together in front of warehouse A, just around the corner from warehouse D, waiting for the court order. "The patrol officer arrived here fifteen minutes after you called," the SWAT commander said. "No one has come in or out since then except for the Kung Pow delivery driver."

Fadiman shrugged. "Either we're in great shape or we're screwed. We're assuming the worst. Go in hard and hot. Maybe the body is still there."

Bigalow answered his phone. "The warrant is in transit."

Fadiman nodded at the commander. "Let's roll."

The warehouse went black. The truck crashed through the garage door, its headlights illuminating the room. SWAT officers wearing tactical gear rushed in hollering "Police."

Frankie pushed Big Jim to the concrete floor. "Lay down, guys, lay down."

The SWAT officers swarmed them. When the lights came back on, Big Jim, Frankie, Eddie, and two of the crew were handcuffed behind their backs. Two others were receiving medical attention. An ambulance rolled into the warehouse.

"Mr. Rollins," Fadiman said, "we have a warrant to search the premises."

"For what? This is one hell of a lawsuit."

"Where's Buddy Ray?"

"I don't have any idea who you're talking about."

A helmeted SWAT officer kicked down the door to the office.

"Hey, you can't go in there."

"We can search any area where a man might be hiding," Fadiman said.

The SWAT officer brought a cardboard box over to the table. "It was sitting open, sir."

"You've got no right to look in that box," Frankie said.

Bigalow pulled out a bundle of hundred-dollar bills, ruffled it, and handed it to Fadiman.

"Mr. Rollins doesn't have anything to do with that," Eddie said.

"Except that it's in his warehouse." Fadiman turned to Bigalow. "Malcolm, take two of the guys and count this money so we can issue a receipt."

"Is that it?" Big Jim said. "You found a box of money? Can we all go home now?"

"We're almost done."

The SWAT police finished their search, but they found nothing: no blood, no clothing, no personal items. The warehouse was completely clean. "There's nothing here, Rusty. The money is it," Bigalow said.

"How much is it?" Fadiman asked.

"Hundred thousand."

"Get the cuffs off them." Fadiman wrote out a receipt and handed it to Big Jim. "You're free to go. Contact the D.A. in the morning about this money."

"You'll be hearing from my lawyers." Big Jim motioned to his assistant. "Let's go, Eddie." They got into the gold Cadillac. Frankie and the other men walked out through the hole where the garage door had been.

"Christ," Bigalow said, "this is a clusterfuck. Do you think Marcie was telling the truth?"

Fadiman nodded slowly. "Yes, I do." He took one last look around the warehouse. "We better get this money turned in." They walked out into the street. Big Jim started to pull away. "Somebody searched the Caddie?"

"Yeah."

"What about the other car?"

"What car?"

"The rest of those guys walking home? They didn't get in the Caddie."

Fadiman and Bigalow trotted off in different directions. Around the side of the warehouse, Bigalow saw Frankie's black Avalon creeping down the alley between two other warehouses. He pulled a walkie-talkie from his jacket pocket and talked with the SWAT commander. A team of SWAT police stopped the Avalon under a streetlight just inside the gate to the industrial park. Fadiman called Big Jim on his cell phone and ordered him to drive around and meet them there.

"I'm sorry for the inconvenience, but I just want to clear something up so we don't have to deal with it tomorrow. I know the Caddie is yours, Mr. Rollins. Who owns this car?" He gestured toward the black Avalon.

"That's a company car."

"You guys get out and stand by the fence." Frankie and four others got out of the Avalon. Two police officers in tactical gear stood on either side of them.

Another officer pulled the keys from the ignition and handed them to Fadiman. He opened the trunk. Empty and freshly vacuumed.

Big Jim shook his head. "Are you finished wasting my time? I'd like to go home and get some sleep."

Fadiman shrugged. "Okay, guys, what can I say? Let them go."

They all started moving toward their vehicles. Fadiman's phone rang. "Yeah."

"Rusty," Bigalow said. "I found Marcie Tolliver's car on the other side of warehouse D. There're two shovels in the backseat."

Fadiman put his phone to his shoulder. "Hold it. Nobody's leaving."

Big Jim turned back to Fadiman. "Is this never going to end?" Frankie and the four others standing by the fence began shuffling around like drunks waiting for a liquor store to open.

Fadiman put his phone back up to his ear. "Keys?"

"In the ignition."

"Open the trunk."

"We don't have a warrant for this car."

"Exigent circumstance."

Fadiman heard the trunk pop open. "Jesus." Bigalow said. "I've got Buddy Ray and a woman in here. It might be—she might be Patty Brown. They're not moving."

"Check for a pulse."

"I'm doing it."

The line was quiet for a few moments. "Rusty, they're both still alive."

"Get the EMTs," Fadiman said.

Frankie and his four men scattered into the shadows between the warehouses, the police officers chasing after them. Big Jim and Eddie stayed where they were. Big Jim dug a cigar out of his shirt pocket. "You finally done with me, Detective?"

Fadiman almost laughed at the absurdity of Big Jim still trying to brazen it out. "You're under arrest, Mr. Rollins, for kidnapping and attempted murder."

"I don't know what you're talking about."

Fadiman turned to the SWAT officer who had handed him Big Jim's car keys. "Read them their rights and take them in." The officer handcuffed Big Jim and Eddie and loaded them into the backseat of a police cruiser. Fadiman took off, jogging between the warehouses back toward warehouse D, where he found Bigalow standing by the ambulance. Buddy and Patty lay on the pavement next to Marcie's open trunk, two EMTs working on them. In the weak light of the streetlamp, they were barely recognizable messes of welts and contusions. "How are they?"

"EMTs say it looks like we found them in time."

"You did that, partner," Fadiman said. "You did that."

Bigalow shrugged. "You got the lead that brought us here."

"Find anything else in the car?"

"There's a .38 in the glove box. Wonder whose prints are on it?"

5

THE GETAWAY

A week later, Patty stood under the hunter green awning in front of the city hospital entrance, waiting for a cab. It was a beautiful autumn day, but she couldn't feel it. Her nose was taped, and deep bruises still showed on her face and arms. She was wearing the dirty golf shirt and tan skirt she'd had on when she was kidnapped. She had $127 and a maxed-out MasterCard in her handbag. Her plan was to stay at the rental apartment until the end of the month. She hoped by then she would feel strong enough to shake the cops and move on. She wasn't going to be in town for the trial.

A gray Cadillac pulled up. The passenger-side window lowered. "Get in."

She took a step forward and peered into the car. Tom was behind the wheel, only now he was clean-shaven and had silver hair combed back from his face. "I thought you were gone."

"Yeah, well, I guess love really is blind."

"Not blind enough to go to the warehouse."

"You should have listened to me."

"How about if, sometimes, you listen to me for a change?"

He shrugged, nodded. "How about when you're not trying to get me killed? Guess what? I've still got the money."

"A hundred and ninety-eight thousand, between the checks and the escape money. Tell me something I don't know."

"So what are you waiting for? Get in."

"How do I know you won't kill me?"

"Honey, I'm probably the only person who knows you who doesn't want to hurt you."

She climbed wearily into the passenger's seat. "Jesus, I feel terrible."

"You ought to feel terrible."

"Buddy could talk a lot more game than he had going on."

"You thought I was washed up."

"You were whining and complaining instead of making things happen. What was I supposed to think?"

"What do you think now?"

"I'm thinking of looking in the want ads for a straight job. I could probably make a living selling real estate."

He pulled away from the curb. "Making money at it is harder than pretending to do it. You need a vacation. Some rest, some relaxation, in a month you'll be ready to ride that horse again."

"You think so?"

"I know so. Tell the truth. You were pretty much beat unconscious before you gave up hope."

"I wouldn't go quite that far."

"That's what I'm talking about, honey." He drove gently down the street, easing up to the stop sign at the intersection with the main thoroughfare. "We're just not quitters."

"You hear how it turned out?"

"Yeah. Buddy agreed to testify on the kidnapping to beat the drug charge, and Big Jim's looking at the counterfeit money and the kidnapping."

"And you didn't have anything to do with that?"

"I was very, very lucky with plan B." He turned right, heading toward the freeway. "And I still don't want to be here when Big Jim finds out how bad the toxic cleanup is going to be."

She lay back in the seat and closed her eyes. Her hands trembled in her lap. "I'm going to need much longer than a month."

"I know. We'll be living off this money a long time."

"So what are our names?"

"I'm Robert Johnson and you're Pamela."

"Rob and Pam. Pleased to meet you." Out the window the houses shot by like cardboard cutouts. "My nose is a little crooked."

"You're beautiful. It'll give your face some character."

"Yeah, right."

"We can afford for you to have it fixed, if you want. It's no big deal."

She turned from the window to watch him in profile driving the car. "So why did you come back for me, really?"

He pulled over onto the shoulder and put the Caddie in park. "I came back for you because I love you."

"But I shot you."

"You didn't shoot me very hard, and you dialed 911. Besides, if I had been with you, I might have been scooped up by Big Jim's guys." He smiled. "I could have been in that trunk, and then there would have been no one to call the cops." He put his hand on her shoulder. "It's going to be a while before I trust your judgment, but I think I can trust your heart."

She dabbed at her tears with a handkerchief. "I feel so ashamed. And I felt so helpless in that warehouse. I hadn't realized how much I'd come to depend on you."

"That's the pain meds talking." He pulled back into traffic.

"No, really."

He smiled and shook his head.

"Just do me one favor." She squeezed the balled-up handkerchief in her fist.

"Okay."

"Next time, baby, please, please, please beg for me to stay with you a lot harder than you did this time. I don't care how embarrassed it makes you feel."

"Next time?" He glanced at her for a second. "What? Do we need a safety word?"

PART II

NINE MONTHS LATER

6

ROBERT AND PAMELA JOHNSON

ob Johnson ran a hand back through his silver-gray hair and took a sip from his whiskey and water. He was dressed like an off-duty insurance agent: dress shirt, no tie, black dress pants, shined shoes. He kept his eyes on Tony, who sat across the booth from him. Tony was huge, his shoulders bursting out of his blue department-store blazer, his neck bulging from his blue oxford shirt. His boyish face was half-hidden by shaggy brown hair and a goatee. "So why do you need us, Tony?"

Tony shrugged. Pamela smiled flirtatiously and patted her husband's left hand, her dangly gold earrings swaying slowly through her long, dark brown hair. She was wearing a tiger-stripe spaghetti-strap dress that could have been sprayed on. The three of them were sitting in the back booth of a small, dark honky-tonk on a country road in the early afternoon. At the scarred-up plywood bar at the front, two men in leather jackets sat nursing beers. The bartender, greasy hair and biker tattoos, glanced down toward the booth every now and again. Rob continued in a quiet, even tone. "Let me get this straight. Guy comes to you. Wants the money laundry in his business robbed. He's supplying the alarm codes, the safe combination, etcetera. You're the tech guy. That's your area of expertise. All you have to do is walk in and out. If you weren't Stella's cousin, I'd think you were a cop."

"Stella told me you were the guy to see."

Pamela smiled her thousand-watt smile. "You're not in the game, are you, baby?"

He looked at her dismissively. "Tony. My name's Tony."

Pamela continued. "You tell me where I'm wrong. You're a hard guy; I'm guessing ex-military, maybe Special Forces technical trained. Add on college computer."

"Maybe."

"You're up against it. Wedding ring says family man. Guy comes to you out of the blue. You got to have the money. You go to your outlaw cousin; she says she knows some folks that will treat you right."

"Something like that. Look, I've got no choice."

Rob shook his head. "You think you're falling back on what you know, but this isn't what you know."

"A minute ago you're saying I could do this alone."

"It's not the doing, it's the getting clear."

Pamela leaned toward Tony. She spoke in a whisper. "We need to hear you say that you can go home from a murder, make love to your wife, and never tell her."

"I can do that."

"I don't know that I believe you."

"I bet I've killed more people than either of you."

Her eyes sparkled. "You kill them for money? To stay out of jail?" She tapped Rob's shoulder. "Let me out."

He shifted out of the booth so that she could slide out. In her four-inch heels she was as tall as he was. She glanced at Tony. "Want anything?"

"I'm good."

She sauntered up to the bar, all willowy curves. She bought a pack of cigarettes, shifting her body so that the bikers at the bar could get a good look at her without seeing the long white scar on her left shoulder, and sauntered back.

Rob let her back in. "Enjoying yourself?"

"Just like to know I've got a ride if I need one." She lit a cigarette and set the pack on the table.

Rob gave Tony the hard look of a man appraising a tool. Tony hadn't paid any attention to Pamela at all. He was all the way married. Probably hadn't even screwed the hookers on active duty. Had his sweet little girl at the house. Saving it up for her. Wanting to make her happy, not go to jail. Right push at the right time, and he'd kill everyone if that's what it took to get home. But what was the right push and would there be a right time? And why was Stella helping this greenhorn at all? She was always safety first. So either she thought he had the skills to make it, or she didn't care if he took a bid on a cell upstate. "Will you do what I say and save the arguing for when we're safe?"

Tony nodded.

"Really? 'Cause you strike me as the stubborn type."

"Yeah, really."

"Then let's start with that. Stella's an old friend. Let's see if we can keep you out of jail." Rob stuck out his hand. They shook. "Okay, let's have the details."

"Jim LaBell, the guy owns LaBell's Super Discount Pharmacy, moves money through his store for some independent mob guys. Twice a month they drop off around a hundred thousand dollars with a bundle of fake prescriptions; the drugs get sold somewhere else; the money and prescriptions get blended in over the two weeks. LaBell got himself in some financial trouble—didn't go into it—so we steal the hundred thousand, split it four ways, robbery covers up his involvement. The money comes in tomorrow, so we have to go tomorrow night."

Rob tapped his index finger on the table. "Hold up, Tony. We don't go until the details are right."

"Jim has got to have his money. Christ, *I've* got to have this money. I'm behind on my mortgage."

Rob smiled. "You're already arguing. Prisons are full of guys who 'got to have.' One step at a time. We do this right, there're no cops and no crooks chasing us. We do this wrong, and best case we're on the run. Worst case your family is dead."

"How's that going to happen?"

"You think LaBell's partners are going to fold up?"

"Look, LaBell told me if we couldn't go tomorrow, he'd have to get someone else. I need this score. That's why I went to Stella. It just took me longer to find you guys than I thought it would."

"You're lucky we were in the neighborhood."

Pamela crushed her cigarette butt in the ashtray. "Couldn't hurt to take a look, Robby. Seems pretty simple."

Rob swirled the ice in his drink. "We'll give it the once-over. If it looks okay, we'll give you a call. If not, you're on your own."

ROB AND PAMELA, fully clothed, lay side by side holding hands on the queen-sized bed in their furnished rental apartment. It was still early. The translucent white curtains were open. The babble of street noises filtered through the window. They'd eaten supper at an Italian restaurant in the neighborhood, a place that served a light, almost fragrant tomato sauce, and had made conversation like the couples seated around them, talking about nothing, particularly not Tony or the job. Afterward, they'd driven across town to LaBell's Super Discount Pharmacy, located in an established strip mall adjacent to an old, upscale neighborhood just inside the city limits of the suburb of Crestview. Everything about the strip mall said brand new in 1988, with every promise for prosperity achieved. Coffee Joe's coffee shop, Chef's Supplies cooking store, Robert's Cards and Stationery, Adeline's Dresses, and, the anchor, LaBell's, all had the self-satisfied gleam of a picture postcard. It was easy to see why LaBell's partners had chosen him. The cops here would be well trained at writing tickets and kissing up to the merchants. Everything about the drugstore was typical. The electrical and phone lines came in through normal junction boxes. The doors and windows were alarmed. The shopping aisles ran from front to back with the usual assortment of items: makeup and hair care, candy, beer and wine, small appliances, toys, household products, snacks, stationery, paperback books and magazines. The pharmacy and over-the-counter drugs ran across the back of the store. Four round shoplifting mirrors hung in the corners of the store to keep the sticky-fingered middle-schoolers in line. The backdoor emptied out into the delivery alley next to the Dumpster. At seven in the evening there was a pharmacist, a tech, and one teenaged cashier. It wouldn't have been all that risky to come through the front door in a ski mask. Rob and Pamela drove home. Rob made some phone calls to his local law enforcement contacts.

So now they lay on the bed holding hands and staring at the ceiling. Rob squeezed Pamela's hand. "Let's talk about the downside. Will Tony fold up?"

"He's got himself convinced. He'll want to prove to us he's hard, knows how to put the 'T' in team. LaBell's the one I'm worried about. He's the wild card," she said.

"All we know about him is that he's up to his asshole and eyeballs. The Feds, the State, the County—nobody's working him. He really is laundering money."

"So he's a fuckup who just happened to fall over our boy Tony." She snickered. "We should take the money and stiff him. Teach him to fuck with crooks. We'd be doing him a favor."

"I'd do it if it wouldn't jam up Tony, but he's got to live here. Stella's too valuable to cross for an extra twenty-five thousand."

Pamela let go of his hand and turned toward him. "Do you think we're ready?"

"We're just about out of money. We better be ready; this is all we know." He put on his customer service voice. "You want fries with that? You need a cart?" He shook his head. "I don't think so. The only people who would hire us to do anything we're skilled at are people who want to get robbed."

"I don't know if I'm ready to take my clothes off."

He rolled toward her. Her eyes were soft and empty. There was no doubt that she was still broken. "I know that last gig was hard on you.

That's why we've waited so long. But have you ever been hurt on a job where I called the shots?"

"No, baby, you've never steered me wrong."

"That's right. Buddy Ray screwed the pooch, dragged you in. Who pulled you out?"

"You did."

"That's right." He ran his hand up and down her arm. "I love you, honey. You know I'm always going to be there for you. This is just a simple heist. It won't send us on vacation, but it will give us enough cash to find a real score. There're no skills involved here, no one to set up. The only person you're going to be taking your clothes off for is me. Besides, your scars are all healed. You're in fighting trim. You're a beautiful, ball-busting bitch. You saw the guys at the bar. They couldn't take their eyes off you."

Her mouth crumpled into a smile. "I'm not taking any prisoners."

"That's right. You're not taking any prisoners. You just got to climb back on that horse. It'll all come back to you."

"You're right, Robby, you're right. Let's get this done. Let's put the past in the past."

He reached for her hand and then leaned over and kissed her lips. "Okay. Last chance."

"I'm in."

He pulled his cell phone from his pocket and dialed Tony.

7

THE ROBBERY

Tony, Rob, and Pamela sat in a stolen gray Suburban with tinted windows directly under the streetlight at the far end of the strip mall parking lot, waiting for the barista at Coffee Joe's to finish cleaning up and to go home. Rob, sitting behind the wheel, sipped his Diet Mountain Dew. He wore a black nylon jacket over a blue dress shirt and black dress pants. A .38 revolver was holstered at his waist. Pamela, lying back in the passenger's seat, wore a black zip-up jacket over a light blue T-shirt and black yoga pants. Her hair was pulled back at her neck. Tony, sitting behind them, wore a dark blue zip-up hoodie with black cargo pants and black workout shoes. He carried a nine-millimeter pistol in a shoulder holster under his sweatshirt. He was nodding his head and tapping his fingers on his leg as if he were listening to music on a music player. The lights in LaBell's Super Discount Pharmacy were on, but the drugstore had been closed for over an hour, and they had counted the employees as they left. A goateed twenty-something wearing a red and white striped shirt and a red cap on backward came out of Coffee Joe's, locked the door, and then collected his bike from the bike rack. Rob turned back to Tony. Tony shook his head. "Nothing on the police scanner."

"Let's get it done." Rob started the truck. They drove out of the lot, circled back into the neighborhood, driving slowly past neatly kept ranch-style and split-level houses illuminated by porch lights, until they reached the open gate of the access alley to the delivery parking behind the stores. Rob cut the headlights as he turned in, easing quietly along the back until they came to the delivery door for the pharmacy. He put the Suburban in park and switched off the interior lights. Tony got out, one arm cradling a black nylon shoulder bag, pulled his hood up, and walked casually over to the electrical and phone junction boxes. He took out a penlight, held it in his mouth, opened the boxes, and disconnected the phone lines just in case there was a problem with the alarm code. He motioned back toward the truck. Rob and Pamela got out, pushed the doors gently closed, and met him at the pharmacy door. He input the alarm code on the keypad, and then unlocked the door with the key that Jim LaBell had provided.

Inside, they turned on their flashlights. They were in a storage area behind the pharmacy counter. Shelves loaded with boxes of inventory sat to the right. To the left was a janitor's sink with a string mop, a strainer bucket, and a vacuum cleaner standing beside it. Beyond that were a gray steel office desk with a computer on it and a four-drawer file cabinet with a DVR machine sitting on top. They went to the computer. Tony moved through screens until they were watching the live feed on the security cameras. There were no outside cameras. Inside, the store was quiet and empty. They pulled on their black ski masks and walked out into the well-lit pharmacy area behind the counter. Pamela searched the aisles until she found the locked cabinet where the narcotics were kept. She knocked the flimsy lock off the door with a hammer and chisel. It was just meant to keep honest people honest, and they had all gone home for the day. She reached her arm into the cabinet and slid the bottles off into her small duffel without bothering to check what they were and then went to the shelves where the syringes were kept and jammed some packages into the top of the duffel. Tony and Rob went straight to the safe located under the customer counter. Tony got out the combination. Rob shook his head. "Can't remember the last time I saw one this old." Tony worked the combination and pulled open the door. Stacks of banded bills sat next to rolled coins and the bank deposit bag. Rob turned to him. "The money's short."

They counted the bundles into their bag: $55,000.

Tony shook his head. "That can't be right."

They dumped everything out of the safe onto the floor. There were maybe a hundred dollars in coins, nothing more. A roll of quarters rolled under a nearby shelf. "Is there another safe?" Rob asked.

"This is all he told me about."

The glass front doors rattled. Rob glanced back toward Pamela, who was kneeling between two shelves. The doors rattled again. They crawled back out into the storage area. On the computer screen, they could see a gray-haired man wearing a long raincoat peering through the picture windows as if he were hoping to see an employee inside. Then he turned and walked away. "Okay," Rob said, "Pamela, pull the disc and break the DVR machine. Tony and I will fuck this place up so it looks like a drug crew."

"What about the other forty-five thousand?" Tony asked. "I've got to have my full share."

Rob tapped his watch. "We've got to stay on task."

"We can't just walk away from the cash. It's got to be here somewhere."

"You want to stay? You're on your own."

"I didn't say that."

"Then let's finish up here and go find LaBell."

Rob and Tony knocked over a Dr. Scholl's display, used a broom to empty a shelf of first-aid supplies, raked their arms through the baby food shelves, pushed the pharmacy cash register onto the floor, and threw open bottles of Coke against the walls. Pamela came to the door. "Let's go."

They went out the back. Tony reset the alarm systems, and then tripped them. He jumped into the backseat of the Suburban. "Cops are on their way."

Rob put the Suburban in drive. He saw a flash to his left, heard a gunshot, and felt the side rear window shatter all at the same time. Pamela yelled, "Go, go, go!" Tony flipped around in the backseat and reached into his sweatshirt for his pistol. Rob stomped on the gas pedal, and the Suburban shot forward. The gunfire chased them, following them down the back of the pharmacy, the bullets punching into the rear end of the truck. Tony brought his pistol up over the seat, looking for a target. "Don't shoot toward the houses," Pamela said.

The truck bounced over the curb. Tony gripped the seat back. Rob swung the wheel, and the rear end of the truck slid around. He turned on the headlights, illuminating the six-foot-high picket fence beside the pharmacy, floored the gas pedal, crashed through a fence panel, and bounced down into the strip mall's parking lot. Pamela scanned the lot. "All clear."

Tony looked out the back window. "Clear behind."

Rob cut diagonally across the empty parking lot, gaining speed as he went. In the distance they could hear dogs barking and the traffic on the main highway. "Hang on." The tires squealed as he turned onto the access street. The truck rocked side to side. Tony lost his grip on the seat and his shoulder banged the door. Rob remembered that there was a stop sign at the next intersection. He glanced both ways as he sped through. Two more blocks. Oak trees and streetlights. No one in the rearview mirror.

"Great driving, baby."

"That wasn't the cops. This job's in free-fall."

Tony turned around in his seat and put his seat belt on. "What do you mean?"

"Somebody was waiting to ambush us. They could have called the cops, they could have trapped us in the store, but they wanted us to take the cash."

Pamela nodded. "Or they didn't want to expose the laundry."

"Even worse." Rob turned right at the next intersection, driving into the peaceful darkness of a residential neighborhood. They all sat quiet, listening, watching the driveways, mailboxes, and well-kept houses slowly slide by, noting the odd dog walker or the person moving between a car and a front door. The houses stopped. Up ahead was the crushed limestone parking lot of a community soccer field. As they pulled into the poorly lit parking lot, they heard police sirens in the far distance. A silver Camry was waiting in the corner of the lot under the maple tree where Pamela had left it.

They climbed out of the shot-up Suburban. Pamela hurried over to the Camry, unlocked the doors and popped open the trunk. Tony carried his backpack and the duffel bags over and laid them in. Rob emptied a five-gallon gas can over the interior of the gray Suburban and dropped a match. The flames licked up over the doors as Pamela drove back onto the street and turned in the direction of the main highway. "So who do you think was on us back there?"

"Don't know," Rob said, "but judging from the firepower, there was only one or two of them."

"Undermanned for the job." Pamela adjusted her rearview mirror. "So what was their job?"

"Tony," Rob said, turning to look into the backseat, "what do you know about LaBell?"

"His daughter, Rachel, babysits for us."

"Which means what? He wouldn't fuck you, or you're the patsy to cover over this dirt with his partner?"

"What are you implying? I don't know this guy. He's nothing to me. Right now, I'm pissed because the money isn't right."

"So we're going to tell him our sad story and get the money squared away?"

"Yeah. What was your plan?"

"Just checking."

JIM LABELL LIVED IN A LARGE, two-story redbrick home on a double lot in Crestview's premier neighborhood. All the streetlights on his slowly winding street seemed to illuminate the ends of the driveways, where security service signs were prominently displayed. The trees, shrubs, and lawns were all manicured to show to the best advantage and the fencing was in immaculate repair. Rob guessed that this neighborhood would have a stopwatch police response time. Pamela parked the silver Camry at the top of LaBell's driveway, near the doors to the two-car garage. They all got out and walked up the brick sidewalk to the white columned porch. Tony rang the doorbell. LaBell opened the door with a cell phone up to his ear. He looked momentarily surprised, then held up one finger and motioned them in. He was about six feet tall, with a fringe of brown hair and a few strands combed over the top. He wore black dress pants and shoes, and a white shirt with a floral print tie hanging loose at the collar. Sweat was beaded on his forehead. Rob could smell the fear on him. They stepped into the entryway and shut the door. Straight ahead, the terracotta tiled hallway led to the kitchen. To the left were the living room and the stairs to the second floor. A coat closet was on the right.

"Yes, Officer, I understand," LaBell said into the phone. "I've got a family emergency right now. I'll have my manager meet you there."

"Hold on," he said to no one in particular, then hit the speed dial. "Becky? It's Jim. There's been a break-in at the store. Can you go down? I hate to ask, but I'm having trouble with Rachel. Thanks." He put the phone in his pants pocket and looked at Tony. "Had to call my store manager. What are you guys doing here? We're supposed to meet tomorrow. And why did you trip the alarms? The cops are all over everything."

Rob pulled the .38 from his holster. "The cops are the least of it. It was the Wild West in the parking lot."

"What are you talking about?" LaBell asked.

Pamela gave him a shove. When he didn't respond, she pushed him toward the wall and started patting him down.

"Hey, now—" LaBell protested.

"Shut up," Rob said. "Someone was shooting at us and it wasn't the cops."

"Where's the rest of our money?" Tony asked. "You said there was going to be at least a hundred thousand, but there was only fifty-five in the safe."

"Guys, guys." LaBell turned around. "That can't be right. The money was there. Just take it all and go. The cops can't find you here."

"We're supposed to have seventy-five thousand for our end," Rob said. "We're twenty thousand short. So we don't much care how much trouble the cops cause you."

LaBell's phone rang. "I have to answer that. It might be the cops again."

"Put it on speaker."

"Hello?" LaBell said.

"We know you got the money," a man's voice said. "Bring the fifty thousand to Cabot Park. Put it under the bench closest to the trash can by the paddleboat kiosk."

LaBell put his free hand on his chest. "Let me hear her voice."

"Daddy—"

"Rachel, are you okay?"

The man's voice said, "Bring the money. If it's right, we'll drop off your daughter tomorrow. You've got an hour. We won't call again." The line went dead.

Rob snorted. "So you pulled fifty thousand from the safe before you left work."

The color drained from LaBell's face. "I've got to save my daughter."

"Were those the bastards who jumped us at the drugstore?" Tony asked.

"Maybe." Rob holstered his gun. "Working all the angles. They knew where the money was going to come from, so they know about us. We've got to tie up loose ends."

"What are you talking about?" LaBell asked.

"Those mopes saw us. We're going to use your money drop to put them in the ground."

"Wait, wait, wait," Tony said. "This is a pretty big step."

Rob pointed his finger at him. "This is the part where you keep quiet until we're in the clear."

"The penalty for murder is pretty steep."

"So a little robbery among friends is okay with you, but eliminating witnesses—not civilians—who've already proven they'd kill you is a step too far?"

"I've just got to think."

"Think all you want; that bus has left the station."

"Hey, guys," LaBell said. "Stop talking crazy; you'll get my daughter killed."

Pamela frowned sympathetically. "No, you'll get her killed. You want her back? Whole, undamaged, with just a few weeks of bad dreams? She's what? Fourteen? Fifteen?"

"Sixteen."

"I'm going to give it to you straight. Chances are they're already tasting the goods. They're going to get your money, party with your baby for a few more days, and dump what's left in a ditch. You want her back, you've got to take her."

LaBell's face crumpled. He suddenly looked twenty years older. He looked from Pamela to Rob and Tony. Rob shrugged. "You've got a tough situation, but this has got nothing to do with us. You should have called the cops to begin with."

"But I got you the money."

"You tried to stiff us. So we take our twenty-five thousand each and clean up the mess you made."

"Okay, okay," Tony said. "We're going to kill those guys—"

"Turn the page," Rob said.

"I know, I know. But I've got a GPS tracker we can put with the money."

Pamela smiled. "Track the money back to the whole crew."

"Exactly. We find all of them and Rachel. The money's never at risk." Tony pointed at LaBell. "We keep his end."

Rob shook his head. "Another twenty-five thousand in the pot? Killing them is different from rescuing the girl. This is the getting-clear part, not the risking-my-life part."

"There you have it," Pamela said to LaBell. "We're going to kill this crew. Can you pay us to save your daughter while we do it?"

"You think I'd rob my store—double-cross my partners—if I had any money? My ex-wife gambled and pissed away everything we had."

"Oh, well," Rob said. He turned to Tony. "Let's get his fifty thousand and rig the GPS in the bag."

"Wait a minute. Just wait a minute." LaBell mopped his head with his handkerchief. "I've still got Rachel's mom's jewelry. I was saving it for her."

"But you'd give anything to get her back," Pamela said. "That's what her mom would want."

"It's all I've got left."

"Okay," Rob said, "let's see it."

Tony followed LaBell upstairs. In a few minutes they came back down and everyone went into the kitchen: maple cabinets and black granite counters that opened onto the family room at the back of the house. LaBell laid the jewelry out on the black granite counter: a diamond ring, a pearl necklace, two gold bracelets, and a few gold chains. Rob poked through it with his index finger. "Not much, is it?"

Tony looked from Rob to Pamela. "But added to his twenty-five thousand?"

Rob looked hard at Tony. "This isn't an action movie. There's no medevac and no medals. And there can't be any dead civilians. Dead civilians means police investigation. Understand?"

PAMELA, Tony, and LaBell were standing in the open garage, out of sight of the neighbors, when Rob pulled into the driveway in a tan Honda minivan. Rob pulled on his black nylon jacket after he got out of the van. The clouds had moved off during the evening; the air was crisp, but the radio still said there would be rain before morning.

"Where did you get the minivan?" LaBell asked.

"Do you really want to know?" Rob said. "Smart money is on not asking questions and ignoring what you see." He turned to Tony. "We all set?"

"GPS tracker concealed in the lining of the bag. No way we can lose it."

"Okay." Rob looked from Pamela to Tony to LaBell. Pamela he knew he could count on. Even at 50 percent, she could do this in her sleep. Tony—all that military training—might be out of rhythm with them, might screw up trying to do the right thing. But LaBell . . . Criminals who thought they were still civilians were absolutely unreliable. His original plan, stealing from his partners to pay the kidnappers, was an invitation to his own funeral. And he'd given no thought as to how his daughter would be changed by being manhandled or gang-raped. He thought he'd go back to his sitcom life as soon as he got through this night and got his baby back. He'd just keep laundering money and filling prescriptions; his daughter would go back to worrying about the prom and flipping through college applications. His troubles were just beginning. It might be better for all of them if he and his daughter both died tonight. "LaBell, you take the Camry to the drop. Pamela, you go with him. Tony, you're with me in the van. LaBell makes the drop and drives away. We follow the bag, call you guys; you follow us. When the bag stops, we ease up, check it out, see what we got to do. No loose cannons. We all work together, we all walk away. Questions?"

"Rob," LaBell asked, "which way do I drive when I leave the park?"

"Drive like you're driving home. They may be watching. We want them to take the bag and get away. You won't see us because we don't have to be close."

Tony handed the bag to LaBell. "We got your back. No worries."

Rob and Tony climbed into the tan minivan, belted in, backed out, and waited for LaBell to drive away. LaBell slid behind the wheel of the silver Camry and set the black duffel in the passenger's seat. Pamela glanced at Rob. He waved at her from behind the wheel and watched as she lay down in the backseat of the Camry. She had plenty of air. She was in control of herself. She should be fine. And she was definitely the one to babysit LaBell after she set him up for the jewelry. Shame there wasn't more.

Tony pulled a small laptop computer from a waterproof case, turned it on, and watched the screen. "I'm turning on the tracker, just to double-check."

"Well?" Rob asked.

"Looking good."

"You certain? Half our money's riding on it, plus a gang of unreliable witnesses."

"No doubt."

PAMELA LAY in the backseat as LaBell piloted the Camry down the road as if it were a rolling living room. "Hey," he said, "do you want me to turn the radio on?"

"Do what you would normally do. So if you don't talk to yourself in a loud voice while driving alone, don't do it now."

"I'm sorry," he said, lowering his voice. "I've been a nervous wreck ever since the kidnappers first called me."

"Only natural."

"So is this how you make a living? Or is this a sideline?"

"Rescuing kidnap victims is definitely a sideline."

"No, I meant burgling."

Pamela rested her head on one arm. "I know what you meant. How did you end up money laundering? Your store must do well."

"Right after we opened the pharmacy, my first wife—Rachel's mom—was diagnosed with cancer."

"That must have been hard."

"We were heavy in debt on opening the store, had an aggressive payback schedule, but it was doable. In fact, we were going to be out from under and on with our lives in record time. But the extra medical bills, day care, expenses were adding up, and the economy . . . well, I couldn't refinance."

"And then a friend appeared to save the day."

"Yeah. He's never asked too much. That money made all the difference. Now I've got the store, the house, Rachel's college fund."

"I thought you were cleaned out."

LaBell shrugged. "My ex-wife, Rachel's stepmom—she was joint on all the personal accounts. Somewhere she made a bad turn—

gambling, drinking, drugs . . . I don't know where it started, guess I was too busy working. But I know how it ended. She was lying to me, stealing out of the house. I had to divorce her. She's the only mom Rachel's known, so you can imagine how that worked."

"You're trying to save her from the kidnappers. That's got to mean something."

"I hope so."

He pulled into a parking place. "We're here." He glanced into the backseat as he reached for the duffel bag. "What if they find the GPS tracker?"

"They won't."

"But what if—"

"Jim, this is the best chance you've got. You were going to give them the money anyway."

He sighed. "You're right. You're right. I suppose I should thank you for helping me get my daughter back."

She smiled in the dark. "Good luck."

LaBell got out of the car. The streetlamps lit the parking lot, but Cabot Memorial Park itself was all shadow. He stood for a moment, looking for the sidewalk and letting his eyes adjust to the dark. The bag felt heavy in his hand. The wind gusted through the trees, giving him that Halloween feeling of ghosts on the prowl. But when the clouds moved, he could see moonlight reflected on the pond and the shadowy outline of the kiosk. He started down the sidewalk, wondering if he were being watched, wondering if the kidnappers would intervene to save the money if he got jumped by muggers. The area around the paddleboat rental kiosk felt surprisingly open. During the day it was elbow-to-elbow grade-schoolers and grandparents. He walked up to the wooden slat bench nearest to the trash can, bent down, and slid the duffel under. After he stood up, he looked around to make sure no one was watching him, as if he could tell the difference between the kidnappers and some lucky park thief. Then he walked back to the car, occasionally looking over his shoulder to see if the bag had disappeared while his back was turned.

After he got back into the Camry and slammed the door, Pamela said, "Everything okay?"

"Yeah, nobody was there."

"Let's head back."

"What if someone else gets the bag?"

"Look, Jim, the sooner we leave, the sooner you get your daughter back. Don't let all the 'what if's' cascade through your mind. Start the car."

"Okay." He started the car and backed out of the space.

"You're doing good, Jimmy. It's almost over."

ROB AND TONY sat in the tan minivan on a quiet residential street two blocks away from the park. Tony was watching the bag on the monitor. "They've dropped it off."

Rob looked in the rearview mirror and then up the street. A few houses kept their porch lights on, and a few had front room lights on, but there were enough cars parked on the street to provide camouflage. "So, Tony, how you going to explain the money to your wife?"

Tony kept his eyes on the monitor. "Temporary consulting job. I ease the cash in week by week until I find a job."

"Good plan."

"You don't want to know what Emily gets like if she thought I was even talking to my cousin Stella. Yelling, banging, crying, doghouse way in the back of the yard, if you know what I mean. She's never going to hear about this."

"You married guys on the straight life, what you got to put up with. It's worth it, though, isn't it? Don't deny it. You can't help nodding."

"I left the army because of her. She was worried all the time. And now there's the baby. Anthony Jr."

"So you got it all."

"Yeah."

Rob smiled. "But you miss the show."

"I won't lie. Regular folks would be going crazy right now. We're just talking, waiting for the firefight. Sure, it'll be a little scary going down, but you know what to do and when to do it. In civilian life, it's nothing but unknowns and loose ends. Everybody says it gets easier, you pick up the patterns after a while, but . . . If I could just find a job, everything would get on track." He glanced up. "The bag is moving to the northeast."

Rob started the van and pulled out.

"Take your first right, that should bring us around the east side of the park. Take it easy; the bag is cutting across the park toward the north parking lots."

Rob got out his cell phone and speed-dialed Pamela. "Bag's moving. We're on Berkshire, heading north. No hurry; it's all copacetic."

Rob and Tony rolled around the east side of the park, moving from streetlight to streetlight, the landscape clean and neat in the dark. Up ahead, at the first intersection, a heavily rusted white Dodge Charger drove through headed west. "Follow that car."

Rob turned left. On the right side were mansions, tall hedges, wrought-iron fencing; on the left were park picnicking areas, picnic tables, trash barrels, and built-in barbecue grills. "The bag is a block ahead of us, heading west." They drove through the next intersection. Up ahead was a flashing red light above the center of the four-way stop. "Take a right."

Rob turned the wheel, gravel spinning out from under the back tires. He called Pamela again. "We're north on Carter, above the park, heading into town."

They rolled along for fifteen minutes, the houses getting smaller and closer together. Up ahead, the street split to the left and right. "Which way?"

Tony glanced up. "This Y isn't on the map. Stay to the right."

The houses gave way to apartments and corner convenience stores. "The bag is moving away from us. Take a left."

Rob turned at the next intersection. "Are we losing them?"

"No. We're good. We don't want to be too far away in case of signal interference, but we're only eight blocks out. Two more blocks left, then take a right and we should be behind them again."

They were heading away from downtown now. They drove past an auto body shop, a recycling center, and a salvage yard. The houses were mainly rental duplexes interspersed with tiny old houses set back on gravel driveways. On the left was a closed-down metal fabrication plant. "Slow down. There's a side street here somewhere."

A gravel road on the right went north into a wooded area. "That's it. The bag stopped moving up there a few hundred yards."

Rob turned onto the gravel and pulled over behind some evergreen bushes. He took out his phone. "We're just off Grant in the old industrial zone next to Unionville. Gravel road on the left just past Beaumont's Metal Fabrication. Van's behind some bushes. Wait for us there. We're going to pin down the location."

He turned off the van, but left the keys in the ignition. "The GPS any help this close in?"

Tony shook his head.

"There's a sports bag with some shotguns in it in the back."

"I thought we were just having a look."

"That's the idea."

They pulled down their black ski masks and tread carefully up the darkest side of the road. Scraggly, dust-covered bushes grew on both sides. The gravel was thin, the road was just dirt and potholes in some places, and the path narrowed until it was only one car wide. Sweat trickled down their necks. No-see-ums and mosquitoes buzzed around their heads. In a clearing up ahead they saw two little tourist cabins, one completely dark and the other fully lit within. They approached the dark cabin first. The door hung off its hinges and the windows were broken glass. They slipped over to the lit cabin. They could hear voices. The door was shut and the front windows were boarded with plywood. Through a dirt-smeared side window, they could see that there were two rooms inside. In the nearest room, a living room kitchen combo, three men dressed in flannel shirts and worn jeans sat on a green plaid sofa with holes in the arms, smoking a joint and nodding to the hip-hop music coming from an old boom box. Two other men sat on folding chairs at a card table, drinking cheap vodka out of a bottle they passed back and forth. Pistols lay on the table in front of them as if they were supposed to be on guard. To the right, the back door was directly opposite the front door. A rusted white refrigerator, a stove, and four feet of cracked Formica countertop that contained a sink ran from the back door to the corner. Over the sink was an open window. Trash, old blankets, and empty bottles and cans were strewn everywhere. The duffel bag sat on the floor by the refrigerator. Through the interior doorway, they could see two women, one young and blond, lounging on a naked mattress in the next room. Tony pushed Rob's shoulder to get his attention and then nodded toward the women.

Rob and Tony made their way back down the gravel path to the minivan. Pamela and LaBell were waiting on them. "Well?" LaBell asked.

Tony pulled up his mask. "She's there. Looks fine."

"Thank God."

Rob pulled up his mask. "Let's not start the celebration yet. They're in an abandoned tourist cabin. Five guys in one room, two women in the other room, so it's definitely doable."

"What you thinking?" Tony asked. "Fish in a barrel? Concentrate our fire so the guys can't get into the bedroom with the women?"

"Yeah. After we improve the odds, LaBell can slip in for his daughter; that way she won't get confused and run into the cross fire."

"I want one of those shotguns," Pamela said.

"There's also Kevlar vests," Rob said. "Let's get geared up and get this done."

They put on the Kevlar vests and loaded their weapons. Rob, Tony, and Pamela carried shotguns and nine-millimeter pistols. Rob checked a pistol and handed it to LaBell. "The safety is off, so don't put your finger on the trigger unless you intend to fire."

"I probably won't need this."

Rob studied him for a moment and then shrugged. It was hard to believe he was as entirely clueless as he appeared. "Okay. When we get up there, Pamela, you and LaBell go around to the left-side window. Tony and I will check the right-side window. If everyone is still where they were, we kick down the front and back doors, firing hard, driving the guys toward the right wall—we should get a couple right off the bat—you break the left window, deal with the other woman, and collect your daughter. We finish up, collect the money. And everybody," Rob said, pointing his finger around the group, "no heroes. We let our guns do the talking. Let's go."

They moved quietly up the gravel path back to the cabin. Rob motioned with his hand, and Pamela and LaBell went around to the left. Rob and Tony went back to the right window. The three guys were still nodding on the filthy sofa. The two guys were still at the card table. Nothing had changed except the level in the vodka bottle. Rob nodded. Tony slipped around the back. Rob crept around to the front door.

Pamela and LaBell looked in the window into the bedroom. Rachel, dressed in faded jeans and a red "Go Gators" T-shirt, sat on the bed. Beside her sat an emaciated woman with short, bleached-blonde, dark-rooted hair and elaborate arm tattoos who was dressed in a sleeveless green top and a long, loose skirt that belonged on a completely different woman. LaBell looked at the woman hard. There was something about her and the way Rachel interacted with her that seemed strikingly familiar, but the glass was so dirt-caked that it was like looking through cheesecloth. Then it hit him. It was Rachel's stepmom, his ex-wife Kyla. LaBell felt dizzy. He sat down in the dirt under the window. She must have put her divorce settlement in her arm and up her nose. She was a wreck. She looked like she belonged in hospice. Tears started down his cheeks. So now she was using Rachel to extort him. And Rachel was helping her. He crept back up. They were talking. He strained to hear what they were saying. He couldn't quite make out Rachel's voice, but then he heard Kyla say, "Honey, you've got to tie off tight to get the vein up."

He was running around the side of the cabin before he realized he wasn't at the window anymore. Rob swung his shotgun around, paused when he saw who it was, and waved him off, but LaBell kept coming. He grabbed the doorknob, turned, and pushed. The door swung in. He charged in after it, yelling, "Rachel, don't do it! Don't do it!"

The guys on the sofa and at the table scrambled up, grabbing for their guns, the back door crashed in, and everyone was yelling and firing weapons. LaBell backhanded Kyla off the bed, grabbed Rachel by the arm, looked back and forth like an animal in a trap, picked up a heavy, half-full ashtray, and threw it through the window. Then he realized that Rachel was yelling, "Dad, you're crazy; let go of me!"

"Shut up," he said.

"Jim!" Pamela yelled from outside. "Out the window!"

Kyla ran out into the gunfire in the living room. LaBell unlatched the window and pushed it up. Rachel broke free, trying to follow her stepmom, but he grabbed her around the waist. She kicked and punched, but he held on.

"Hurry up!" Pamela yelled.

LaBell swept the broken glass off the windowsill with the back of his hand and then pushed Rachel out the window to Pamela. "I screwed up," he said. "I screwed up, but I couldn't wait."

Rachel swung at Pamela, but Pamela ducked, slapped her face, and got a grip on her wrist. "Let's get back to the van."

"What about the others?" LaBell asked.

"We can't do anything here. Let's go."

LaBell climbed out of the window and they ran back to the van, LaBell dragging Rachel along in the dark.

"Let go of me!" she yelled. "Let go of me! Mom! *Mom!*"

"I came to save you."

"I want to stay with Mom!"

"She kidnapped you."

"Kidnapped? Are you crazy? I ran away. You wouldn't give her a chance."

"I did everything I could to help her. I paid for rehab. She got a big settlement in the divorce. Where did that go?"

The gunfire stopped. The woods were abnormally quiet. They turned and looked back down the path. They heard running.

"Mom!" Rachel yelled.

Tony appeared, his ski mask pushed up on his head. "Rob here?"

"No."

"I better go back."

Sirens squealed in the distance. Pamela glanced toward Grant Street. "Rob will be fine. Let's get out of here. Where's the money?"

"I think it got away."

"Maybe Rob has it. Let's take the van." Pamela and Tony climbed into the front. She started the van.

"Let's go," LaBell said, pushing Rachel toward the side door of the van.

"I don't want to go with you!"

He pulled her close and gripped her shoulder with his other hand. "Are you high? You're coming with me. You don't know what you're saying. You're a drug addict."

"I'm going to tell the cops what you did. You hired people to shoot at Mom."

"You're going to tell the cops you were in a crack house with your ex stepmom, where she was giving you heroin when your dad burst in? You're going to rehab."

He shoved her into the minivan, climbed in behind her, and slammed the side door. She moved to the third row, put on her seat belt, and turned to the window. "I won't do anything for you."

LaBell sat in the second row. His hands were shaking. "Fuck, fuck, fuck, fuck, fuck," he muttered.

Pamela glanced over her shoulder. "Hard part's over, Jim. Breathe."

"But the money—"

"Now's not the time to worry. You got your baby. Everything will be okay." She got the van turned around. "Tony, text Rob. Tell him we'll meet him at the apartment."

ROB SAW the red of the minivan's taillights disappear onto Grant Street as he was chugging down the gravel path. There were at least two junkies shot back in the cabin. The woman had run right through the firefight, grabbed the bag, and climbed out the window over the sink. You can always do amazing things if you don't care if you'll die. God only knew where those other three mooks were. Their car must have been off in some other direction. He placed the shotgun, his pistol, and the Kevlar vest into the trunk of the Camry, got into the car, and adjusted the seat. LaBell was more trouble than he was worth. If there were any justice in the world, that stunt he pulled would have gotten him killed. They should have stiffed him back at his house and dared him to go to the cops. Instead, he'd let Pamela's and Tony's emotions get the best of them and they'd hit the bullshit trifecta. Now they couldn't kill LaBell without drawing the cops down, they'd lost the $50,000, and most of the witnesses were still loose. At least the $55,000 and the jewelry, whatever that was worth, probably a night on the town, were back at the apartment, so the night wasn't a total loss.

The sirens sounded closer. His phone vibrated in his pocket. He saw the text message from Tony. *Meet at the apartment.* He backed out onto Grant Street. The street was empty for miles. He could see the stoplights changing at the intersections until they were little more than green and red twinkles in the far distance. No cars anywhere. But the police sirens were louder and louder, obviously on a parallel street. He drove away driving-school safe, both hands on the wheel, egg between his foot and the gas pedal.

After Rob rolled into his and Pamela's apartment complex, a buffer zone between a shopping mall and an upscale neighborhood by a golf course, he parked in front of their furnished apartment, an end unit in a row of tan clapboard town houses, and sat for a minute enjoying the quiet. Pamela had drawn short straw on the getaway. That father-daughter reunion was not going to be one for the scrapbook. And it would probably play into her weakness. Even though she'd been strong tonight, she was still emotionally scarred from that last job. She'd thought his love for her had limits. Now she knew better. But she was still afraid to go off the high board into the deep end. Being the victim herself made her feel sorry for the amateur crooks they preyed on. That had to change. She needed to toughen up, see the marks for the cash machines that they were. Milking LaBell for the jewelry was a start, but she still had a ways to go.

Rob got out of the car and went to unload the trunk. While he was reaching in, he saw something glint in his peripheral vision and turned his head just in time to catch a fist in the eye. The blow knocked him sideways, but he turned as he fell, trying to get a punch in or at least make contact with his assailant. A kick folded his knee; he protected his face from the pavement with his arm and rolled across the asphalt, trying to gain space to get up. Too late. He got a kick in the diaphragm while he was on his knees. The guy standing over him said something, Rob couldn't make it out, but the voice sounded familiar. He turned his head. Buddy Ray.

"Hey, 'Rob.' Surprised to see me?" Buddy smiled down on him, his blond head framed by the parking lot light. He wore dark-colored slacks and a khaki jacket. "I needed to separate you from your new boy toy." He gave Rob another kick, knocking him onto his back.

Rob wretched and snorted, trying to catch his wind. Finally he said, "Buddy, you're looking good. You stop doing your own thinking?"

"Thought you could fuck me on our last job?"

"That was you fucking you, thinking you could screw me."

"Well, I want my share."

"All spent." Rob sat up.

"I got the money and jewelry out of your apartment. We'll call that a down payment. I'm going to dog every game you play until we're even."

"That's a mistake."

"I don't think you're in a position to judge mistakes."

Rob started to get up. The last thing he saw was Buddy's shoe coming toward his face.

"ROBBY, ROBBY." Rob opened his eyes. Pamela was crouched over him. Tony, glancing around like a bodyguard, was standing behind her with one hand in his hoodie pocket on the butt of his pistol. "You okay?"

"Fucking Buddy Ray. The gift that keeps on giving." He tried to sit up. "Did you see anything when you got here?"

"Let's get you inside." Pamela and Tony each grabbed one of Rob's arms and pulled him to his feet. He tried to stand, but his legs wobbled under him. They half-carried him into the apartment and laid him on the sofa. Pamela went into the kitchen, wet a dishtowel under the tap, and got a bag of peas out of the freezer. Tony had his pistol out in his hand now. He walked through the apartment to make sure it was empty. Pamela came back to Rob, wiped his face with the cold towel, and put the frozen bag of peas on his eye.

He put his hand over the bag and sat up. "I'm okay."

Tony came back into the living room. "So who's this Buddy Ray?"

"Guy we used to partner with." Rob said. "Tried to cheat me on our last job together. Almost got Pamela killed. Ended up screwed. Should have killed him."

"So what happened?"

"He was waiting on me. Said he got the loot. That he's going to keep after us until he gets what he's owed. Christ. Look in the bedroom closet."

Tony went into the bedroom. "Nothing here."

"Look everywhere. Pamela, you help him."

Tony came back into the living room. "You know where you left it."

"Yeah, but I want to prove to you it's not here."

Tony sat down in a chair facing the sofa. "So the money's gone."

"If it's not in the house, it's gone." Rob shifted the bag of peas on his face and felt his ribs with his other hand.

Pamela set a glass of water on the end table next to Rob. "How you doing, Robby?"

"I don't think my ribs are broken."

Tony shoved the pistol back into the holster under his arm. "I've got to have that money. I can't lose my house."

"Guys," Pamela said, "we have to think this through. The cops are on the drugstore. The junkies got away. Buddy got the rest of it. Who was shooting at the drugstore?"

Tony shook his head. "Doesn't matter. The tracker in the ransom bag still works. There's only three of them left, three and the woman. We find them, kill them, take the cash."

Rob set the peas down and looked Tony in the face with his good eye. "Where you bury your dead? We already missed once. There's no element of surprise. It's a straight up shoot-'em-up. If we take them, can we get away from wherever they're at? Is Buddy gone, or is he tailing us? Will he try to jack us or call the cops on us? This hole is too deep. The money's no good if we're dead or in jail."

"So you won't make a try for it? You lost the money and you won't help me get it back?"

"Oh, yeah? And who wanted the jewelry and the extra twenty-five thousand for the kid? Don't play that bullshit with me. There's plenty of blame to go around." Rob leaned back and put the bag of peas back on his eye. "Tell you what. Let's sleep on it. If a plan comes to mind, fine. Otherwise, we're out of here in the morning."

Tony got up. "I can't leave. I live here. You guys were supposed to be experts. You owe me some help making this right."

"Tony, Tony, relax," Pamela said. "We'll figure something out."

"Fuck you both." He slammed the door on his way out.

Pamela sat down next to Rob. "That went well."

"Actually, it did. Didn't have to shoot him. He believed Buddy got the money."

"I feel sorry for him."

"Sure. But that doesn't change what happened. You know what Buddy's like. He knows us too well."

"How you feeling?"

"Like I need something to eat."

"Can you get around? There's nothing here, but we can hit that all-night diner on Stapleton by the Quick Trip."

"I believe I can. We've got to dump that Camry anyway. Can't leave it until tomorrow."

She helped him up. "You know, you never had a chance to kill Buddy after the double cross."

"I know. Should have made the time."

JIM LABELL PULLED up the police tape, stooped under it, and pushed through the double glass doors to his drugstore. A police technician dressed in white coveralls was packing her gear into a hard case. His manager, Becky Ramirez, a forty-something black woman with big hips and accountant's glasses, wearing a raincoat over cow pajamas, stood talking with two people who must have been the police. She waved him over. "Jim."

As LaBell made his way to the back of the store he surveyed the damage: four shelves of baby food and formula strewn across the floor, brown liquid splattered up the wall by the soft drink coolers, the Dr. Scholl's display knocked over, the insoles scattered over the floor, shards of broken glass everywhere, and the cash register lying open on its side in front of the pharmacy counter. Rob and his crew certainly made a lot of mess for the amount of time they were here.

An athletic-looking blonde in a black pantsuit held out her badge. "I'm Detective Peterson. This is Detective Rubella." She indicated her partner, a dark complexioned man in a suit and no tie.

"I'm Jim LaBell. Sorry I couldn't be here earlier." He turned to Becky. "Thanks for coming in. This is really above and beyond. I hate to ask, but could you lead the cleanup in the morning? I've got to get Rachel to rehab—"

"Is she okay?"

"Considering everything?" He nodded.

Becky rubbed his shoulder. "We'll be praying for you. Don't worry about tomorrow. You just do what's best for Rachel."

"Thanks."

Becky headed for the door. LaBell turned to the detectives. "Sorry for the interruption. It's been a crazy last couple of days."

"Have you ever been robbed before, Mr. LaBell?" Detective Peterson opened a palm-sized notepad. As she looked down, a lock of blond hair fell down in front of her eyes and she tucked it behind her left ear.

"Never. We hardly ever even have a shoplifter."

She glanced up. "Really?"

"This is a good neighborhood. We take care of it with the parents."

She scribbled something on the notepad. "Well, this looks like a straight-up drug robbery. The techs are done, so you can clean up."

"Do you think you'll catch them?"

"Honestly? Hard to say. Depends on if they left fingerprints, or slip up trying to sell the drugs."

LaBell looked from Peterson to Rubella. "Anything else? I'd like to lock up."

Detective Rubella rubbed his forehead as if he were warding off a headache. "Your daughter run off from rehab?"

"No. She ran away from home. Surprised the hell out of me. Found out where she was this evening. My ex—her stepmom—had some drug problems, so I'm just covering all the bases."

Rubella and Peterson exchanged a glance. "What's your ex-wife's name?" Peterson asked.

"Kyla."

"Kyla LaBell?"

LaBell nodded.

"When was the last time you saw her?"

"Honestly? I couldn't say. We're not on speaking terms."

Rubella continued. "But your daughter keeps up with her. Right? That's why you're putting her in rehab?"

"I don't know. She's sixteen. She's been gone for a week. Maybe I'm overprotective, but that sounds like rehab to me."

Peterson nodded. "Well, I'm glad you found your daughter. And I hope she's not on drugs. We may need to talk to her later about her stepmom, though; we'll be in touch."

LaBell DROVE HOME. The light was on in the kitchen, but Rachel wasn't in there. He backtracked into the entry, turned on the lights to the carpeted stairwell and upstairs hall, and walked up to her bedroom. He knocked on the door. "Rach. Rach." No answer. He opened the door slowly. She was lying on her bed in the dark fully clothed.

"Get out of here!" she yelled.

He stood at the door. "They sent me a kidnap note. I didn't know you'd run off with your stepmom. I was worried sick they would hurt you if I didn't get the money in time."

"Worried sick? You don't care about me." She turned her face to the wall.

"Then why did I give them the money?"

"You were never fair with Mom. You just threw her away."

"She got half of everything we made together. Where did it go? She could have bought a house, a car; she could have gone back to school."

"I hate you."

"Rachel, you helped them try to extort me. You talked to me on the phone as if you'd been kidnapped."

"I'm not talking to you anymore."

LaBell walked back down to the kitchen, poured himself three fingers of Scotch, added a couple of ice cubes, and sat down at the counter. He rubbed his face with his hands, took a drink, and looked at the refrigerator door as if there were still kid's artwork magneted there—stick figures of princesses and horses, construction paper cutouts of Thanksgiving turkeys, watercolor scenes of nature repro-duced from vacation pictures. Where was the little blonde girl who yelled "Daddy!" when he came to get her from day care? When had their relationship turned? Had he always been such a clueless bastard? He sighed. The past—not changeable. He'd like to throttle the two-dollar wise man who came up with that. The past should be changeable, needed to be changeable, because that's where the mistakes were. His cell phone rang. It was his partner, Mr. Wendell. "I did what you told me. How did the thieves end up coming to my house?"

Mr. Wendell spoke with an eastern European accent. "Complications. Don't worry about it."

"I had to play along with them or they would have known."

"Did you get your daughter back?"

"Yes. Why didn't you tell me it was Kyla? I could have found her on my own."

"Didn't want you doing anything stupid."

"Stupid? We were almost killed. Kyla got the ransom and now those thieves are hanging around."

"Relax. I've got people on this."

"But the money—"

"Play your part and it will all work out."

Mr. Wendell hung up. LaBell held his phone in his hand, looking at the front of it as if he could read something there. Then he laid it on the counter, put his face in his hands, and started to cry.

TONY DIDN'T WANT to wake his wife by opening the garage door, so he left his white Dodge truck parked in the driveway in front of their suburban ranch, one like many on his street, half-brick front, two-car garage, three bedrooms, two baths. It would be another ten years before any of the trees were large enough to shade the houses. He slipped quietly in the front door, letting his eyes adjust to the dark so that he wouldn't step on any baby toys or knock into the swing, wherever it had moved to during the day. The nightlight was on in the hall bathroom. He took his clothes off and laid them over the back of the sofa, walked down the hall naked, and peeked into his son's room—there he was, wrapped in a blanket, lying on his side in his crib, his breath barely audible. Tony's face lost its purpose, went completely blank, and then a smile slowly crept across. Some unformed childhood half-memory had flinted through his mind. He shook his head, closed the door, and crossed the hall. When he opened the door, his wife, Emily, turned on her bedside lamp. She looked at him through squinty eyes, her light brown hair all pillow head. "How did it go?"

He sat down on the bed beside her and turned off the light. "It was fine."

"I was surprised they kept you so late on your first day."

"Another guy was sick."

"Did the boss like you?"

"It's just a temp job, honey. What they like is me getting the job done."

"If it works out, maybe they'll offer a permanent job."

"I don't think so."

"Mortgage company called again. I talked with my mom. We can stay there if we lose the house."

"We're not going to lose the house." He stroked her hair. "I've got this temp thing. And I'm developing some leads. You remember Terry? There's a start-up where he knows some guys."

She rested her head on his leg and hugged his waist. "No matter what happens, it's better than the army. At least you're here with me."

Tony's phone rang in the living room. "I thought I turned that off. I better get it before it wakes the Ant."

He jogged back into the living room. "Yeah?"

"It's Rob. Somebody set up on our apartment while we were out getting something to eat. Anybody follow you?"

Tony went to the front windows and pushed aside the drapes just enough to peek out. "Nobody tailed me. And there's nobody extra on the street. Around here they'd stick out."

"Were the cameras off at the drugstore? Could there have been any security we didn't know about?"

"That was all clean."

"We're going to a motel. We'll be in touch tomorrow. Watch yourself."

Tony turned off his phone and went back to the bedroom.

"Who was that?" Emily asked.

"Supervisor. They're going twenty-four seven there. Looks like I'm on call tomorrow." He got into his side of the bed.

Emily snuggled up against him. "See, they do like you."

8

THE DAY AFTER THE ROBBERY

The next morning, Pamela stood in the bathroom looking at herself in the mirror. Her dark hair was wet, and she was wearing the black yoga pants and light blue T-shirt she'd been wearing the night before. "Have you got a comb?"

Rob moved his head out of the shower spray. "What?"

"Comb."

"Left back pants pocket."

She found his comb and started working out the tangles in her hair. He stepped out of the shower, toweled off, and put on yesterday's black slacks and blue dress shirt. "Let's get some coffee."

They had spent the night in a cheap motel by the interstate. There were cigarette burns on the furniture and porno on the pay-per-view, thin towels and tiny bottles of generic shampoo/conditioner, and a complimentary coffeemaker supplied with enough coffee to make dark brown water. Out of habit he peeked out the window before he unlocked the door. "Christ. Isn't that the tan Corolla from last night?"

Pamela took a peek. "He thinks we can't see him on the other side of that truck."

"Amateur." Rob got out his phone and called Tony. "Hey, Tony, how you doing?"

Tony was sitting on his sofa in sweatpants and a T-shirt with his onesied son in his lap. "Doing great."

"Anybody watching your house?"

"No."

"Our tail found us. Can you go to our apartment? If it's clear, get our gear, or at least the guns."

Tony glanced toward the kitchen, where he could hear Emily emptying the dishwasher. "We still on?"

"I'll make sure you get something."

"I need more than something."

"I'll pay you to do the job, okay? I'll give you five thousand dollars to get our gear. Give me a call when you're done."

Tony hung up his phone. Emily, wrapped in her furry pink robe, looked at him over the granite-brown Formica counter peninsula. "Who was that?"

"They called me in for another shift."

"Let me make you a hot breakfast before you go."

"No time. Got to get there ASAP." He kissed his son on the head and set him on the floor. "The Ant's on the loose." He walked down the hall to their bedroom to get dressed.

IN THE UNIONVILLE neighborhood just south of the old industrial zone, a neighborhood whose broken-down and abandoned houses were once the homes for the workers who left after the plant closings in the 1980s, a man in his midforties with a stubbly-black crew cut, dressed in a charcoal-gray suit with a silver tie, sat in the front passenger's seat of a black Avalon. His driver was a retired boxer with a tightly trimmed brown beard and scars down the left side of his face. He wore a blue tracksuit. In the back was the driver's partner, an equally large black man with a shaved head and a diamond earring. He also wore a blue tracksuit. Next to him sat a small, skinny junkie who smelled like sour milk and day-old diapers. The junkie indicated the boarded-up house sitting between two burned-out ruins. "That's where they stay, Mr. Vincent."

"You sure? You want to be sure before you make White James and Keith get out of the car."

"What you described you're looking for, that's them. Talking big, buying party weight, woman, three guys."

Vincent peeled a few bills off of the wad in his hand and handed them to the junkie. "Forget this morning."

"Yes, sir."

The black man looked at him. "That means get out the car and walk away."

The junkie got out. Vincent looked at his driver. "Why are we here, James?"

"To get the money back."

"So don't kill anyone until we have the money."

They drove up in front of the boarded-up house. The white paint had peeled away in hand-sized sheets; the bare wood was cracked and weathered gray. There were several holes in the roof. The windows had boards nailed across them, but someone had pulled the plywood sheet off the front door frame. White James and Keith got out carrying shotguns, ran up the steps onto the rickety porch, and kicked the door in. Vincent followed in their wake with an automatic pistol down at his side. Light fell into the living room through the doorway and the cracks between the boards covering the windows. Food trash, old clothes, plastic bags, and vials littered the floor. Two men started up from an old mattress in the corner. They wore loose jeans and worn-out flannel shirts. White James and Keith smacked them with their shotgun butts and dragged them into the middle of the room next to the charred remains of a fire. Vincent shook his head in disgust. "Where's Kyla?"

One of the men pointed. In the gloom under the window, Kyla lay half-naked. Her face was a mass of bruises, dried blood ran from her mouth, her skirt and panties were missing, and her legs were splayed as if she were unconscious when they had finished with her. Vincent motioned with his head. Keith checked her neck for a pulse. "She's alive."

Vincent looked down at the two men on their knees in front of him. "You guys really fucked her up."

The one on the right, the one with no front teeth, said, "That was Will's idea."

Vincent looked at the other one. "You Will?"

"No sir. I'm Donny. Will's not here, I don't guess. I don't know."

"You lie to me and you're going to think she looks pretty good."

White James kicked Donny in the stomach. "Pay attention."

"Where's the bag of money?" Vincent asked.

The junkies looked at each other. Vincent sighed. "James, go get the sledgehammer and the bolt cutters out of the trunk. There's no need to take these two anywhere."

White James caressed the scars on the side of his face. "Can I work the bolt cutters, sir?"

"Just go get them." James ran out the door. "What do you think, Keith? You think these two will do the smart thing and be scamming for dope this afternoon, or do you think they're going to die right here?"

Keith grinned, his teeth bright in the gloom. "I think one of them's smart enough to limp away, maybe make it to the emergency room, but I haven't decided yet who that's going to be." Keith hit Donny in the side of the head so that his head whacked into the head of No Teeth.

White James came back with the bolt cutters and the ten-pound sledge. Vincent looked down at the junkies. "What's it going to be? Cut-off toes or broken bones? I know. You." He pointed at Donny. "You decide for your buddy. Smash his foot or cut off his big toe?"

He smiled. "Smash his foot."

"You bastard," No Teeth said.

Keith put the shotgun barrel up against the side of No Teeth's head. "Hold still."

White James swung the hammer back over his shoulder.

"Wait!" No Teeth yelled. "The money's in the kitchen. There's a hole in the wall behind the fridge."

White James dropped the hammer and crossed into the kitchen. They could hear him dragging the refrigerator out from the wall. A few minutes later, he came back with a black duffel bag. "Here it is, boss."

Vincent squatted down and counted through the cash in the bag. "It's about forty-eight thousand. Where's the rest?"

"That's all we got left. Her old man and his friends busted in and we almost lost that."

"That sounds screwed up enough to be true." Vincent transferred the money to a plastic grocery bag. "Thank you, gentlemen." He stood up. "Kill them."

White James pulled a nine-millimeter pistol from his jacket pocket and turned toward Donny, who covered his face with his hands. James shot him through his hands and caught him just above his mouth, and then put two bullets in his chest as he fell sideways.

"Please," No Teeth said, "I'm nobody. You don't have to do this."

White James smiled. "If you were somebody, it might have saved your life." He shot him in the head, and then in the chest.

Vincent took one more look around the room.

"Burn it?" White James asked.

"That would just draw the cops. There's nothing to tie us here. Pick up our tools."

Keith motioned toward Kyla with his head. "What about her?"

"She's not going anywhere."

JIM LABELL AND HIS DAUGHTER, Rachel, followed Dr. Gregory Joseph into his office at the Hope House of the Regional Resource Counseling Services. On one side of the room was a large cherrywood office desk with two black leather chairs facing it. On the other side was a cherrywood coffee table surrounded by a black leather love seat and two matching chairs. The back wall was a series of windows overlooking the park-like grounds. Dr. Joseph, a fat man with thinning, sandy-gray hair combed carefully back from his red face, motioned them to the love seat. Then he unbuttoned the jacket of his carefully tailored suit and sat down in one of the chairs facing them. Rachel's eyes were red from crying. Her blonde hair, pulled back at the nape of her neck, was still wet from the shower. She wore sandals, pink jeans, and a gray hoodie that sported the logo "Clemens High Cheer Squad." LaBell was dressed for work, wearing black slacks and a blue-stripe oxford shirt open at the neck. His face looked as if he hadn't slept; his fringe of brown hair was slightly tousled and his jaws were tense.

"Thanks for fitting us in, Greg," LaBell said.

Dr. Joseph sat back in his chair and smiled softly. "How can I help you, Jim?"

"Well, Greg, I'm going to tell you some things that may not be surprising to you in your line of work, but were really surprising to me. I'm just going to tell you what I think I know. The truth might be somewhat different."

"Okay."

LaBell told Dr. Joseph what had happened the previous evening, leaving out only the money laundry and his involvement with the robbery. While he spoke, Rachel looked down at her feet, shaking her head when she seemed to disagree with one of his points.

"Did you report what you thought was a kidnapping to the police?"

LaBell shook his head.

"Are you going to report it now?"

"No. I just want to forget about all that. I got Rachel back, and now there's this drug thing."

Rachel's head snapped around. "I didn't take any drugs."

"No, but you were going to. Kyla was coaching you on tying your arm off. The loaded syringe was on the bed."

"I'm not a drug addict."

"I hope not."

"You just want to keep me away from Mom."

"Honey, she's not your mom."

"Why? Because you threw her away when she wasn't perfect enough?"

"I didn't gamble away our savings and lie about it. I didn't scam the rehab. I didn't take dope and screw junkies in my family's home."

"Because you're so perfect."

"I didn't say that." LaBell turned to Dr. Joseph. "You see what I've got here. Can you put her in your program?"

"We can do an assessment, see what's appropriate."

LaBell shook his head. "I mean right now, today. If I'm going overboard, we can always dial down."

"Dad, you can't leave me here."

"Are there any papers I need to sign?"

"Jim, we can take Rachel in on an emergency basis, do drug screenings, observe her, but if she does have a problem"—he looked at Rachel—"and I do mean 'if,' you know better than most that people only get better who want to get better."

"I know. I know."

Rachel stood up. "I won't stay here."

Dr. Joseph shrugged. "This isn't a prison, Rachel."

"I'm leaving."

LaBell pointed his finger at her. "Rachel, if you won't cooperate and put my mind at ease, I'll report Kyla to the police."

"You won't do that. Your friends would get in trouble."

"I don't care. You're the most important person to me. I'll do whatever I have to do to make sure that you're well. I want to be fair. You show me you don't have a drug problem, I'm open to you having a relationship with Kyla—just not one that involves skipping school and taking dope."

Dr. Joseph shook his head. "Jim, I don't know if using Rachel's relationship with Kyla as leverage is such a good idea."

"Just help her, for God's sake."

TONY DROVE his Dodge truck into the parking lot in front of Rob and Pamela's apartment building. His nine-millimeter pistol was in the pocket of his jacket. He parked out in the lot where he had a good view of the area. To the right was a playground surrounded by a chain-link fence: two swing sets, a monkey bars, and three cypress benches. Empty. To the left, across the parking for another set of apartments, was a lightly traveled intersection with only two or three cars waiting for the lights to change. Most of the reserved parking spots next to the sidewalk in front of Rob and Pamela's building were empty, but there were two cars parked in front of the apartment: a red Ford Fusion on the left and a gold Chevy Malibu on the right. The Fusion was empty. The Malibu was not. The man in the driver's seat was watching the door to Rob and Pamela's apartment as if he were trying to make up his mind.

Tony called Rob. "There's a guy watching your place. Blond, regular features, maybe thirty-five."

"Sounds like Buddy. Anybody else around?"

"He the guy who took the money?"

"Yeah."

Tony took his pistol off safety and walked up on Buddy's car from behind, moving fast, staying out of the Malibu's rearview mirrors until he came up between the Fusion and the Malibu as if he were trying to get to the sidewalk. Then he pulled his pistol, stepped up beside Buddy's window, and tapped the barrel against the glass. "Get out of the car."

Buddy glanced toward the glass, saw the pistol, dropped down in the seat, and turned the ignition. Tony grabbed at the door handle. Locked. Buddy jammed the gold Malibu into reverse and squealed back into the parking lot. Tony jumped to the curb to avoid being crushed between the cars. Buddy spun the steering wheel, scraped the side of the Malibu on the back bumper of the Fusion, and sped away.

Tony put his pistol back in his jacket pocket and glanced around. There was no one in sight. He stood for a minute, his heart pounding, at a loss for what to do. He wanted to run to his truck and chase after Buddy, but he knew that was completely stupid. He felt like a fool. He almost had the $55,000 in his hands. Almost had his mortgage caught up and his bills paid. Now it was gone. He should have waited for Buddy to go inside. Then he could have searched the car for the money or gone into the apartment after him and dealt with him there. Too late now. He went up to Rob and Pamela's apartment. The gray steel door was locked, but easy to pick. He went back into the bedroom and got the large black duffel bag he remembered from last night down off the closet shelf. He unzipped it just to make sure. Shotguns, pistols, and ammunition. He peeked out the door before he went outside. The coast was clear. He locked the door on his way out, and carried the duffel back to his truck.

LaBell was fuming by the time he finished getting Rachel processed at Hope House. Why was he the asshole? Why did Rachel always take Kyla's side? He was the one providing the home and the love and the future. He pushed through the front doors and started down the limestone steps. How long would it be before Rachel lied to him again and ran off to do something stupid with Kyla? Taking drugs or having unprotected sex was bad enough, but what if she got HIV, or got beat down and raped? He had to stop thinking like that. He had to get in control. He had to protect Rachel from Kyla and herself. He'd already tried paying Kyla off. Fat lot of good that had done. She'd never leave on her own. She'd have to be dead or in jail. Dead or in jail. To keep Rachel out, Kyla had to go in. But if he reported Kyla, testified against her, Rachel would just be more pissed off. He sat down in his Toyota Highlander. But maybe she could be scared off. Even if she were only gone for six months or a year, maybe that would be enough time. He got out his phone. "Tony, it's Jim LaBell. How are you? I need to talk to you. Can you meet me in the Buy More parking lot on Fulton Road? Great. See you there in ten minutes."

The Buy More grocery store parking lot was about half full of cars, so it wasn't difficult for LaBell to find Tony's white Dodge truck. He pulled up beside him. They both got out and walked around to the tailgate of the truck.

"What's up?" Tony asked.

"I just got Rachel into rehab."

"Well, I'm sorry about—but that's good, isn't it?"

"Step at a time. Can you still use the GPS tracker to find that bag?"

"Sure. Rob wanted to wait, though."

"I don't care about the money. Help me to get Kyla to go away, and you can have the money. We don't need to tell Rob or Pamela about it."

"Get Kyla to go away? If she had somewhere easier to go, she'd be there. What you're really talking about is killing her."

LaBell held his hands up. "I didn't say it."

"Look, Jim, I understand how you feel. Kyla's a train wreck heading towards the crossing, but I'm no murderer. You want her dead, that's for you to do. I'll help you track the money, and if some of them get killed because they won't give up the bag, well, that's the way it goes, even if it's her. But I'm not Rob or Pamela. I'm not killing them just to be sure."

"Fair enough. You got your equipment with you?"

He nodded. "I've got Rob's guns, too."

They moved the gear over to LaBell's Highlander and drove across town into the old industrial area by Unionville. It didn't take very long to home in on the duffel bag. They pulled to the curb in front of a burned-out ruin next door to a boarded-up, abandoned house. Plastic trash bags blew like tumble weeds across the street and between the abandoned houses.

Tony put the tracker back into its protective case. "You sure you want to do this?"

"I have to do this."

"You ever shot anyone before?"

"No."

"You have fired a weapon?"

"Before last night? I took a class a long time ago."

"Okay. My first priority is my safety. My second priority is the money. Don't walk into trouble you can't walk out of."

"Okay."

Tony loaded two shotguns, handed one to LaBell, and took his nine-millimeter off safety. "Let's go. Don't lift the gun if you don't intend to fire."

Tony led the way up onto the porch. The loose boards squeaked. The front door was ajar. He kicked it all the way open and charged through, LaBell at his back. Directly in front of him, in the light falling through the door, lay two blood-soaked junkies, the duffel bag at their feet. Tony stepped around them and walked back through the gloom into the kitchen. LaBell stopped up short. He looked down at the junkies, crumpled in their own blood and brains, and gagged. He took a step back. As he turned to look away, he saw a woman lying on the floor under a boarded-up window, the light crisscrossing on her body and dividing her into more or less equal-sized sections. The lower half of her body was naked. Her arms and legs were splayed out like a manikin knocked over on the floor. Her face was a bloody pulp. He strained his eyes to see. He wanted to believe it wasn't Kyla, but the sleeveless green top and the arm tattoos left no doubt. "Jesus." His head swam. He felt as if he were losing his balance. He dropped the shotgun, jerked his hands up beside his face, and bent over.

Tony reappeared. "You okay? This place is empty." He squatted down at the black duffel. "Money's gone. These guys were executed. Blood's fresh." Then he noticed what LaBell was looking at. "Christ. That Kyla? Somebody worked on her a long time."

"Not like that. I wanted her dead, but not like that."

Tony found her blue print skirt and tossed it over her hips. He felt her neck for a pulse. "She's not dead. What you going to do?"

"I can't do anything. She looks so . . . I don't know what I was thinking. I'm not a killer."

"Good for you. Let's get out of here." Tony picked up the duffel with the GPS tracker in it. LaBell just stood there. "Hey," Tony said, "fresh blood, middle of the day. We got to go." He waved his hand in front of LaBell's face. LaBell looked at him. "Follow me." He picked up LaBell's shotgun and led LaBell back out to the car.

"You drive," LaBell said.

LaBell sat in the passenger's seat, looking straight out the windshield, as they rolled away from the house. When he'd first seen her and thought she were dead, he'd been happy, horrified and happy. Happy to be free of her, happy to be rid of her influence on Rachel, but horrified by what had happened to her, and horrified by his own happiness. He looked back over his shoulder. The abandoned house got smaller. When had he become that sick fuck who took pleasure in another's pain? Was that the father he wanted to be? He looked back out the windshield. His lips were moving, but he didn't know why. He looked at his hand. He was holding his phone. He dialed 911. "I heard shots fired and screaming from an abandoned house on Hoover Avenue in Unionville, just north of Casey Street. Number three-twelve, I think." He hung up and laid his phone in his lap. Tony didn't say anything. He just drove the car.

AFTER TONY DROVE Jim back to the Buy More, they got a call from Rob to meet at the Sup 'N' Cup diner on Houston Street. The lunch rush was over. Waitresses in sunflower yellow polyester uniforms were wiping tables and laying paper placemats and napkin-wrapped stainless for the early-bird dinner. Rob, Pamela, Tony, and LaBell sat in a corner booth far from the door, a thermos of coffee in the center of the table, various kinds of pie on plates in front of them.

"What's up with him?" Rob asked, looking from LaBell to Tony. "We expected to hear from you earlier."

Tony set his forkful of banana cream pie back on his plate. "Why you asking me?"

"Because you came in together, and he looks like he just got notice of an IRS investigation."

"I got your equipment."

"What took so long?"

"Jim called me. Wanted to find his ex."

"And?"

"We found her. Somebody else found her first. Package gone. Her friends really gone. She might have made it to the hospital. I don't know."

Rob looked from Tony to LaBell and back to Tony. "You call that careful? Cowboying in the middle of the day? I'd expect it from him, but you should know better. I thought she was on our to-do list anyway."

"I'm just trying to make a living," Tony said.

"Man needs a score card to keep track of the players in this game," Rob said.

"You think it was what's-his-name—the guy who used to work for you?"

Rob shook his head. "Not his style. He'd wait until after the gunfight and bushwhack whoever was left."

Pamela sipped her coffee. "There's got to be more bad news."

LaBell drummed his fingers on the table. "I called my partner last night. He already knew about the robbery; said he had somebody on the job."

Rob rubbed his forehead. "So it could have been them at the store and cleaning up today. Wonderful. What's your partner's name?"

"Calls himself Mr. Wendell, but he speaks with an East European accent, so I always thought it was phony."

"What does he look like?" Pamela asked.

"I've seen him twice. Both times he was wearing golf clothes. Big guy, military mustache, hair and mustache dyed black, jowly pinkish face."

Pamela looked at Rob. He shrugged.

LaBell nodded. "Yeah, you guys need to get gone."

Rob ate a forkful of chocolate pie and washed it down with coffee. "What did you tell the cops?"

"That Rachel ran away and I was putting her in rehab."

"Where were you during the robbery?"

"Charity dinner for high school athletics. Plenty of witnesses." He looked at each of the others. "You done with me? I need to get to the store."

"Sure," Rob said. "We've got the check. I hope everything works out for your daughter."

They watched LaBell walk away. "So," Rob said, "give me some good news on Buddy."

Tony shook his head. "He got away. I couldn't take the risk of shooting him in the parking lot, and he was willing to risk getting shot."

"But you got our gear," Pamela said.

"I got the guns. I didn't know what else mattered, and I didn't want to stay there."

"So we've got to go back."

"But you won't be empty-handed."

The waitress, a middle-aged woman with dyed-blonde hair pulled up into a hairnet, set down a fresh thermos of coffee and the check. "Thank you," Pamela said.

Rob pushed his fork down into his remaining chocolate pie. "I have to admit I'm a little disappointed in how this turned out, but a deal is a deal. We'll give you five thousand for retrieving the gear. But it's going to take us a few hours to get it."

Tony smiled. "No problem."

"We need our gear now, though, if we're going to get your money for you."

"Why? Is the money under surveillance at your apartment?"

"Something like that."

"Need any help?"

Rob shook his head. "This job's cost us too much already."

ROB AND PAMELA pulled into the parking place in front of their apartment. The red Ford Fusion with the scraped bumper was still there. There were children on the swing sets now and moms on the benches. The intersection was becoming busier and busier as people were starting to get off work.

"Tony's on his own," Rob said. "There's crooks in this and there's cops in this, but there's no money in this. The last time I was on a job this expensive I went to jail."

"Let's get our stuff," Pamela said. "I want a shower and clean underwear. We can go out to dinner, relax, sort out the future."

Rob opened the front door and turned on the light. The sofa lay on its back. The bottom had been slashed open, exposing the springs. The drawers on the media center were all out and flipped over. The kitchen cabinets hung open. Rob ran through to the bedroom, Pamela close behind him. The closet had been emptied out onto the bed and the dresser onto the floor. Shirts, pants, underwear, and socks were scattered and tangled across the carpet. Rob knelt down and reached under the bed. Nothing. He sprang up and went into the bathroom, while Pamela lay down on her back and looked up at the bottom of the box springs. A note was taped to the bathroom mirror. On the outside it said, "Tom and Patty." Rob snatched it off the glass and peeled it open. "I got your escape packet. Ten thousand, cash. It won't be long before I get back what you owe me. Then I start on the interest payments. Get used to working for me."

Pamela stood in the doorway. He passed the note back to her. His face was neutral; his eyes were empty; his hand shook slightly. She read the note. She knew better than to say anything. They walked back into the hall.

"We've got to clear out of here," he said.

"We've got guns."

"We're not robbing convenience stores until we have enough money to set up a score. We're too old for that shit. We shouldn't have gotten greedy. We should have robbed LaBell and left him to solve his own problems."

"We did the best we could."

"Bullshit. That was our fucking B game. Our A game doesn't suck." He walked into the bedroom, her trailing him. "Let's just shove our clothes into the suitcases. We can sort it later." He pulled two empty suitcases out of the closet floor and opened them on the bed. Pamela scooped up an armload of clothes, dropped them on the bed, and started folding them into the suitcases.

"Buddy's dogging us," Rob said.

"He knows our program."

"He's having too much fun rubbing our noses in it. We've got to use that."

Pamela looked up from folding a blouse. "I thought we were running."

Rob straightened the creases on a pair of dress slacks. "With what? We have to get our money back. At least enough to set up shop somewhere else."

"At least we know who's tailing us."

"We still have to be careful. LaBell's wobbling."

"He can't crack. He's got his kid. If he spills, his partner will probably kill him."

Rob laid another pair of slacks into the suitcase. "Let's say we stay a little longer, deal with Buddy. Risk factors?"

"The cops."

"We've got a little distance there. They mostly come at us via LaBell."

"Tony?"

"He's married to us; he just doesn't know it."

"LaBell's partner?"

"LaBell's the weak link all the way around. He's on the high mountain without a Sherpa or oxygen. Somebody pinch him until he squeals and the avalanche starts. Did you soften him up a little yesterday?"

Pamela smoothed a crewneck shirt into her suitcase and closed it. "I gamed him up a little."

Rob stopped folding the dress shirt he had in his hands. "Can you keep an eye on him?"

"You care how far I go to cement it?"

"Do what you got to do."

"'Cause I don't want you pissed at me for fucking him, if that's where it goes."

"Do I seem insecure to you?"

"I'm just saying, baby, that you're my only one."

He laid the shirt on the bed, took her in his arms, and rubbed her back. "Honey, that's all behind us. I trust you. Right now we have to focus on the future, be all we can be."

"Okay," she said.

"Okay." He kissed her and went back to folding the shirt. "So you good with this?"

"Yeah, I'm good."

He laid the shirt into the suitcase. "Is this the end of it?"

"Yeah, I think so."

He closed his suitcase. "Let's put Tony in play." He got out his phone. "Hey, Tony, what's up? You still need to make some real money on this job? Something's about to pop. You on board? Excellent." He hung up the phone. "What have we got left here?"

"Bathroom and a sweep of the kitchen and living room."

"Let's hurry it up. We need to start scouting a place to stash Buddy after we take him."

LATE IN THE AFTERNOON, LaBell stood at the back of aisle twelve by the pharmacy counter in his drugstore. A few customers were walking up and down the aisles with red plastic baskets. His manager, Becky Ramirez, and Martin, a teenager who worked part-time, were standing beside him. The yellow police tape was gone, the broken glass had been swept up, and the first-aid section had been dusted and reshelved. The only real loss was the computer in the pharmacy cash register, which wouldn't reboot, forcing customers to take their pharmacy purchases up to the front registers to check out. LaBell had just finished inspecting the surrounding shelves and floor. "Thanks, Martin," he said to the teenager, "you can take off."

"See you tomorrow, Mr. LaBell." Martin pulled a ball cap out of his back pocket, put it on his head with the bill pointing back, and unhooked his belt so that his jeans fell to his hips, exposing his polka-dotted boxers. LaBell and Becky watched him slouch away.

"Seeing him on the street," Becky said, "you wouldn't know what a good kid he is."

"How was business this morning?"

"Sightseers from the coffee shop mainly, but we might have sold a few more items."

"Well, thank you, Becky, for last night and this morning."

"Jim, come on, you've always been there for me. How are you doing really? You don't look like you slept at all."

"It's been a hard twenty-four hours."

"How about Rachel?"

"She hates me and loves Kyla. I ruined her life. I turned against Kyla, which"—he shrugged—"is true. I did turn against her after she betrayed us."

"But she went into rehab?"

"Oh, yeah. Hope House. Greg and I are on a board together."

"They're the best. Remember Tyler Promsett? Flamed out first semester of college? They got him squared up."

"It was touch and go for a minute there. They don't have a hard lockdown, and if she wouldn't agree, I was going to have to take her to county and sign her in."

"But she did."

"Yeah."

"See? It's all going to work out, Jim. Teenagers—their bark is worse than their bite."

"You're right. You're right."

"Ten years from now this'll all seem like a blip in the road."

LaBell sighed. "You're a good friend, Becky. I'm lucky to have you here. You should take off Friday and make a three-day weekend."

He looked up the aisle. Detectives Peterson and Rubella were coming toward him, Peterson leading the way. "Excuse me, Becky." He walked toward the detectives.

Peterson smiled. "Mr. LaBell, how are you, sir?"

"I've been better. It's Detective Peterson, isn't it?"

"Good of you to remember, sir." She pushed her hair out of her face.

"You have a son in freshman football?"

"I do."

"Looks like his career is off to a good start."

"We'd like to see a little more studying."

"Wouldn't we all. Have you got any news?"

"We have a few items we'd like to clear up." She got out a small pad. "You were at the high school athletic awards dinner last night; then you were searching for your daughter?"

"That's right. She'd run away."

"You put her in rehab?"

"Hope House. Got her in this morning."

"Did you know that your ex-wife is in the hospital?"

"Hospital? No. Like I told you last night, I don't have any contact with her."

Detective Rubella was watching LaBell's face. "But you're afraid that your daughter has been seeing her."

"My first wife died when Rachel was a baby. Kyla's the only mom she's known."

"Kyla was found in a shooting gallery, just about beaten to death."

LaBell's mouth dropped open. He looked from Peterson to Rubella. "Is she going to be okay?"

Peterson shrugged. "She's in intensive care."

Rubella continued. "So, your store was broken into, drugs were taken, your junkie ex is in the hospital, and your missing daughter's in rehab?"

"Do you want me to pee in a cup? Look in the records. I got divorced because my ex wouldn't seek help and I didn't want her around my daughter. She was dangerous. You couldn't believe anything she said." His eyes teared up. "Before the gambling and the drugs, you should have seen her then. Night and day."

Peterson nodded sympathetically. "I sorry this is so hard, Mr. LaBell. But our focus right now is on your ex-wife and her crew. You may have found your daughter in the nick of time. If you think of anything, give us a call. We'll be in touch when we know something new."

. . .

Rob and Pamela were standing at the window by the door to their dark motel room, peeking through the closed mini-blinds.

"The tan car is back," Pamela said.

"That guy is settling in like he's expecting to make an evening of it. We keep at this, he'll be pulling a sandwich from a lunch box and opening up a thermos." He turned on the lights in the room and opened the blinds a crack. "Let's give him something to look at."

Pamela got out her phone. "Tony? You're on."

Rob and Pamela stood in the room, gesturing at each other as if they were having an argument. Tony, dressed in blue cargo pants and a gray hoodie, crossed from the motel rooms across the parking lot, took a deep breath, and focused his mind. He had one chance. He had to do this right. This guy wasn't going to get away. He came up on the parked Corolla, opened the driver's door, and stuck a .38 snub-nosed revolver into the driver's face. "Keep quiet and get out. Keep your hands in the air."

He grabbed the man by the collar of his green golf shirt and pulled him out of the car. The man was fortyish, pudgy, with brown hair receding back onto the top of his head. "Hey, hey," he said, his hands up in front of him, "I think we have a misunderstanding."

"Another word and you're wearing dentures." Tony pushed him toward the motel room. Rob opened the black metal door and pulled him in. Rob held a nine-millimeter handgun to the man's head while Tony frisked him. "No weapons." He handed the man's wallet to Rob. Rob holstered his gun.

"Sit down." Rob pushed the man into the easy chair under the window. He looked in the man's wallet. "Vince Zella, Paramount Investigations. The picture sucks. Where's Buddy?"

"Who? Mister, I'm not looking to get hurt. I'm just doing a divorce surveillance."

"Pay attention," Rob said. "Blond guy, athletic, thirtyish."

Zella nodded. "That would be Mr. Sawyer."

Pamela sat on the edge of the bed and tugged her skirt down her thighs. "Divorce surveillance? Who's supposed to be the cheater?"

"You are, ma'am."

She jumped up. "My God, you've got pictures of us in bed?"

"Sorry, lady, they're evidence and I don't have them with me. You'll have to wait for your lawyer to get them back."

Rob handed Zella his wallet. "You've been played, Vince. We're married to each other. Honey, show him your driver's license." Rob and Pamela handed their driver's licenses to Zella.

"Jesus Christ." Zella handed their licenses back. "Look, I'm not wanting any trouble."

"How are you going to make this right?" Rob asked.

"What you got in mind?"

"Let's call the police, baby," Pamela said. "What this guy did is illegal. He should be closed down."

"Hey, a guy hired me to do a job; that's all I know."

Rob turned and looked at the wall for a few seconds as if he were thinking. Then he turned back to Zella. "I don't care if you get paid, okay, but we need to confront this Mr. Sawyer. I don't know what this guy's game is—blackmail, Internet porn, who knows? We should be filing charges."

Pamela cut in. "Robby, I'm the one who was walking around here naked. I want him in jail."

"Hold on," Zella said. "I'm sorry about this whole thing, ma'am. I don't need any bad publicity. How about if I set up a meeting with Mr. Sawyer? You get him and I walk away."

"If you're lying, we're going straight to the police," Rob said.

"I just want this fiasco over with."

"Good. Call up Mr. Sawyer and set up the meet. My guy"—he pointed to Tony—"is going to keep you company until we're all done. You got a problem with that?"

Zella shook his head.

"Okay, then. Get going."

Tony left the motel room with Zella. Rob sat down on the bed. "You haven't lost your touch. You played your indignation just right."

"You had plenty of game yourself." Pamela sat down beside him. "And what about Buddy? Using civilians."

"He's got brass balls."

"He learned from the best."

Rob lifted her hand to his lips and kissed it. "But he didn't pay enough attention. We need a new motel. Let's clear out of here. You go check on LaBell. I'll find a nice, remote place to stash Buddy. Then we'll connect with Tony."

"He didn't ask for the five thousand."

"No, he didn't."

PAMELA STOOD on the white columned porch of LaBell's house. Her hair was pulled back at the nape of her neck, and she wore a pink short-sleeve silk V-neck and a white jean miniskirt with white cowboy boots. She was cradling a bouquet of flowers wrapped in green paper. LaBell answered the door, still dressed from work. He looked out the door both ways.

"Can I come in?" Pamela asked. "I brought you some flowers. Thought your day could use some brightening."

"Why are you here?"

Pamela smiled sheepishly. "Just wanted to make sure you're okay. How's your daughter?"

"Rehab."

"It's been a tough go." She handed him the bouquet. "You should probably put these in water."

He turned and she followed him in. "I know she's angry now, but one day she'll thank you," she said, trailing him back to the kitchen.

"Is that right?"

"Yeah, that's right."

LaBell looked at her hard. "What makes you think you know so much about it?"

Pamela turned around and lifted the back of her pink V-neck, revealing a crosshatching of scars running from her shoulder blades to the top of her skirt. "Rob saved me from the guy who did this." She dropped her shirt and turned back around. "I was a runaway. Got in with this guy who I thought loved me. Well"—she shrugged—"long story short, he wasn't very good for me."

"I'm sorry," LaBell said. "I'm kind of touchy right now."

She indicated the bouquet. "I think you're supposed to cut off the bottom of the stems and put them right into the water."

LaBell set the bouquet on the black granite counter top and unwrapped it, revealing a cacophony of soft, springlike colors. "Very pretty." He took a glass vase out of an upper cabinet and trimmed the flowers with the kitchen shears. "So you're Rob's wife?"

"No, he's just a good friend. The wedding rings just make life easier. Why do you ask?" She leaned toward him on the counter, pushing her cleavage forward.

He placed the flowers into the vase. "There." He centered the flowers on the counter. "I'll be able to enjoy them whenever I'm at home." He turned toward her. "I was just curious."

She put her hand on top of his and looked into his eyes. "You like bad girls, Jim?"

He looked at her sharply. "What's your game?"

"I'm not playing a game, Jimmy." She ran her index finger back and forth on his wrist while she spoke.

He looked from his wrist to her face. She smiled with her eyes. "It's nothing to be ashamed of." She patted his hand and then took her hand away. "I don't know what your first wife was like, but I know what your second wife is like. I think she ended up being just a little bit too bad."

"Really?"

"School me where I'm wrong. You like to walk on the wild side, but you want to keep it all in the bedroom—you've got your reputation and your daughter to consider. You met your ex; the pieces of the puzzle fit together and it was all good until she started rodeo riding in public. You got worried about the effects on your daughter. You tried to push the genie back into the bottle, but it just wouldn't go, so you had to turn your ex loose, even though part of you didn't want to. Now you're trying to get off your bad girl diet for the sake of your daughter. Don't worry, it's not catching." She stood up from the counter.

LaBell looked at her as if he wanted to tell her to go to hell. But

Pamela's intuition told her that he felt empty and alone, that he wanted to be able to talk to someone who actually knew what he'd been going through. She took a slow breath and waited.

LaBell looked past her toward the front door. Then he glanced at the banister to the stairs. His expression changed. "You got part of it right," he said.

She smiled. "Which part?"

"Right up until the reason I got a divorce."

"Oh, yeah, I'm sorry. It was a late night. Gambling and drugs."

He nodded. "Would you like a glass of wine?"

"I'D LIKE to get a few more days of surveillance," Buddy said. He was sitting in a coffee shop at a corner table with his back to the wall. He was dressed in his "Mr. Sawyer" outfit: gray slacks, blue blazer, white shirt, and regimental stripe tie. Vince Zella sat across from him: jeans, green golf shirt, and a sports coat. A file folder sat on the table between them with a billing statement on top.

"That's fine," Zella said, "but I'm going to need a payment to cover current expenses before I move forward."

Buddy got out his "Mr. Sawyer" checkbook and wrote a bad check.

"Thanks," Zella said. "Any changes?"

"Just keep recording what they're doing. My lawyer will evaluate what you've got thus far and tell me when we've got enough."

"Okay." Zella got up and left. Buddy put the lid back on his coffee, picked up the file folder and his coffee, and wove through the square wooden tables and out the door. It was starting to rain small soft drops onto the cars in the parking lot. Buddy hurried over to his car, a gold Chevy Malibu, unlocked it, and slid into the seat just ahead of the cloudburst. He heard the hammer on a gun click back just as he was flipping open a cup holder. In the rearview mirror he saw the face of the guy who'd confronted him in the parking lot at Rob and Pamela's that morning—and the business end of a nine-millimeter automatic.

"Keep completely still and I won't splatter your head onto the windshield."

Buddy felt the end of the barrel push into the hollow at the base of his skull. The driver's door opened. The wind blew the rain in. "Hey, Buddy." Rob handcuffed Buddy through the steering wheel. Then he came around and got in on the passenger's side. "Man, that rain came up fast." He frisked Buddy, taking his pistol, his knife, and his wallet. "It's all good, Tony."

Tony sat back. Rob put Buddy's seat belt on him; then put on his own seat belt. Buddy's pistol lay in Rob's lap. "Don't worry, Buddy, I'm not going to kill you. Unless, of course, you call attention to us. We're just going to go somewhere where we can have an uninterrupted chat. Start the car and head east. Headlights and wipers, please."

They drove through the early evening traffic by the megamall—drivers talking on cell phones and eating out of sacks while kids in car seats watched DVDs—got on the beltway headed away from town, got off two exits later where the development hadn't yet reached the highway, and drove down a two-lane country road lined with honeysuckle bushes until Rob indicated a dirt road on the right. The rain had stopped. They rolled down the damp road, pitching through the potholes, until they came to a clearing.

Out of sight of the road among some old pine trees stood a ramshackle barn, the red stain worn off the north side and the east side caved in. The main doors were locked with a heavy chain and padlock, but two missing boards in the vertical siding allowed access on the south side. Rob unlocked one of Buddy's handcuffs, Tony jerked him out of the car, and Rob recuffed him behind his back. The crickets were loud and the road noise seemed far away. Rob led the way into the barn, stepping through the missing boards. He walked to a battery-powered lantern hanging on a rusty hook and turned it on. Inside, the barn was post-and-beam construction, with what used to be a loft in the collapsed area. A few crushed cigarette packs, empty plastic bags, and used condoms were strewn across the dirt floor. A large post stood in the middle of the barn, supporting the weight of the beam that spanned from one side of the barn to the other.

"Tony," Rob said, "bring him over here."

Tony pushed Buddy over to the post. Rob ran a piece of chain through Buddy's handcuffs and padlocked him to the post. Buddy sat on the ground, his arms behind him, his blue blazer pushed back on his shoulders. Rob dragged over one of the folding chairs he'd leaned against the wall earlier. "Where's the money?"

Buddy smiled. "On our last job, they almost killed me and I wouldn't tell them, so why should I tell you?"

"You couldn't tell them what you didn't know." Rob rolled up his sleeves. "I tell you what. I'll make you a promise. Give us the money. I won't kill you. Pamela won't kill you. Tony won't kill you. You hold out, Tony will definitely kill you, and he doesn't even know you."

"Mexican standoff. You can't kill me if you want the money."

They heard a car drive up. Rob grabbed a fistful of Buddy's hair and shoved his handkerchief into Buddy's mouth. Tony stood to the side of the opening with his pistol down along his leg. A car door slammed. "Robby?" Pamela called out.

Rob looked out the opening. "Hey, honey."

Pamela came into the barn. "Nice and cozy." She nodded at Tony. "Look who we have here." She took the handkerchief out of Buddy's mouth.

"Remind you of old times?" he asked.

"Only this time I've got a partner who'll watch my back."

"Explain to Tom how this works, Patty. Oh, that's right; it's Rob and Pamela now."

"You think this is some kind of joke." She patted Buddy's cheek. "You're in a world of hurt." She turned to Rob. "Searched his car yet?"

"No, I guess I was hoping for him to make sense."

He picked up a small black duffel bag from next to the other folding chair, pulled out a Taser, and handed it to Tony. "You used one of these before?"

"Sure."

"Tune up our boy while we search the car."

"You sure this will work?"

"Tony, stop listening to his bullshit. Hit him with the juice, and keep on hitting him until he decides to start taking his situation seriously."

ROB AND PAMELA walked out to Buddy's car. "It's a little dark to make a thorough search," Rob said.

Pamela shrugged. "We can at least give it a start."

They looked in the trunk and the passenger compartment, but there was nothing they could see. Rob felt around under the seats. He could almost feel the vacuum marks. It was just a standard stolen car, except that Buddy had been driving it for at least two days. Pamela found the registration in the glove box. "Let's scout out the owner."

Rob went back into the barn. Tony had taken off his hoodie. He was standing with the Taser in his hand; Buddy lay slumped on the ground, his mouth open and drool running down his chin. "Can you hold down the fort for an hour?"

"Yeah."

"We're taking Buddy's car. Here are Pamela's keys." He handed the keys to Tony. "Remember, Buddy used to be one of us. Our bread and butter is fucking with people's heads. Don't let him fuck with yours. Relax, and we'll be back before you know it."

Rob and Pamela drove back down to the highway and then into town, rolling up and down the hills in the dark until they were back under the streetlights of the city. The address from the registration was an older neighborhood of well-kept-up small one-story houses. This particular house was dark inside and the grass needed mowing. Rob pulled up in front of the detached garage by the kitchen door. "I'm betting the other key on this ring fits the door." He turned the key in the lock and they went in. He flipped on the wall light switch. The blinds were closed. They were standing in an eat-in kitchen with a gray Formica-topped table. The sink and butcher-block countertops were loaded with dirty dishes. In the living room there were family pictures taken in the 1960s hanging on the walls and a matching brown plaid sofa and two side chairs. An old nineteen-inch TV sat in the corner. Their getaway driver's licenses lay on the walnut-stained coffee table. Rob picked them up. "Buddy was planning on hanging this on us as a going away present."

"Breaking and entering? The cops have time for that?"

There were two bedrooms, one with twin beds with matching quilt bedspreads ready for company, and one with a queen bed that was rumpled and unmade from someone sleeping in it. They went downstairs to the unfinished basement. The floor was spotless. Neatly stacked and labeled boxes filled shelves on one side of the space. Near the washer and dryer was an old chest-style freezer. Rob lifted the lid. Inside was the old lady who owned the house, still wearing her hearing aids and glasses, a gunshot wound in her head.

"Close the lid, Robby."

Rob dropped the freezer lid. "You okay?"

Pamela bent over and put her hands on her knees.

"Don't get sick."

"I'm fine." She took a deep breath and straightened up. "Killing someone's little old mom for the use of a ride and a crib. And then he was going to pin it on us."

Rob shrugged. "You've got to admire the efficiency, though. He controlled his costs and visibility."

"You're not easing up on him?"

"Don't you worry, after we get our money, I'm tying him up with a bow. I'm way past tired of that fuck sticking his nose where it doesn't belong."

They went back through the house, room by room, tipping out drawers and emptying boxes, but the jewelry and the money weren't there. "Damn it," Rob said. His clothes were sticky with sweat. He stood in the kitchen overlooking the wreck they'd made of the house. "Did we miss anywhere?"

"No," Pamela said. She looked down at her pink V-neck. "Christ, my shirt has dirt streaked on it. Must have been the boxes downstairs." She went to the sink and wet a paper towel. "No, no, no," she said. "The old lady."

Rob looked at her. "Under the old lady?"

She nodded.

"Definitely a classic. It's almost too obvious."

"It's got Buddy written all over it."

They went back down into the basement. Rob had his hand on the freezer lid. "You ready for this? I could probably do it by myself."

"She's what? One hundred ten pounds frozen? You'll put your back out."

"I'm not that old."

She gave him a look that said he wasn't going to win the argument.

"Okay, then."

Pamela moved to the feet end of the freezer. Rob threw the lid up; then moved to the head end. "Let's jiggle her a bit first, in case she's frozen onto something." He reached down under her shoulders; Pamela grabbed her ankles; they jostled her a bit. "Okay, one, two."

They lifted her out of the freezer and lowered her gently to the floor.

"Jesus," Rob said, "I'm weak."

"You're fifty-one, baby."

"Don't rub it in." He looked in the freezer. "Anything?"

Pamela shook her head. A box of frozen fish, a bag of frozen corn, a loaf of bread, a bag of lima beans, three ice trays, frozen blood.

"Why was she even running this freezer? There's nothing in here," Rob said.

"Kind of sad, isn't it?"

"Let's put her back."

"Lift with your legs."

They put the old woman back in the freezer. Rob closed the lid. "I'd like to put Buddy in there with her, the bastard, but it seems somehow unfair to her."

"I'm not opening that freezer anymore."

"Tony could help me." He smiled. "As a last resort, if Buddy won't give up the cash, we cram him in here with her and see how long he lasts."

They drove back to the dilapidated barn. Tony was sitting on the folding chair, playing a game on his phone. Buddy lay crumpled at the base of the post. He'd wet his pants.

"Any news?" Tony asked.

"All bad," Rob said. He explained what they had found.

"So that's what took so long. You could have called. This guy never became cooperative."

"Sorry," Pamela said. "We haven't messed you up with your wife, have we?"

"No, it'll be okay. What're we doing with him overnight?"

"Don't worry," Rob said, "nobody has to stay. You got the syringe, honey?"

Pamela took a loaded syringe out of her handbag. "The main advantage to robbing a drugstore." She handed it to Rob.

Rob gestured at Tony. "Watch my back." He squatted down in front of Buddy, felt his pulse, and then injected him in a neck vein. "That should take care of him until morning. Let's get out of here." He handed the syringe back to Pamela. "Come on, Tony, we'll give you a ride to your truck. We're not driving the old lady's Malibu anymore. It's bound to get hot eventually."

LATER AT THE NEW MOTEL, a Value Inn at the interchange nearest the barn, Pamela stood in her robe in the bathroom looking in the mirror. She had just finished brushing her hair, which hung loose on her shoulders. Rob, still dressed, came into the bathroom and stood behind her.

"You haven't asked me about Jim," she said.

Rob pulled her robe down to her waist and put his arms around her from behind, his arms wrapped just under her breasts, all the time watching her face in the mirror. "I know." He rested his head on her shoulder. "Is he bought in?"

"He's bought it. I told him the runaway story." She tried to turn around, but he held her tight. She closed her eyes.

"Look at me."

She shook her head.

"Look at me."

She opened her eyes and found his in the mirror. "That's better. I know it's hard mind-fucking LaBell." He ran one hand along the scars on her ribs. "I wouldn't ask you to do it if it didn't have to be done."

"I know, baby."

"So if you can't do it, tell me now."

"I can do it."

"You sure?"

She nodded.

He kissed her neck. "I know you're feeling emotional—LaBell's daughter, the little old lady. Don't deny it. Just remember, we've got control of this one. If anyone's going under the bus, it's not going to be one of us. We're getting out of here without a scratch."

A tear started from the corner of her eye. He loosened his grip. She turned in his arms and held him tight.

9

HUNTING FOR THE MONEY

The next day at 8:00 a.m. LaBell was at the pharmacy doing some paperwork ahead of the 9:00 a.m. opening. Someone knocked on the front doors, not an unusual occurrence: a trade rep, an employee a few minutes early, a longtime customer in an early morning hurry. But this was a man LaBell had never seen before: midforties, crew cut, charcoal-gray suit, hard, veiny hands. "We're not open yet."

"Mr. LaBell? I'm Mr. Vincent. I represent your partner, Mr. Wendell. I believe he told you I was in town. Can we speak privately?"

LaBell glanced out into the parking lot. There were cars clustered by the coffee shop. A few dark clouds drifted across an otherwise blue sky. The weather report had indicated sunny, but maybe he needed to check again. He nodded and led Vincent down the center aisle into the storage area at the back of the store. "The early employees will be in shortly."

"I understand." Vincent smiled. His face crinkled in a way that was almost violent. "I'll get to the point. Your new best friends— where are they staying?"

"I don't know."

"Find out."

"Can't you find them?"

"We're working on it."

"They're still trying to find the money."

"So are we. And so are you. After all, you're responsible for paying it back."

"Wait a minute. You guys brought the thieves in."

"Take it up with the boss. You're a family man. Just keep your little girl in the front of your mind. How is she anyway? I here she's twelve-stepping it."

"My daughter's got nothing to do with this."

"Hell of a thing for a sixteen-year-old. Already on the treadmill. It's a delicate time, they tell me, a time when parental support is important." He tapped a finger on the side of his head. "Think it through, Mr. LaBell. Think it through. Do what's right for your family. Find out where your friends are staying. I'll be in touch."

LaBell followed him back through the store and watched him push through the glass front doors. He wanted to tell Vincent that he wasn't afraid, that Vincent could fold his threats into five corners and shove them where the sun didn't shine, that he was the master of his own fate, but he knew in his heart that Vincent wouldn't believe him and wouldn't care even if he did believe him. They both knew he had limits, limits defined by pride and love and fear, limits that men like Vincent didn't have. So he was stuck in the middle between Vincent on the one side and Rob, Pamela, and Tony on the other side. If either side found out the depth of his relationship with the other, there'd be hell to pay. And he couldn't call the police because, besides the fear of death, he didn't want to go to jail or to lose his pharmacy or his reputation in the community. He turned, his shoulders slumped, and tried unsuccessfully to smile. He'd just have to keep his head down and muddle through. He'd gotten Rachel back, and this was the price he had to pay.

Tony, still wearing a white T-shirt and blue-checked camp pants, sat on a metal stool at the peninsula of the kitchen counter, drinking coffee. Emily sat across from him in her furry pink robe with the Ant in her lap, her light brown hair brushed back from her face. "You had another late night."

Tony nodded. "Expedited job. Overtime pay."

"That's great, Tone." She patted the Ant on his back. "I'm not trying to pressure you," she continued. "I'm just trying to figure out how far our money has to stretch. You started this job last week, so when is your first paycheck?"

"It's a temp thing, so it doesn't follow the usual sort of rules, but I ought to have something by the end of the week."

Emily nodded. "Okay, so I can buy more groceries. Maybe we could catch up the electric."

"Why don't you get a sitter for Friday?"

"Can we afford that?"

"We won't shoot the moon. Go to a movie or something."

She smiled. "I'll call Rachel, see if she's available."

Tony set down his coffee cup, brought his hand up to his face, rubbed his goateed chin, and turned his head. "That's probably not a good idea."

"Why? She's our best sitter. The Ant loves her."

"I ran into Jim while I was picking up diapers. Rachel's in rehab. Jim's pretty broken up about it."

"My God. After what happened to Kyla, I bet he's crushed. I should give him a call."

"I wouldn't do that. He blurted it out and then made me promise not to tell anyone. You know how wound up he can get."

"Rachel's such a good kid. How did this happen?"

Tony shrugged.

"We should put her in our prayers."

Tony looked at his wife holding his son. They were so perfect. They deserved to be safe and cared for. But the $5,000 Rob had promised him wasn't enough. He'd started out with a sure $25,000 for the robbery. Enough money to get the mortgage and bills all squared away. That had turned into $18,000 after LaBell skimmed off $50,000 for the kidnappers. That was a shitty thing to do, but he couldn't really blame him for trying to save his daughter, and there was still enough money left to create some elbow room. But after Buddy Ray took the $55,000 and the jewelry from Rob, Tony had kissed his hopes good-bye. Well, they had Buddy Ray now. There was no turning back. Tony had robbed a store, gone gunning for Rachel's kidnappers, helped capture Buddy Ray. All to keep his family off the street. He knew Rob and Pamela wouldn't go soft. They would do whatever it took to get Buddy Ray to cough up the $55,000. And he'd give up that cash before they were done with him. So all Tony had to do was stay strong until the payday came. It was strangely like being deployed in a war zone.

He picked up his coffee cup. "That's exactly what we should do."

"I'll call Susan and see if she's free Friday."

LaBELL STOOD next to Dr. Joseph behind his desk in his office at Hope House. Dr. Joseph was in his shirtsleeves, his suit jacket on the back of his chair, wide red suspenders holding his pants up. On the computer screen in front of them, they were watching video footage from the facility's closed-circuit surveillance system.

"This is what we've pieced together." Dr. Joseph stooped over the desk to work the mouse. "Rachel is going down the hall here. Right there is where she looks over her shoulder. Okay, this is on the grounds at the front of the building. That's her climbing over the stone wall. And this is from outside the wall on the street. There's the car she gets into."

"Red Mustang. That's Billy Cruz from around the corner. He's always seemed like a good kid."

"They're all good kids, Jim."

"His dad's going to hear about this."

"And he'll politely say something about how your motherless, oversexed, addicted daughter scrambled his son's mind."

"You're not helping, Greg."

"I just helped you to keep from making an ass of yourself. Ryan

Cruz? City council? If you can't calm down, you need to stay out of this."

LaBell took a deep breath. "Okay, Greg, I'm hearing you."

"Good. We called the cops. We don't think she's gone far. What you should do if you can keep your inner bastard under control is call her friends and check places she might go to. When you find her, you need to be gentle. She needs help, not judgment."

"You're right." He walked back and forth in front of the picture windows. "She's not a bad person. She's just going through a bad patch." He came back to the desk. "Is she an addict?"

Dr. Joseph hemmed and hawed. "She acts like a person who's used to taking drugs—manipulative, secretive, personal control issues—but a full-blown addict?" He shrugged. "We didn't have her here long enough to find out. Get her back here and we'll do what we can."

LaBell sat in his car in the parking lot of the Hope House, making a list of places to go and of Rachel's friends to call. It was peaceful and quiet here. With the window lowered, he could hear birdsong and the muted traffic noises from beyond the wall. It was like being parked at an elementary school while class was in session. His mind kept cascading through the past, trying to hang on imaginary points in time where he could have saved Rachel, stopped her, turned her around, kept them from ending up here, but he knew it was all just bullshit. If he had cleaned up one spot, it just would have created another spot. That's the way reality worked. And who knew? Maybe this spot they were in right now was the simplest, most fixable of the possible catastrophes in store for them. He looked out the windshield at the main entrance to the building: the limestone steps rising up to the two massive oak doors with their eight glass panes. The wheelchair ramp fitted in on the left side so it almost looked as if it were built there originally, back when this was the old county hospital. Stairs and ramp. This was the world we lived in. Thinking about bad things only made them worse. The trick was to find solutions without thinking about the problem.

He dialed his phone. "Kari? This is Jim LaBell, Rachel's dad. She forgot her phone this morning and I'm trying to get a hold of her. You haven't seen her, have you?"

"No, Mr. LaBell. We don't have class together this term and our lockers are in different halls. If I see her at lunch, I'll let her know."

LaBell made three other phone calls with similar results. He drove to the Burger Barn, Ed's Billiards, Koala Coffee, and the nearest mall. No Rachel or friend of Rachel's or teenager he knew well enough to talk with. Why was he surprised? He was looking for her in her cover life, and she had escaped into her underground life. Where was that? Mr. Wendell had pulled him down the rabbit hole. Now he had Rob and Pamela and Tony and Vincent and a world of trouble. Who had pulled Rachel down her rabbit hole?

His phone rang. "Hello?"

"Jim? It's Pamela. How you doing?"

"I can't really talk right now."

"That's okay. I was just thinking about our visit yesterday—"

"I don't mean it be rude. Rachel ditched rehab. I'm trying to find her. I've got a lot on my mind."

"My God, that's terrible. Do you need help? Someone to keep you company?"

"Thanks, but no. I got a visit from an associate of my partner this morning. I don't think we should be seen together. I'll talk with you later." He hung up.

Kyla. That's who opened the door for Rachel, got her started on all this stupidity. At least she was safe from her. LaBell took the next left turn and headed downtown toward the neighborhood where they had found Kyla. He didn't know where Rachel might be, but he could drive a grid looking for Billy Cruz's red Mustang. It was a long shot, but at least he would feel like he was doing something.

. . .

Rob and Pamela were driving down the commercial strip by their motel. Pamela put her phone away. "Did you hear all that?"

"Yeah." He took a right turn into a McDonald's restaurant. "Wendell's either going to think LaBell's one unlucky bastard, or that his daughter was in on the robbery."

It was lunchtime before Rob and Pamela got back to the broken-down barn where they had left Buddy. Tony was already there. Buddy was naked, sitting on an old red blanket, one wrist handcuffed to the chain locked around the post, a plastic bucket on the dirt floor beside him.

"Hey, Tony, you getting started without us?"

"He had some needs that I didn't want to provide personal assistance for."

Rob turned to Buddy. "Brought you some food." He handed the McDonald's bag to Buddy.

"Have we got another blanket for him?" Pamela asked.

Buddy looked up from the sack. "Why? See something you like?"

"Shut up," Pamela said, "and eat your lunch."

Rob went over to Tony. "Find anything in his clothes?"

Tony pointed to a pile on the floor by the folding chair. "Nothing out of the ordinary: cash, nothing written on the bills, keys, wallet, cards and license."

"Put the cash in your pocket," Rob said. "Go ahead, he won't need it." He glanced at Buddy, who didn't even look up from his French fries. "Okay, the loot has got to be somewhere. Let's start by tearing down the old lady's car."

They went out to the car, which was parked out of the shade of the barn. Nothing in the glove box, cup holders, or map pockets. They pulled the floor mats, shoved their hands down between the backseat cushions, laid their shoulders onto the carpet and looked and felt under the seats. Down in the crevice between the passenger's seat and the front console, Pamela fished out a receipt from a garage dated yesterday. So they popped the hood and trunk. They examined every reservoir and compartment with a removable cover. Nothing. They opened the gas tank cover to check for a string or chain running down into the gas tank. Nothing. Finally, they got out the spare tire, bounced it, deflated it, and pried it off the rim. Empty.

Rob looked over at the barn as if Buddy were laughing at him. "We could pull all the tires off."

Pamela shook her head. "There's nothing there, Robby. The receipt is just a bullshit receipt."

"What now?" Tony asked. "Back to the Taser?"

"No," Rob said. "We have to try something a little more convincing. He won't give the money up if he thinks he has a chance of keeping it."

Rachel and Billy were driving his red Mustang around in the Fish Hook—a collection of old stilted cabins on a peninsula jutting into a wide spot on Spotter's Creek, down in the flood plain. Rachel knew a junkie who squatted in one of the old cabins, an old man everyone called Perfect, but she'd only been down there at night with someone else driving, so she wasn't quite sure which cabin was his. Billy drove with the seat tilted back to keep his head from rubbing the ceiling. He was gym muscled, with his black hair trimmed close to his head. He wore black basketball shorts and a red golf shirt. Rachel was leaning back into the corner of the door and the passenger's seat with her feet up on the dash. She wore gray sweatpants, sandals, and a baby blue T-shirt. Her hair hung loose around her face. She put her feet down. "Cut down this next little alley on the right."

They bounced through a mud hole. "Don't let me go home without washing this car," Billy said. "Dad doesn't care if I cut school, but he'll never quit bitching if I bring this car home dirty."

Rachel laughed. "Give me a cigarette."

He tossed a box of Camel filters at her. "That old guy really live down here?"

"Yeah. And he knows where the best dope is. Have to pay for the info, but it's worth it. There." She laid the cigarette pack on the seat and pointed to a cabin with a yellow door. Billy pulled up in front of it. "Get the tire iron."

"I thought you said you know this guy."

She looked at him as if he were entirely clueless. "I didn't say I trust him. Besides, there might be some other guy in there."

"Game face," Billy said. He climbed out of the car and stretched. Rachel waited by her car door while he got the tire iron.

"You ready now?" she asked. "Watch and learn, baby cakes." They climbed up the rickety steps, careful of the missing boards. "Perfect!" Rachel yelled. "Perfect, you there?"

She glanced up at Billy. "Bang on the door."

"You are high maintenance." He pounded his fist on the door, rattling it in the frame.

"What's up?" a voice called out.

"Perfect?"

"Who is it?"

"Rachel. Kyla's daughter."

The yellow door swung in. A skinny old man, shirtless, bruises on his ribs, his gray hair hanging in his face, stood in the way. He peered at Billy, at the tire iron, at Rachel and smiled, showing two black teeth in an otherwise empty mouth. "Hey, girl, you here to give me a blow job?"

Billy gave him a push. "Shut up, you old fuck."

Rachel put a hand on Billy's arm. "Relax." She turned to Perfect. "Who's got the best weed down in the Corners?"

"How does that help me?"

"Twenty bucks?"

"Let's see it."

Billy pulled a twenty-dollar bill out of his pocket.

"I'd rather have the blow job."

"Twenty bucks before you even cross the threshold," she said. "Sounds like the start of a great day."

"You know Milt?"

"Phone number?" She turned to Billy. "Give me your phone."

Perfect rubbed his chin and rattled off a number. She dialed.

"Milt? Rachel, Kyla's daughter. Where you at?" She nodded, hung up, and looked to Billy. "We're good."

Billy handed Perfect the twenty-dollar bill.

"See you later," Rachel said.

Perfect stretched the twenty out in his hands, then looked over the top of it at Rachel. "White meat chicken sure taste sweet."

Rachel gave him the finger.

They drove back out of the Fish Hook the same way they came in, splashing through the mud holes and sliding around the corners.

"Hell of a day," Billy said. "I just want to score some weed, but first I've got to bust you out of jail."

She rolled her eyes. "I wasn't in jail."

"Then we have to go see some crackhead wizard from *Deliverance*."

"You majoring in drama?"

"I'm just trying to get ready for whatever comes next."

"Relax. We'll find your weed, and you'll be back in the burbs before school lets out."

"I thought we were going to hang out."

"I've got to find my mom."

"So? Your mom knows me. No big deal."

She shrugged. "Where's your iPod?"

They rolled down into the western part of Unionville, the part everyone called the Corners, found the abandoned row house Milt was working from, and bought a quarter of an ounce of marijuana. Then they crossed back east, traveling via the side streets, until they were on the street behind the tourist cabin she'd been at with her mother.

"Pull over," she said. "I'll be right back."

Billy pulled over to the broken curb. Rachel ran down a dirt path that meandered through the overgrown bushes and volunteer saplings between two abandoned houses. She slipped through a gap in a rotten board fence, and came up on the cabin from behind. She peeked in the back door. It looked different in the daylight: dirtier, more dilapidated, less safe. The table and chairs had been knocked over. Bullet holes were sprayed across the walls. But there was no one there. No one had been there since her dad had come for her. Her smartphone was where she'd left it, under a loose floorboard by the bed where she'd been sitting. She picked it up. Still had plenty of battery. She slid her hand between the corner of the mattress and box springs and pulled out the $35 her mom had put there. Why had she left the money there?

Rachel ran back down the path and out between the houses to the car. "She's not there. Let's try another spot."

"Doesn't your mom have a phone?"

"No."

"No phone?"

"She's off the grid. She's not tied down by owning things. She doesn't have places to be or things to do. She's completely free."

Billy put the car in gear. "What's that got to do with having a phone?"

They drove deeper into the old industrial zone, the uninhabited houses replacing the inhabited ones, until they arrived at a boarded-up house where Kyla sometimes squatted.

As soon as Rachel saw the yellow police tape, she pointed and yelled, "There, there, there!"

Billy squealed up in front of the house. Rachel jumped out of the Mustang and ran up the steps and onto the porch. She stopped at the tape, trying to see into the gloom, and then ducked under it.

"Mom!" she yelled, "Mom!" Inside, three chalk lines shaped like people were drawn around dark brown stains soaked into the old wood floor, just like the kind she'd seen on TV crime shows. She couldn't breathe. She got down on her hands and knees.

Billy was behind her. He knelt and put a hand on her back. "You okay?"

Her lungs filled in a rush. She turned and grabbed him. "Something's not right. Something's not right." Tears started down her face.

He rubbed her back and then pulled her to her feet. "This place is fucked-up, Rach. There's nothing else here. Let's go out to the car." He led her outside.

At the door, she turned and looked back in. "Hospitals."

They got back in the car. Billy pulled away from the curb. "Where do you want to go?"

"Just get away from here." Rachel wiped her tears away with the palms of her hands. She got out her phone and looked up the numbers for the hospitals in the city. She called the first hospital. "Hello? Could you connect me with Kyla LaBell's room?" Nothing. She called the second hospital. Nothing. The third hospital. "I'm sorry," the receptionist said. "Kyla LaBell is in the ICU. No visitors are allowed except family."

She hung up her phone. "County General. Mom's at County General. That's where we need to go."

"That fucked-up hospital where poor people go? Is she okay?"

"I don't know. She's in the ICU. All I know is she's alive."

LaBell drove back and forth through Unionville, from the river on the west, past the row houses and closed corner stores, past the abandoned houses and weed-choked empty lots, down to the old Consolidated Metal Fabrication plant, over a block and back to the river, over a block and back to the plant, but he never saw Billy and Rachel. He'd decided he'd make one final pass when his phone rang. "Yeah?"

"Mr. LaBell? Detective Rubella. We found your daughter."

"Where is she?"

"Not to worry. She's okay. She's with her mom at County General."

"Thanks."

"We'll wait for you."

LaBell took the second-floor walkway from the concrete parking deck into the hospital. He knew where he was going. The cool quiet of the hallways was comforting. He walked by ambulatory services, where family members read magazines or watched TV while they waited for patients to finish their procedures. He took the second right, rode up the left-side elevators, turned left, and pushed his way through the ICU doors.

Detective Peterson, holstered pistol at her hip, was leaning on the counter of the nurses' station. She straightened up when she saw him. "Mr. LaBell, we need to talk."

"I want to see my daughter."

"This will just take a minute." Peterson took him by the elbow and guided him into a side hall. "Over here."

"What is it?"

"You're the one who made the nine-one-one call about your ex-wife."

"I don't know what you're talking about."

"But your phone does. Nine-one-one makes a record of all incoming calls. Why were you looking for Kyla?"

He took a deep breath. "I knew Rachel had been seeing her on the sly. I couldn't blame her. But Kyla—you've seen what happens in her world—I wanted to warn her off. Appeal to her conscience, if she still had one."

"So you found her and her associates."

LaBell nodded.

"But you didn't want to be there when the uniforms arrived."

"Not my proudest moment." He sniffed and looked away.

"The other two?"

"They were dead, exactly like you found them."

Detective Peterson motioned with her head. "Go see your daughter."

LaBell saw Detective Rubella standing outside a room. Inside he found Rachel sitting on a plastic chair, hunched down in her sweatshirt, her face in her hands. Kyla lay on the bed unconscious, an IV in her arm, an oxygen mask half covering the green and purple bruising on her face, cabling leading from her body to a bank of monitors near the head of her bed.

Rachel looked up. "Daddy."

"Hey, baby," LaBell said. He crossed the room to her and took her in his arms.

Rachel cried on his shoulder. "Look what they did to Mom, Daddy. Look what they did to Mom. Look what they did."

"I know, baby. I know." He rubbed her back.

"What's going to happen?"

"I wish I could say that everything's going to be all right. I wish I could. But nobody knows right now how things are going to turn out."

"But why? Why did this happen to Mom?"

LaBell started crying. "Her life went off the rails. The addict took her over. This is what I've been afraid of. This is what I've been wanting to protect you from." They held each other and cried, standing there next to the bed, the only sound in the room the monitors and their crying.

Finally, they let go of each other. LaBell gave his handkerchief to Rachel and wiped his face on his sleeve. "Let's hope she gets better," LaBell said, looking at Kyla. "Let's hope this is the bottom of her pit, and she can really start on recovery." He turned to Rachel. "Can you see now why I want you at Hope House? I just want to keep you safe."

"Can I come visit Mom?"

LaBell nodded. "We'll work it out. But no more of this sneaking."

"Okay, Dad."

"I'm going to take you back to Hope House."

"I want to stay here."

"She doesn't know you're here, Rach."

"When she wakes up, she'll be by herself."

"The nurses will be here. They'll call us. I'll bring you right away."

"You promise?"

"I promise."

She nodded.

"You can order Kyla some flowers. Then she'll see flowers when she wakes up."

Rachel bent down over Kyla and kissed her forehead. "I love you, Mom."

LaBell put his arm around Rachel's shoulder and walked her out of the room. Her bond with Kyla was as strong as ever. Maybe even stronger. Kyla was going to be in their lives indefinitely if she pulled through. He was going to have to find a way to deal with that. He wondered what Rachel would think if she knew he was the one who made the phone call that brought her stepmom here. Would she be suspicious of his motives, or simply happy he'd saved Kyla's life? Either way, he wasn't going to say anything. He didn't want the credit or the trouble.

Peterson and Rubella were standing at the nurses' station. "We'll be in touch," Peterson said.

LaBell nodded.

When he and Rachel were in the elevator, she said, "Dad, when I first got here, before I went into the room, there was a guy who acted like a cop but wasn't a cop."

"Really? What did he look like?"

"Like a TV tough guy."

"What was he doing?"

"He checked on Mom, looked at her chart."

"Well, the cops are there now. I'll tell them. They can handle it."

They both were quiet on the ride back to Hope House, but LaBell felt a closeness with his daughter that he hadn't felt recently, as if their shared tears had washed away the strife between them. He knew it wouldn't last, but right now he needed the respite of that closeness, and of the feeling that the world could be made right that the closeness embodied. He'd made a mistake asking for Wendell's help. Now Vincent, Rob, Pamela, and even Tony were all after the laundry money. He couldn't change that. But Rachel was his priority. He had to find the simplest way forward that would keep her safe. If he helped Vincent find Rob and the others, could he be sure Vincent would take care of them before they found out he had snitched on them? Take care of them. Well, Rob and Pamela were professional criminals; he owed them nothing. But Tony . . . well, even he didn't have to say yes. He could have walked away at any time. They had all chosen to go after Wendell's money. He glanced at his daughter. Finally, there was a glimmer of hope that their lives were getting better; that she was going to see Kyla's lifestyle for what it really was and choose the future over addiction and death. There was no backing down now. He had to do everything he could to protect their life together.

At Hope House, Dr. Joseph was standing in the lobby talking with the receptionist, a young woman with a nose ring and three eyebrow rings who was on her last week of treatment. His face was red and he was puffing as if he needed to use an asthma rescue inhaler. They hadn't called ahead, but he didn't seem the least bit surprised to see them. "Jim, Rachel. Have you decided to give us a little more cooperation?" He turned to the receptionist. "Sally, mark in Rachel LaBell."

Rachel looked down at her hands. She was worrying the silver friendship ring she wore on her right index finger. "Dr. Joseph, I'm sorry I've been such a pain in the butt."

"What made you change your mind?"

Her eyes teared up. "I saw my mom at the hospital."

"I'm sorry to hear that. How is she?"

"They don't know. She's in intensive care." She wiped her eyes on her sweatshirt sleeve.

"Have you had lunch?"

She shook her head.

"Come along, we'll find you something. You're missing afternoon group."

"Thanks, Greg," LaBell said. "I'll take you to see Kyla tomorrow, Rachel."

"Unless she wakes up."

"Unless she wakes up." LaBell took a deep breath, exhaled, and then turned and left. As he was walking across the parking lot, his phone rang.

"Jim? It's Pamela. How's it going?"

"Better, much better."

"Find your daughter?"

"Yes. Thank God. That's a load off my mind."

"Can I stop by to see you after work?"

"I don't know if that's such a good idea. Vincent was at the hospital."

"He talk to Kyla?"

"Kyla can't talk to anyone yet." He stood by his Highlander with his keys in his hand. What could Kyla tell if she were conscious?

"I bet she doesn't know anything. He's working the money trail, and the money left after she went down."

"You think so?"

"Why else is she alive?"

"I've got to go to work."

"I'll see you this evening."

LaBell unlocked his car. All the positive emotion from reconnecting with his daughter had evaporated. Rachel was safe for now. But if the police found out about the kidnapping plot and went after Kyla, they would drive a wedge between him and his daughter. If Vincent didn't find the rest of the money, he'd threaten to harm Rachel to make him pay it back. And if either the cops or Vincent found Pamela, Rob, and Tony, all hell would break loose, and he'd end up dead or in jail. LaBell sat in his car and looked at the stone wall at the front of the grounds, the running bond pattern of cement and limestone, as if it were a maze that would show him the way out.

MIDAFTERNOON, out behind the broken-down barn, the smell of rain in the cooling breeze, Rob, Pamela, and Tony stood by Buddy, who was naked, kneeling beside a freshly dug casket-sized hole, his wrists tied to his ankles.

"You can't be serious," Buddy said.

Rob gave him a push with his foot. He fell into the hole, landing on his side. He spat dirt out of his mouth. "You can be buried dead or alive," Rob said. "It's up to you."

Buddy twisted his head, trying to look up. "We used to be friends."

"So I should piss on you now instead of on top of your grave? Where's the money?"

"They got it. I got it from you; Vincent got it from me."

"Who're 'they'?"

"You just don't get it, do you? I was supposed to kill you at the drugstore break-in the other night. This gig is all bullshit. LaBell's partner has always been after you."

Pamela put her hand on Rob's shoulder. "So this was a setup from the beginning."

Rob shook his head and laughed. "But you had to steal the money from us first."

"Like you wouldn't."

"But Vincent figured you out."

"He's nothing but a bastard."

"So LaBell's partners got the kidnap money and our money? They got all the money and LaBell's jewelry?"

"Yeah."

"So where's the escape packet? The ten thousand that went with our new driver's licenses?"

"I had to give it up."

"We've got to get that back."

"Let me up. I'll help you. Vincent probably kept the extra. He's the detail guy. You can probably get that back."

"Where's Vincent staying?"

"He's at the McKinley downtown."

"Room?"

"I don't know, but I can find out."

Rob glanced at his partners. Neither of them said anything. "Tony, get him out of there."

Tony dropped into the hole, cut Buddy's ankles free, and pulled him to his feet. Rob and Pamela pulled him out by his shoulders. He sat on the ground, dirt smeared down his face and shoulder, breathing hard. "I'm in with Vincent. He trusts me. I'll find out everything you need."

"I'm sure you will." Rob helped him to his feet. They walked him back to the barn, chained him back to the post as they had before, gave him a bottle of water, and went back outside. Rain was beginning to spit.

"So," Tony said, "kill him, leave him, or free him?"

"You got to keep your sense of humor in this business. Let's put him back in the old lady's house."

"What about Jim?" Pamela asked.

"What about him?"

"Wendell has all the drugstore money, plus Jim's jewelry. Should we tell him?"

"Why? He brought us into this. We're not responsible for him. Our original plan was to stiff him. Let him take his ride. Besides, we don't know how far he's in. Has he been playing us?"

"Come on, Robby, you saw him wig out. That guy wouldn't leave his daughter with drug addicts."

"But he might leave us swinging. If Buddy's not lying, if these guys have a grudge against us, then they used Tony to rope us in." He looked at Tony. "How do you know LaBell?"

Tony shrugged. "Like I said, Rachel babysits for us. He knew I just got out of the army; that I'm looking for work."

"But you reached out to your cousin Stella. Stella steered you to us. So LaBell has to know something, and Stella has to know something."

Pamela shook her head. "That's an awful lot of ifs."

"Honey, if it looks like shit and smells like shit, chances are it tastes like shit."

Tony looked from one to the other. "All that's great, but the money's still gone. Where does that leave me?"

Rob shook his head. "We don't know if the money's gone. We're going to tie off some loose ends. We're going to do everything we can to get all the money back. We're going to at least pay you the five grand we promised." The rain started in earnest. "It's time to stop being surprised and start being surprising."

ROB DROVE the old lady's gold Malibu back to her house, the windshield wipers whacking evenly across the windshield. Buddy was drugged out and trussed up in the trunk. Tony followed in his Dodge truck. Rob wore latex gloves and a rain suit. They'd vacuumed and wiped down the car before they loaded Buddy. The rain was lucky. It made the night darker, which made it less likely that any neighbors or dog walkers would see them. Rob pulled to a stop in the old lady's driveway, in front of the detached garage with the car trunk closest to the back door. Tony parked on the street and cut across the yard. Rob unlocked the door and swung it open, but he didn't turn on the lights. Without speaking, they heaved Buddy out of the car and carried him into the kitchen. Tony went back out to shut the trunk.

As he shut it, he noticed a white-haired man with a pipe between his teeth, holding a red and white umbrella and being pulled along by a tiny light-brown dog whose hair was plastered over its body. The dog turned and yipped. Tony knelt down between the kitchen door and the rear tire. The old man turned and glanced up the driveway. The trunk popped open. He started up the drive. Tony scampered around to between the front of the car and the garage. The old man slammed the trunk lid shut with his leash hand. The dog was pulling the leash, sniffing around to the front of the car. The old man tugged on the leash.

He started to turn, but the kitchen door caught his eye. He took a step toward it, his eyes squinting. Lightning cracked and the rain suddenly pounded down, causing water to rush from the downspouts. Inside, Rob saw the old man standing in the threshold. He dragged Buddy deeper into the darkness.

The man poked his head into the kitchen. "Hello?" he yelled. He peered about. "Wind," he muttered, and shut the door.

Rob crawled over to the door and watched the old man through the glass as he walked back down the driveway. Then he opened the door.

Tony scurried in. "Thought the dog would give me away."

"Let's make it quick." Rob took a bottle of prescription painkillers and some syringes out of his pocket and put them on the counter. Tony cut Buddy loose and arranged his arms and legs to make it look as if he'd passed out in the floor. Rob put the syringe they had injected Buddy with on the floor beside him. Tony crawled backward, wiping up the water from where they had stepped. They left the door wide open. The rain was pelting down. They slipped around the other side of the house and down to Tony's truck. The old man and his dog were gone. Rob called 911 on a throwaway cell phone. They sat in the dark watching, until they saw the patrol car arrive and the police officer go inside and turn on the lights.

"We're done here." Tony pulled away from the curb. Rob rubbed his hands together. "I'm finally getting a good feeling about this fiasco. Tomorrow we'll deal with Vincent."

Tony turned at the first intersection. "I know how this helps you and Pamela, but what's in it for me? Thus far, I've got nothing to show."

"Look, Tony, we got screwed just as bad as you. All we can do now is make the best of it. These guys know who you are. You want them dogging you and your family from here on out, or you want to be rid of them?"

"Is that what this is about?"

"You want the truth? We get our traveling money back from Vincent, and I'll pay you the five grand I promised you. At this point, anything more than that is gravy."

10

SETTLING SCORES

The next afternoon, LaBell was working behind the pharmacy counter when Detectives Peterson and Rubella pushed through the glass double doors in their dark suits and highly shined shoes. He'd been trying very hard to have a normal day, to fall into the old rhythm, to forget all the craziness of the last few days, at least temporarily, by just doing the simple tasks he was good at: filling prescriptions, talking to customers, checking the stocking of the shelves, relieving a checker who needed a break, and, except for taking Rachel to visit Kyla at the hospital, he had been mainly successful. The troubles that were now coming home to roost, the troubles he'd caused long ago when he's taken the short cut of agreeing to launder Wendell's money, the troubles that had taken him by surprise when Kyla's broken nature had surfaced in their marriage, and the troubles that shouldn't have taken him by surprise, that of Rachel's divided loyalties and rebellion, had been mainly tamped down. But now, as the detectives came down the aisle toward him, these troubles pushed to the surface and began to swirl in his mind, displacing any temporary peace. He came out from behind the counter and met them near the employee-only door to the storage area.

"Mr. LaBell," Detective Peterson said, "how are you, sir?"

"I'm okay."

Detective Rubella nodded. "How are things working out for your daughter at Hope House?"

"So far, so good. I'm kind of busy. Is there a point to your visit?"

"Yes, sir," Detective Peterson said. "We were just wondering if anything else had come to mind? About the break-in?"

LaBell shrugged. "Nothing."

"Well, two more of your ex-wife's associates have been found dead. Executed. Looks like a drug deal gone wrong. And yesterday a guy was arrested in a home invasion—a walk-off from minimum security; he had drugs that may have been taken from this store."

Detective Rubella stepped in close to LaBell and spoke just above a whisper. "Murdered an old lady. Looks like your ex came out of this better than some others."

"So why are you telling me this?"

"It's looking more and more like your wife was involved in the break-in, even though we don't have any direct evidence yet."

"Ex-wife. Am I missing something?"

Detective Peterson cut in. "You found your ex half-dead in an abandoned house, Mr. LaBell. The day before that, your drugstore was robbed while you're hunting for your missing daughter. Then your daughter skips out of rehab and we find her at the hospital with your ex. In the meantime, four of your ex-wife's associates turn up dead. This is way beyond coincidence. Even if you had nothing to do with any crime, covering it up makes you an accessory. If you know something, you need to tell us."

"My daughter didn't have anything to do with this. As for Kyla, I don't have any idea of what she did or didn't do. I got divorced to get out from under all that crap. I hope you catch whoever broke in here. I want my daughter to get well, I'm upgrading my security system, and I want to get on with my life. If you'll excuse me, I need to get back to work."

"Think about it, Mr. LaBell. Think about what's really best for your daughter." Peterson and Rubella walked away.

.   .   .

IT WAS RAINING AGAIN by the time Pamela got to LaBell's house. She ran from her gray Cadillac to the white columned front porch. She pushed the doorbell and then turned to watch the rain sheeting down, bouncing off the redbrick walk. No one answered the door. She pushed the bell again, this time looking through the sidelights for LaBell's form coming to the door, but he didn't come. She tried the handle. The door was unlocked. She stepped into the front hall. "Hello. Anybody home?"

LaBell appeared at the top of the stairs. "I'm busy right now."

"What are you doing?" She climbed the stairs and walked down the hall, looking in the open doors. He was in a room with pink flower-print wallpaper. There were dance trophies on a high shelf over the bed, an iPod docking station/radio on the bedside table, and a big, mirrored dresser with makeup containers scattered across the top. He was pulling clothes out of drawers and putting them in a suitcase lying open on the bed. "Taking Rachel some things?"

"We're getting out of here for a few days."

"Getting out of here?"

"Vincent was at the hospital when Rachel got there. They blame me for the missing money. They find out I've been talking to you guys, I don't know what they'll do. Then this afternoon the cops came to see me at the store. They think Kyla was behind the break-in. We're going to get out of here for a while."

"Where you going to go?"

"Just a little vacation. Disney World sounds about right."

She looked at the sweaters, shirts, and underwear stacked in the suitcase. "That's a lot of clothes for a short trip."

"I don't know what she'll need."

Pamela started refolding the shirts. "They'll look better it you fold them like this."

"That's great. Thanks." He searched down through the lower drawers.

Pamela repacked the shirts and started on the sweaters. "You telling your partner what you're up to?"

"No."

"He's going to think you've run."

"I don't care."

"How far do you think you'll get before he finds you?"

"What do you mean?"

She smoothed a sweater into the suitcase. "I know it's counterintuitive, but if you run, you're dead. Doesn't matter if you were planning to come back. Your partner won't trust you anymore. If you leave, you can never come back. You can never be Jim LaBell again. You have to start over from scratch and hope he never finds you." She looked up at him. "How will that work for Rachel? What's best for her?"

"Saving her life is best for her."

"You think she'll go with you with her stepmom in intensive care?"

LaBell didn't say anything.

"Keeping her in rehab, getting her some perspective, that's what's going to save her life." Pamela took his hands in hers. "I know you're scared. In the last couple of days, your perfect world has fallen apart. You don't know what to do. You're feeling crazy pressure and you just want out from under. But you've got to remember that Wendell does what he does for a reason. You're his laundry. You have value as long as you don't act in a way that negates your usefulness."

"Like going to the cops?"

"Like wigging out, becoming unpredictable, drawing the attention of the cops. How do you think the detectives are going to view your little getaway? How do guilty people act?" She pulled him close and rubbed his back. "Does this make sense to you?"

"Yeah."

She whispered in his ear. "Just relax. Put these clothes away. Let reality unfold one day at a time. Take care of your daughter and don't concern yourself with Wendell's game. Make the cops work for a living."

"Okay."

"Okay." She let go of him and kissed his lips. "You're not alone in this."

"Really? You know everything about me. I don't know anything about you."

"There's not much to tell." She stood against him, her fingers through the belt loops on the sides of his pants.

LaBell swallowed. "Where do you live?"

She looked into his eyes. She could see the fear and uncertainty melting away. She just needed to seal the deal. The place they were staying wasn't that important. They'd be gone in a few days. "We're at the Value Inn."

"Really? But that place is a dump."

"Just hiding in plain sight." She stood up on her toes and kissed him again.

MEANWHILE, Rob opened the side door of a commercial van with "Cosmopolitan Painting and Decorating" printed on the sides that was parked in the parking ramp of the McKinley Hotel. He was dressed in a McKinley room service delivery uniform. Inside the van, Tony sat in the back, keyboarding on a laptop computer. "Got the info?"

"Yeah. West tower, room 1298. He's booked for two more days."

"You got his car info as well?"

Tony nodded.

"Start looking while I check the room."

Rob commandeered a used room-service cart, neatened the dishes and refolded the napkins, and rolled into an elevator and up to the twelfth floor. The hallway was quiet. Rob examined the door carefully, slipped the lock, and pushed the cart inside. He moved quickly and systematically. He didn't expect to find the money or the jewelry, but maybe there would be a scrap of paper or a business card that might give an indication as to where Vincent's hiding place was. The counters were clear. The dresser contained only underwear and socks. Three expensive suits and four shirts hung in the closet. The shaving kit in the bathroom was unremarkable. Rob made one more walk-through. The room was so clean it was hard to believe Vincent actually slept here. Rob scraped his footprints back to the door and pushed the cart back into the hallway. Four doors down, a housekeeper, a middle-aged Latina in a black dress with a white apron, backed out of a room into the hall.

"Hi," she said.

"Hi."

"You must be new."

He nodded.

"You're supposed to leave the cart."

"They took their food, had me collect the old dishes."

She frowned, pushed a strand of gray-black hair out of her face, and gestured for him to stop. "You're turned around. The service elevator is in the other direction."

He smiled sheepishly and shook his head. "I need to get some coffee. This is my second job. Daytime I work the desk at the condos on Sommerville."

She nodded. "My cousin does maintenance there. He says it's easy work."

Rob shrugged. "Pretty boring at the desk. I don't see the other guys."

"Tell you what. Just leave the cart. I'll get their dishes when I do turndown."

"Thanks." He gestured back in the other direction. "Elevator's that way?"

"You got it."

Rob walked off in the direction the housekeeper indicated, but after he turned the corner in the hallway, he pushed through the door to the stairwell and started walking down. He dug his phone out of his pants pocket. "Tony? I'm on my way to you. Nothing of interest, but he'll definitely be coming back."

. . .

THE NEXT DAY, after work, LaBell stood in his kitchen, trying to decide what to do about supper. He could make something simple and just happen to have enough for Pamela when she turned up. Or maybe he should just wait for her and ask her if she wanted to go out or get some delivery. Maybe go up to the Chinese at Littleton Center. They had things to talk about: the cops, Rachel's rehab, maybe he could find out a little more about her, how she fell into her life, if Rob trained her or if they came up together. She had a funny way of always deflecting the conversation back to him, so that even though she said very little about herself, it didn't seem as though she were hiding anything. He opened the refrigerator and scanned the shelves. Not really much there. They would have to go out. He smiled. He knew she was too good to be true, that she was probably just playing him, but somehow he didn't mind. He needed some human comfort, a soft touch, someone to talk to who really knew what was going on; someone who wouldn't judge him; someone who was on his side. So what if he was being foolish? He wasn't in love with her, and she was taking care of herself, so why shouldn't he take care of himself?

The doorbell rang.

He answered the door. Wendell and Vincent were standing there.

"Well, ask us in, Jimmy," Wendell said in his slightly European accent. He had a carefree, open expression on his face and wore a tailor-made black suit with a white shirt and a bright blue silk necktie.

"Were you expecting someone else?" Vincent asked. The jacket of his gray pin-striped suit hung open, revealing a pistol in a shoulder harness. He clenched and unclenched his hands. LaBell stepped back from the door. They walked in.

"Would you like to sit in the living room?"

"No, thank you." Wendell rubbed his black mustache. "Let's go stand on your patio. The weather's fine."

They walked through the kitchen and den and out the French doors onto the gray slate. The dappled light angling through the tall oaks in the neighbor's yard murmured with the breeze. LaBell attempted a smile. "Can I offer you a drink, at least?"

"No, thank you." Wendell casually surveyed the yard. "Beautiful property. How long have you been here?"

"Ten years."

Vincent stepped to the edge of the patio and watched the street, his hands clasped behind his back.

Wendell continued. "You might remember in the beginning—what? Twelve, fourteen years ago, I told you I was a reasonable man. You came to me when your daughter was kidnapped. A wise choice. We said we'd get her back for you if you helped us with the grifters."

"I did what you asked."

"We didn't tell you to spend fifty thousand dollars."

"But they wanted the money then."

"You should have waited for us. Did you call us?"

"Rob and his crew were standing in my hallway. They weren't supposed to come here. You were supposed to take care of that."

"You should have thought of something else. You spent the fifty thousand without asking, so you owe fifty thousand. What happened to your ex—maybe we gave her an opportunity, but she had addiction in her blood; the endgame, that was the animals she took up with did that to her. Not us. We're reasonable men. Her partners wouldn't give us our money, so Mr. Vincent had to insist. Do you understand?"

LaBell nodded.

"So you owe me fifty thousand. We've got a good deal here, so we'll take the fifty out of your end in payments with interest. When you're done paying us off, we'll go back to our original arrangement. We on the same page?"

LaBell nodded.

"I need to hear you say it."

"Yes, we're on the same page."

"Good. I don't want any misunderstandings."

Vincent rejoined them. "Did you find out where your friends are staying?"

LaBell looked from Vincent to Wendell and back again. "They're at the Value Inn at the north beltway exit."

Vincent nodded.

Wendell patted LaBell on the shoulder. "I like you. You don't want to find out what happens if your daughter gets a taste for dope. A family man like you should know better. We've had a long relationship. Just keep paying your debts and everything will be fine."

PAMELA SAT IN HER CADILLAC, watching LaBell's house. She could see Vincent on the back patio, but she was down in the seat, in the deep shade of a large oak, so she wasn't concerned about being discovered. She'd reconnoitered the neighborhood. She knew Vincent and the old guy with the mustache were by themselves. She imagined they were giving Jim a good talking to. That would be the place they were at in the program: re-cement the relationship with greed and fear. Because Jimmy was definitely a keeper. If they didn't need him, the visit would have been at night, and Vincent would have been by himself to set up Jimmy's suicide. The front door opened. Vincent and the old man stepped out on the porch. Pamela ducked down farther in the seat. She counted slowly to ten, then peeked up. She watched their backs as they got into a gray Volvo S80. She got out her phone. "Rob. Vincent and some old guy are leaving LaBell's. You want me to follow them?"

"No. You figure out LaBell. We're going to set up on Vincent at the hotel."

She watched them drive away. Then she walked up LaBell's brick sidewalk, rang the doorbell, and went in. "Yoo-hoo."

LaBell glanced down the hall from the kitchen. He already had two fingers of Scotch in a glass. "Wendell and Vincent were just here."

"That was Wendell?" She went through to the kitchen and sat on a stool at the black granite counter. "Aren't you going to offer a lady a drink?"

He took down a glass and poured for her.

"Thanks." She took a sip. "I saw Vincent's car pull into your driveway as I was driving up, so I circled around and waited."

LaBell drank from his glass. "Don't even tell me it was that close."

"So that was Wendell with Vincent? What did they want?"

"I have to pay back the fifty thousand dollars that you guys took from my safe."

"That's bullshit."

"You're telling me. I've got to pay interest, too."

"That's so messed up. They've already got their money and your jewelry."

"What are you talking about?"

"We tagged one of their associates. A guy who jumped Rob. They got our fifty-five thousand and the jewelry from him. I'm guessing they also got the fifty thousand from Kyla's crew."

"Wait a minute. The cops told me—was that the home invasion guy?"

She shrugged.

"You put some drugs on him?"

"Of course. Throw the cops off us."

"Then why do they still want money from me?"

"They're crooks. Do you think you're ever going to get paid off? Now you're working for free."

LaBell looked into his glass. "What am I going to do?"

"How did you get roped in?"

"They said they'd get Rachel back if I got Tony to rob the store. They said nobody would get hurt."

"They probably told Kyla to take Rachel to get drug money out of you."

"I'm doomed."

Pamela poured LaBell another drink. "You got in bed with crooks, Jimmy. I know it's hard to believe, but this is a good result. You're alive, Rachel is safe, and they need you. All you can do is keep quiet and hope they screw themselves."

Tony sat behind the wheel of the Cosmopolitan painting van, watching the entry to the McKinley Hotel's parking deck. Rob was on foot halfway up the deck, nearest to the doors that were closest to Vincent's hotel room. They each wore utility worker coveralls. Rob wore a heavy tool belt. He had the doors open on a telecommunications access box, and he was working his way up the panel as if he were checking the connections. He'd positioned himself so that his face wasn't visible on the security cameras. When the time came, and he needed the Taser hidden in his tool belt, the cameras would conveniently go on the fritz.

"How long we wait?" Tony said into his radio.

"As long as it takes. Eventually he's going to use the bed or come for the suits. He won't leave those suits. Spent way too much on them for them to be throwaways. He's a snappy dresser."

Tony called home on his personal cell phone.

"Hey, Tony, I was starting to worry," Emily said.

"I should have called earlier, but I just got a break. We're on a tight deadline."

"I saved your supper."

"Put it in the fridge. There's no end in sight here. What did you have?"

"Fried chicken, mashed potatoes, peas."

"I wish I was there with you, sweetie."

"I know."

"At least it's overtime. How's the Ant?"

"He's being a good boy. Took a good nap; just had his bath."

"Give him a kiss for me." A red Honda minivan turned into the deck and drove past him.

"I got a sitter for Friday." A dark blue BMW put on its headlights as it started up the deck.

"Great. I got to go. We'll catch up later."

"I love you."

"I love you, too."

Tony slipped the phone back into his pocket. He had the distinct impression that she didn't believe he was at work, but he didn't want to add to the lie by creating a lot of false details. This job had turned to mud almost from the beginning. A simple little inside job. If he had been by himself, there would have been plenty of money in the drugstore safe. He wouldn't have gone to LaBell's that night, fallen into the schemes that led to sitting in a stolen van in a parking deck, waiting for the chance to shake down a career criminal. But if he had been by himself at the drugstore, would Buddy still have been waiting? Would he have fought his way out or got shot? Would he have had a backup car waiting? He might have been killed at the drugstore, broken Emily's heart. *Out-of-work veteran killed in robbery.* He'd made his choice. He'd stepped over the line. His only option now was to stick with Rob and Pamela, clean up this mess, and take whatever share could be salvaged. A gray Volvo pulled into the ramp.

Tony grabbed his radio. "He's on his way."

Rob shorted the wiring on the security cameras and closed the telecommunications box. He stepped up behind a concrete pillar as the Volvo crept by. He had his hand around the grip of the Taser. The Volvo pulled into an empty spot five cars away. Over his shoulder, he could hear the family that had emptied out of the red minivan as they got near the door to the elevator. The Volvo's headlights turned off.

Rob walked out of the shadows with purpose, walked along the back bumpers of the parked cars, and dropped to a crouch behind the black Cadillac next to the Volvo. The sounds of the family disappeared. Headlights cut down the middle of the deck. A white Toyota Avalon zipped by and turned up to the next level. Rob heard the Volvo's door open. He scurried around the back of the Volvo and sprang to his feet as he pushed the Taser toward Vincent's neck.

Vincent turned, blocked Rob's Taser hand with his forearm, and punched Rob in the groin, knocking the wind out of him. Rob folded up and dropped the Taser. Vincent punched him in the side of the head, but Rob shifted his weight so that it was a glancing blow. He raised up his arms to protect his face, leaned into the car, and kicked Vincent in the knee.

Tony screeched up in the painting van, blocking the view from the aisle. Vincent dug inside his suit coat for his pistol. Rob was on his hands and knees, reaching for the Taser under the Volvo. Tony sprang out of the van, knocked Vincent's gun hand into the air, punched him twice in the face, and knocked him to the pavement. Rob grabbed the Taser and gave Vincent a jolt as he was getting to his feet. He collapsed. Tony opened the side door. They picked up Vincent by his shoulders and feet, climbed into the back of the van, and duct-taped his wrists and ankles.

Rob fished the Volvo keys out of Vincent's pocket. "Meet you at the barn."

Moments later, the painting van and the Volvo were both out of the parking deck.

Vincent was awake when Tony opened the side door to the van back at the dilapidated barn. Rob punched him in the stomach as he lay on his side. "Just give me a reason. I don't need much; just give me a reason."

They carried him around the barn and tossed him in the hole they had dug for Buddy. "You yell and you're going to get shot."

They went back to the gray Volvo and opened the trunk. Two forest green duffel bags, one large and one medium, sat on the freshly vacuumed carpet. Rob unzipped the large one first. Two assault rifles, three machine pistols, and clips of ammunition. "Glad this was in the trunk." He opened the medium-sized one. The $65,000—the $55,000 from the drugstore safe and the $10,000 escape money—was loose in the bag. The jewelry was in a plastic freezer bag.

"Jackpot. You must be living right, Tony. 'Cause it sure hasn't been me."

Tony clapped his hands together and laughed. "So now we're back where we started."

"Except we're cutting down on the number of assholes. You've got a decision to make. Me and Pamela, we've got to try to get the boss. He'll just come after us again. You could take your cut and walk away. Hope he doesn't remember you. 'Course, you've seen his generosity at work. He didn't give a second thought about screwing LaBell, and he was making money with him."

Tony looked back and forth between the bags. Right now he was safe. Rob and Pamela were probably going to get this guy. It didn't make sense for him to take unnecessary risks. He was a family man.

He'd already told Emily too many lies. Still, these crooks knew who he was. What if they took out Rob and Pamela, came back next year or in five years, and demanded his help on some fucked-up crap shoot sure to land him in jail?

"Clock's ticking, cowboy, what's it going to be?"

"Let's finish it up."

Rob put his hand on Tony's arm. "Thanks. Don't worry, no matter what happens, your family'll get your cut."

They walked back to the five-foot-deep hole behind the barn. The sun had passed below the tops of the trees, pushing this area into the shade. Vincent lay on his side in the hole. He shifted his head when he saw them. "You made your point. You got your money."

Rob slid his foot up to the edge of the hole, pushing some loose dirt in. "Who's your boss?"

"Come on, you know I can't tell you that."

"Tony, go get the gas can out of the barn."

Tony nodded and left.

Vincent spat dirt out of his mouth. "You're just talking crazy now."

Rob didn't say anything. He just stood watching Vincent with a neutral expression on his face. Tony came back with a plastic five-gallon gas can. "Looks heavy," Rob said. "Is it heavy?"

Tony handed it to him. "It's full."

Rob unscrewed the cap and poured gas on Vincent. "Out here in the country, no one will notice."

Vincent started squirming. "Hey, I'm just a working stiff like you. You don't have to kill me."

"Who's your boss?" Rob set the gas can down. "Tony, you got a match?"

Vincent shifted onto his back. "Let's calm down here. I tell you his name and you drop me off at the hotel."

"The name and the why and you go free."

"Mr. Korsovo. All I know is he had business with you."

Rob put the cap on the gas can. He and Tony walked out of listening range. "So, you know the guy?" Tony asked.

"Yeah. Piece of shit we robbed a couple years back. Never met him." Rob glanced toward the hole and back at Tony. "So who's going to do him? He's got to go; he'll be after us tomorrow."

"I'll do it."

"I appreciate that."

"One thing, though. You have to give Stella a pass."

"Tony, Tony, Tony, that's a lot to ask. You know as well as I do that she's got to be caught up with Korsovo somehow. You heard Buddy. She didn't accidentally connect me and Pamela with you. She brought us into this on purpose. Fact that we were friends only makes what she did worse."

"Tell me about it. She almost got me killed."

Rob studied his face, looking for the lie. "You should want her dead more than me."

"I don't want any killing in my family."

"You're going to wish you pinched this one off at the bud."

Tony shook his head.

Rob shrugged. "Okay, but she has to know we let her go."

"Definitely."

They walked back to the hole. "Where's your boss?"

"Knowing won't help you."

"Humor me."

"He's at the private airfield on Cummings Boulevard. He's flying out tonight."

"How much detail does he know?"

"He was hoping to get you and squeeze the laundry guy. He had to settle for squeezing the laundry." He gestured with his head toward Tony. "Him and his cousin, I hooked them in. Get me up out of here."

Rob got out his phone and called the airfield. "Yes. I'm supposed to catch a ride with Roberts and Korsovo. Could you tell them I'm on the way?" He listened to the response, then hung up. "No planes leaving tonight."

"What?" Vincent said. "Must be a mistake. Let me try."

Rob looked at Tony and shook his head. Tony shot Vincent in the leg.

"Jesus!" Vincent cried.

"Not bleeding too much. Let's try again."

"You think you're the crazy fuck. Guess who's got your girl?"

Rob shook his head. "I'm supposed to believe that? You're full of shit."

"We snagged her at Jim's house."

"You're lying."

"Then where is she? We own that boy. He says she's some fine house-broke pussy."

"I don't believe you."

"You're staying at the Value Inn. Your only chance of getting her back is letting me go."

Rob looked down into the gloom at Vincent's face and saw the flash of a smile. "Where is she?"

"One thing at a time."

Rob pulled his phone out of his pocket and speed-dialed Pamela. Her phone rang five times and rolled over to voice mail.

"Cut me loose," Vincent said.

Rob's phone fell from his hand. In his mind he saw Pamela's broken body convulsing on the concrete floor of a warehouse, fluid leaking from between her legs. He'd gotten her into this mess. He told her she'd be safe. He jumped down into the hole, grabbed Vincent by the collar of his shirt, and began beating his face. "You bastard. You're going to tell me everything."

"She's still alive. She's still alive."

Tony jumped in the hole behind Rob and pulled him off Vincent. "Christ, you'll beat him unconscious. How will that help?"

Tears ran down Rob's cheeks. "Pamela's already dead. Only satisfaction I'm going to get is watching him choke on his balls." He pulled a lock-back knife from his pants pocket. "Get me the duct tape so he won't be able to spit them out."

"You're talking crazy."

"Listen to your partner," Vincent said. "You can still save her."

Rob looked at Tony. "If she was *your* wife . . ."

Tony's eyes went blank. He climbed out of the hole and hurried back to the van for the duct tape.

Rob punched Vincent in the nose with the fist that was holding the knife and let go of Vincent's shirt collar. Vincent fell back into the bottom of the hole. Rob knelt over him and began cutting his suit pants off of him. Vincent squirmed and kicked. Blood ran from the knife nicks. Tony came back with the duct tape in his hand and stood at the edge of the hole, watching. He saw Rob's phone vibrating in the grass at his feet and picked it up. "Yeah?"

"Tony," Pamela said, "where's Robby?"

Tony reached down and slapped Rob's shoulder. "On the phone. It's her." He passed the phone to Rob.

Rob was standing over Vincent with his knife in his hand. He tried hard to control his voice. "Honey, you okay?"

"Baby, I'm fine. What's wrong?"

"Asshole said they'd got you."

"I'm fine, baby. I'm fine. Just took longer to settle Jimmy than I thought."

"You in the car?"

"Yeah."

"By yourself?"

"Yeah. I'm by myself. They really had you going. You're so sweet when you worry. See you in a few."

"Did you tell LaBell where our motel was?"

She paused. "Yes, I did."

"He told Vincent."

"Robby, that's my bad. I screwed up."

"You were fucking LaBell just now?"

"Yeah. I thought I had him wrapped around my finger. Guess I underestimated him."

"Don't worry about it. I can't wait to see you."

Rob slipped his phone into his pocket and turned back to Vincent, cut-up pants around his ankles, face swelling black and blue. Rob took a deep breath. "Now that I have your attention, where is Korsovo staying?"

"He's in a condo at the Steam Creek Golf Club."

"Address?"

"Twelve-ninety-two Fairway Eight."

"How many?"

"Three bodyguards."

Rob climbed out of the hole. His hands were shaking. His clothes were stuck to him and his hair was slick with sweat. "I hate it when I lose my temper. My clothes stink like gasoline and my hands hurt."

Tony shot Vincent twice in the chest.

Rob glanced at Tony and then looked down at Vincent. "Let's pour the lime and push the dirt in before the light's completely gone."

AFTER MIDNIGHT, Rob, Tony, and Pamela pulled up in a stolen Ford Explorer with tinted windows, just outside of closed-circuit camera range to the service entrance of the Steam Creek Golf Club and Residential Community. They were wearing dark-colored jackets over body armor and carrying the automatic weapons that they found in the Volvo. Beyond the black, six-foot-high, wrought-iron gate, a streetlight shined down on a two-door equipment garage and dump-truck-sized piles of gravel and mulch. Tony got out, slipped in through a blind spot in the camera placement, and disabled the camera and the silent alarm on the gate. He waved them through and closed the gate behind them.

"Anything to worry about?" Rob asked.

"Bargain-basement setup. It's all show."

They crept through the cul-de-sacs surrounding the golf course, learning the layout, getting a sense for the features that weren't on the map. They knew where Korsovo was supposed to be, in the end unit of a two-story condo that was on the golf cart path to the clubhouse. They knew Steam Creek employed four rent-a-cops, none of them moonlighting police, two at each of the guardhouses at the entry streets on either side of the community.

"These are some good-looking condos," Pamela said.

"List of vacationers and a carpet cleaning van?" Rob replied.

They laughed.

"Maybe next year," Rob said.

Pamela looked in the backseat at Tony, who was holding an assault rifle across his lap. He looked so relaxed that for a moment she thought he was asleep. "Thanks for helping us out. It's a lot easier when you got a third guy you can trust."

Tony shrugged. "It was always going to end up like this. I just didn't know it when I signed on."

"Lots of guys would have just run."

"Trust me, this is easier than a job interview."

Rob turned into Korsovo's cul-de-sac. Two streetlights lit the parking circle. Three tan brick condo buildings of four units each faced the parking. Bushes with red berries on them framed the porches. None of the porch lights were on. "So far so good." He wheeled around, pointing the Explorer out of the cul-de-sac, and pulled up to the curb.

Tony rolled out of the side door and lay in the grass, looking through infrared glasses. "Alarms on the windows and doors."

Pamela glanced at Rob. "We're going to make a hell of a racket."

"We stay on schedule, we'll be all right. You go around the side and catch them through the windows. Tony, you got my back."

They crept up on the end condo. Light glowed through the curtains downstairs and through the blinds on an upstairs bedroom. The condo next door was dark. Through a gap in the curtains, they saw two beefy men in suits in the living room watching TV, another one in the kitchen. Pamela scurried around to the side windows, staying below the level of the bushes. Rob and Tony crouched at the front door. Pamela raised her machine pistol and pulled the trigger. The silence was shattered by gunfire, breaking glass, slugs slamming into the walls and the bodyguards yelling. The entry alarm wailed.

Tony kicked in the front door. It snapped back to the wall and bounced halfway back. Rob ran in, fired into the living room, and ran up the stairs. Tony stepped in behind him and sprayed the living room. The bodyguards scrambled for cover behind the sofa and chairs.

Pamela sprang up. The bodyguards in the living room were

pinned down, but the man in the kitchen was running for the patio door. Pamela ran along the outside, firing at she came, chasing him with gunfire. He ran through the shattered patio door. She chased him across the golf course. The night was black in the rough that separated the condos from the eighth hole. Pamela crept along, trying to listen for footsteps in front of her in the pauses of the gunfire behind her. A branch snapped to her right. She fired off three shots and ran to her left, zigzagging toward the fairway. She dropped to the ground, inserted a full clip, and lay still, concentrating all of her energy on watching and listening.

Upstairs, Rob fired through the door that the light peeked under, then kicked it in. Korsovo, dressed in red striped pajamas, with his pants bundled under his arm, dove out the window. Rob ran down the stairs and out the door. Around the side of the condo, he saw Korsovo disappear into the adjoining cul-de-sac. Rob ran through the evergreen bushes and between two condo buildings. A few condos had their outside lights on, and there were two streetlights lighting up the parking. A dozen cars sat empty. The gunfire stopped. The silence was disorienting. Rob dropped his rifle to his side and walked in the shadows, looking in the bushes against the buildings and between the cars as he went. Korsovo couldn't have gotten past this cul-de-sac. He had to be hiding here.

Lying on the edge of the fairway, Pamela saw a large shape creeping toward the low spot between a sand trap and the green. She steadied her arm and fired twice. The shape fell. She scrambled along the edge of the rough until she was at the closest point to the shape. Then she ran out across the fairway, the machine pistol stretched out in front of her. She'd shot—what? Close up, it was clear that it wasn't human. Two shots rang out behind her. Her back felt as if it were on fire. She dropped next to her kill. It was a large black dog. The bodyguard stepped out from the other side of the sand trap, his white shirt glowing in the moonlight. Pamela swung around and fired just as he did.

Tony stood in the middle of the living room of the apartment. The two bodyguards were down. The room looked like the finale of a B-grade action movie: furniture overturned, bullet holes stitched across the walls, the air thick with the smell of gunfire. The noise still echoed in his head. He turned the corner into the kitchen. Empty. Pamela had taken off after the other bodyguard, out across the golf course. Rob had headed off between the neighboring buildings. Pamela might need the help, but Korsovo was the mission. Tony started off in the direction that he thought Rob had gone.

Rob heard the shots echo out of the golf course. He knew he was running out of time. In only a few more minutes, the police would be here. He had walked about two-thirds of the cul-de-sac when he suddenly charged toward the parked cars, hoping to spook Korsovo. Nothing. He walked out into the middle of the cul-de-sac under the streetlights and turned in a circle, looking under the parked cars and through the bushes. Just then, the water sprinkler system popped up through the lawn. In his peripheral vision, he saw a bit of striped pajama disappear between two buildings. He ran through the sprinkler system. Korsovo was standing on the front porch of a condo that had its lights on, ringing the doorbell with one hand and banging on the door with his other hand. He was soaking wet, his pajamas stuck to his soft body and his hair plastered down his face like some sad-sack sitcom character. Rob wiped the water from his eyes. The door was opening. Everything was happening in slow motion. Rob's window of opportunity was closing. He knew he wouldn't shoot the civilians. It was time to walk away, but he just couldn't do it. He pulled the trigger. The gunfire blasted away the quiet. Korsovo flailed around like an inept marionette. Rob dived behind an evergreen bush as Korsovo dropped to the porch. Someone in the condo screamed.

Rob crawled back between the two condo buildings under cover of the bushes, the sprinklers soaking his clothes; then he sprang up and ran. Tony came out of the shadows and joined him. When they got to the truck, Pamela was sitting in the passenger's seat breathing hard.

"You okay, honey?" Rob asked.

"Took a couple of hard rounds into my vest. I'll be okay. You got caught in the rain."

He nodded.

"Did you get him?"

"Took a little effort, but, yeah, he's done troubling us."

They rolled back toward the service entrance. As they neared the black-iron gate, they heard police and ambulance sirens in the distance. Tony jumped out, grabbed the gate and pushed, but it wouldn't budge. Pamela and Rob ran out to help.

"They must have locked down the hinge motors from the main gate," Tony said. "Give me a few minutes."

"Fuck that," Rob said, "we're getting gone. Get the duffels out of the truck."

Rob hunched down and grabbed the bars of the gate. Pamela scrambled up his back, swung over the top, and dropped to the street. "You, too, Tony."

Tony tossed the duffels over the gate and then followed her. Rob went back to the truck, poured gasoline from a five-gallon can into the interior, struck a flare, and dropped it in the open window. Then he ran to the gate. Tony stuck his arms through the bars and clasped his hands together to make a foothold. Rob scrambled over. As they ran off into the neighborhood toward the stolen Ford Focus they'd set in place earlier, the Explorer exploded.

BACK AT THE VALUE INN, Tony sat slouched in the brown easy chair by the door, Pamela sat on the bed leaning back against the head-board with an ice pack behind her back, and Rob was squatting down looking in the mini fridge, his wet gray hair combed back from his face. "There are two beers in here and a bottle of drugstore scotch in the bathroom."

Tony sat up. "Toss me a beer."

Rob glanced back at Pamela. "Scotch." He got up, handed the beer to Tony, and padded barefoot back to the bathroom. He came back with two plastic cups of Scotch, and handed one to Pamela. "To a good night's work."

They all took a drink. Rob sat on the edge of the bed facing Tony. "Two more bits of business and you won't see us anymore." He sipped from his cup. "LaBell's a loose end."

"So what?" Tony said. "You want to kill him? He's all Rachel has."

"He's not an innocent. He knows what he knows. The cops push hard enough and he'll fold," Rob said.

"He's a crook like us."

"No, sugar," Pamela said. "Not like us, like you."

Rob studied Tony's face. "He's proven he can't be trusted. He was playing both ends against the middle."

"No," Tony said. "He just proved he's a coward who's in over his head."

"I'm not asking you to do it. If he's got to go, I'll take care of it."

"You don't need to kill him."

Rob turned to Pamela. "LaBell is unreliable," she said, "but his daughter is everything to him, and to protect her, he's got to keep his mouth shut. If he tells the cops anything, it will end with them finding out about the money laundry and he'll lose everything, so I think Tony's probably right."

"Okay, Tony, he's your problem." Rob stood up. He took a long drink and put his cup down on top of the TV. "Now for the fun part."

He shook out the duffel bag containing the $65,000 and the freezer bag of jewelry onto the bedspread. Tony got up and came over to the bed. Rob picked up a bundle of hundred-dollar bills and set it to one side. "The ten grand was ours, so we keep that." He picked up the freezer bag and tossed it onto the bed in front of Tony. "You take the jewelry to Stella. She knows how to get rid of it; don't keep any of it. That should square us for the five grand we promised you. Of the fifty-five thousand, you take twenty, just in case the jewelry is short. That work for you?"

Tony nodded. "I'm good."

Rob handed him two bundles of ten thousand each. "You want the rest of the drugs from the robbery, to sell back to LaBell?"

Tony shook his head. "No thanks. That just sounds like a new way to get into trouble. You can keep them."

"So they go in the trash." Rob looked him up and down. "You did okay. This all worked out. We'll keep you in mind if we're ever working around here again."

Tony put the bundles of money and the freezer bag in his jacket pockets. "Don't take this wrong, guys, but I'm going to take this job as a sign, get my career going, forget about all this. Your line of work is way too risky for a guy with a wife and kid."

"You sure about that? You were running and gunning."

He grinned. "I just got caught up in the moment."

"Suit yourself. Just don't forget to tell Stella that she got a pass and I expected better of her."

Pamela got up off the bed. "Good-bye, Tony." She gave him a hug.

Rob shook his hand. "What are you going to tell LaBell?"

"That you guys are gone and he needs to keep his head down. Good luck." He went out the door.

Pamela pushed back the edge of the curtain with the flat of her hand and watched Tony get in his truck and drive away. "He must have learned to trust his teammates in the military."

"We all packed?" Rob asked.

"It's all in the car, baby."

"You find the other fifty thousand?"

"The other fifty thousand?"

"Yeah, the other fifty that Vincent took off the junkies."

"You mean the forty-eight he took off the junkies?"

"Yeah."

"It was in Korsovo's luggage. I found it after Tony went to help you."

"Where'd you hide it?"

"It's in a duffel in the trunk."

"So, eighty-three thousand and Buddy in the slammer. And we got our ten grand back. This job went the long way around, but it was worth it."

"What about Korsovo?"

"Don't know. I'll feel a lot better if some new partners don't show up to squeeze LaBell. But only time will tell if somebody's still on us." He took her hands in his. "You did good work on this job, honey."

"I screwed up with LaBell. Misjudged the bastard."

"You held your own. Owned up to your mistake. Nothing is ever one hundred percent."

She smiled. "Yeah?"

"Yeah." Rob pulled her close. "Look at me. I almost lost it when I thought they had you. If I had killed Vincent too soon, God knows what kind of shape we'd be in now."

She whispered in his ear. "That's the problem with love."

Why was he so crazy about her? He wanted to hold her forever. "Let's wipe down this room and get out of here."

"Okay," she said.

"Okay," he said.

"Are you going to let go of me?"

"Just until we get to a new motel room."

He let go of her. She gave him a peck on the lips. He looked systematically around the room, thinking about the surfaces they had touched, and then put the bundles of money that were lying on the bed into his jacket pockets.

Pamela came out of the bathroom with the bottle of Scotch in her hand. "Hey, baby, what are our new names going to be?"

Rob smiled at her. "You choose."

"Okay." She put the whiskey into the duffel bag. "I wiped the faucets and the toilet tank, so the bathroom is good to go." She gathered Tony's empty beer bottle and their empty cups and tossed them in with the whiskey. Rob wiped off the TV and the remote, the top of the counter, and the telephone. Pamela got the last beer out of the mini fridge and wiped the fridge off. "How about . . . Joe and Tess Campbell?"

He nodded his head. "Joe and Tess. Sounds good." He stepped over to the bathroom door, looked in, and then turned and scanned the room. "Is that everything? It will be light soon. We need to get away from here."

"We're done here. What do you want to do with the getaway car?"

"Burn it. I'd burn the barn, too, except it would draw attention to Vincent."

"We've been burning a lot of vehicles here. What about putting it in the river?"

He shrugged. "I can go with that. You follow me in the Caddie." He picked up the duffel from the bed. Out in the half-empty parking lot, a thin red line stretched across the eastern horizon. The birds were beginning to stir. Rob moved the duffel bags containing the money and the weapons from the trunk of the Ford Focus to the trunk of their gray Cadillac. "We've got to hurry. We've only got about an hour until full light and morning traffic."

"Where's the nearest water?"

Rob got out his smartphone. "There's a state park just fifteen miles west. We'll put it in the lake." He showed the map to Pamela. "See? It's down this county road."

"Okay. I'm following you."

He got into the Ford Focus, pulled out of his parking space, and took a left turn out of the parking lot, Pamela right behind him. The morning was clear. At the first intersection, he turned west. Soon, farm fences ran down both sides of the road. Just as the sun began to reflect off of his rearview mirror, he noticed cows wandering out into the pastures from their morning milking. He pulled up at a four-way stop at an intersection with a gravel road. A sign indicated that the park was straight ahead. Pamela was following him. He'd dealt with Korsovo, Vincent, and Buddy. After they got rid of this car, they had nothing else they had to do.

It was going to be a beautiful day.

***

A Note from the Author

So the Travelers have followed their code and escaped with the cash. They've dealt with Big Jim, Vincent, and Korsovo. They've left Buddy in the worst place imaginable for setting them up. They've pushed Marcie out of the game, and they've helped Tony get back on his feet.

And the Travelers are back together, skin on skin, ready to lie to or steal from any criminal they can set up as soon as their money runs out.

What's next?

Leapfrog Technologies in Cloverdale. A data mining program to steal and a new crooked employer to cheat. But things aren't as they seem. Are they ever?

Crooks, amateur crooks, and pretenders: How do they shake out? Crooks know what they're doing, amateur crooks think they know what they're doing, and pretenders haven't got a clue. Mix them together and you've got a quagmire of lies and bad leads, with a little truth sprinkled on top.

The Travelers will have to be at the top of their game, using intimidation and their best gentle persuasion, to find their way through this rat's maze to their payday.

The Computer Heist is a fast-paced, hard-to-figure-out thriller. I'd love to have you along for the ride.

For a sneak peek, turn the page.

A SAMPLE OF THE COMPUTER HEIST

Chapter 1: The Negotiation

On a cold Wednesday afternoon in February, the Traveling Man and his wife, currently going by the names Joe and Tess Campbell, sat on one side of a well-worn green vinyl booth in the back corner of a Perkins restaurant opposite Samantha Bartel, who had contacted them about a possible job. They were all eating pie and drinking coffee, each side sizing up the other, trying to decide how to develop enough trust to begin talking about the details. Joe Campbell was fifty-three, just over six feet, pudgy around the middle, with salt-and-pepper hair, a black mustache, and a nose broken slightly to the right. He had a face that was hard to remember. He wore a blue suit, a white shirt without a necktie, and a simple gold wedding band. His wife, Tess, was forty-four years old, though she looked thirty-nine. She was blonde with brown eyes, all curves on a dancer's frame. Even though her shoulder-length hair was pulled back in a bun and she wore a conservative blue suit with a single strand of pearls, she exuded an infectious sex appeal.

Joe ate a forkful of blueberry pie and washed it down with coffee. He glanced out the window at the cars in the near-side parking lot, searching for anyone who looked like a cop, but all the cars were empty. "So Samantha—it's okay that I call you Samantha?"

She nodded.

"How do you know Marky?"

Samantha looked at him carefully. She hadn't taken off her charcoal overcoat. She sat hunched down in it, looking even smaller than usual, and held her coffee cup with both hands. Her dark hair, cut short, was laced with gray. She had the start of a double chin. She wore no makeup or jewelry. She was plump, apple-shaped, and the tailored gray suit she wore made her look fat. "He used to work for me a long time ago."

Joe rubbed his chin. He didn't like her evasiveness. "As a civilian? That would be a really long time ago."

"Yeah, before he and his girlfriend hacked into the IRS database."

"Ten years in federal prison. And he said I might be able to help you."

Samantha pushed her fork around in the chocolate pie filling still left on her plate. "He said you were the guy to see."

Joe rubbed his hands together as if they were cold and then, prayer-like, tapped his fingers against his chin. He and Tess hadn't committed to anything. They could still get up and walk away. "So he told you how to get in touch with us."

"That's right."

"How did you find Marky?"

"He used me as a reference to get a job."

Joe smiled. "And you helped him out?"

"Sure. He's a talented guy. A good worker."

Joe glanced at Tess. She was stirring sugar into her coffee. "What did Marky say that we do?"

"He said you could"—she looked around and then lowered her voice—"collect materials that others weren't able to collect without drawing attention to yourselves."

Tess chuckled. "That's an interesting way of putting it."

Joe watched Samantha's eyes. "Let me apologize in advance if this seems indelicate, but I want you to go in the ladies room with Tess and prove you're not wearing a wire."

Samantha blinked, clenched her teeth, and shrugged out of her overcoat. Her face colored pink. "Okay." She started to get up.

Joe and Tess exchanged a glance. Tess reached across and patted Samantha's hand. "You're okay. Sit down."

Joe pushed back in his seat to keep a better eye on two men wearing jeans, insulated work coats, and ball caps who were sitting four tables away. "You think you're in our price range?"

"I don't have any idea."

"We start at one hundred thousand plus expenses. Fifty thousand up front. Or half the action, assuming that it's more than a hundred thousand plus expenses."

"That's a lot of money."

"We offer a lot of value."

"I'll give you twenty-five thousand up front."

"We have to hear the job, but if it's simple enough, we'll take twenty-five up front, twenty-five on the day, and fifty on delivery."

"Okay."

"So let's hear the details."

"Are you familiar with Leapfrog Technologies in Cloverdale?"

They nodded. "Software company, isn't it?" Joe said.

Samantha continued. "That's where I work. I'm the assistant director of new development. We've just developed a new data-mining program for small business applications. It's called Lilypad 5. I want you to steal it and wreck the computer server in a way that will look like an accident."

Tess tapped her manicured fingernails on the table. "You want us to steal a computer program?"

Samantha nodded. "You go in, transfer the program to a portable drive, mess up the server. The next day, everyone thinks there's been some sort of bizarre computer malfunction. No one knows the program is gone. That's what I want."

"So there's only one copy?" Tess asked.

"I know it sounds crazy, but yeah, there's only one right now."

Joe wrote in a small notepad. "I've got a good idea for damaging the server, but I don't know how difficult it'll be to transfer the program."

"No problem," Samantha said. "My nephew, Brandon, is a programmer. He'll go with you to do the transfer. You take care of the in and out and messing up the server."

The workingmen went up to the front counter to pay their bill. Joe scanned the room for other suspicious faces. "Strangers and amateurs. I don't go on the job with them."

"Neither do I. If you screw up the transfer, we'll have nothing. If you highjack the program, I have nothing. So you take Brandon."

Joe smiled. "I'm feeling the love here. Okay, you pay the upfront money; we'll take your boy for a ride." He sipped his coffee. "One more thing. We have to get a look at the ground, so you have to provide Tess with a cover for the duration."

"What do you mean?"

"Tess needs complete access to your offices."

"She'll draw attention to me."

"You need your nephew to transfer the program; I need my partner to scout the job."

Samantha looked at Tess. "Have you got any skills?"

"Not the kind you mean. Don't worry. I know how to look busy."

"Looking busy won't be good enough. We're just the new development group. After a security breach a few years back, the board of directors got paranoid and moved us off of the main campus, so we're a small shop. There has to be a reason you're suddenly there." Samantha closed her eyes and rubbed the bridge of her nose. "What will work? Ah," she opened her eyes and pointed at Tess. "You're a temporary intern from the local college. You know, an adult learner on a job shadow. Brandon can drop you into Orion College's database."

Tess nodded. "Sounds good."

Joe rubbed his chin. "So you're at a separate location? Just how tight is your security?"

"Security counter in the lobby by the elevators, surveillance cameras throughout our offices, random security checks, that's about it." Samantha looked from Tess to Joe. "We done here?"

"Almost." Tess smiled softly, showing her perfect white teeth. "Okay, we know what it is. Now we need to know why."

"Why you're doing it is because I'm paying you."

"But why are *you* doing it?" Tess asked.

"That's none of your business."

"Yes it is. The why is often the reason somebody gets caught. And we're not getting caught."

Samantha looked between them out through the picture window. A yellow front-end loader was scooping up the dirty snow that had been piled up in the back parking lot and was dumping it into a dump truck to be moved across town. "I've been with Leapfrog fifteen years. My boss is a jerk. He always steals credit for what I do, claims my ideas, so I get cheated on bonuses and salary. I'm tired of being a doormat. I just want my fair share. Lilypad 5 has a lot of commercial uses. In the right hands it could also be used for industrial espionage. I'm going to sell it to a competitor."

"Already lined up?" Joe asked.

She nodded.

Joe continued. "So your bosses have been screwing you and now you're going to get paid."

Samantha looked into her empty coffee cup. "That's about the size of it."

"What time do you get to the office in the morning?" Tess asked.

"Eight a.m."

"I'll meet you there. After I look around, I'll know whether it's doable."

Joe and Tess watched Samantha leave the restaurant and trudge across the icy parking lot to her car, a silver Camry. Joe motioned to their waitress, a skinny, gray-blonde woman with a smoker's mouth. "This looks like easy money. A couple of days of light work and we're out of here."

Tess blotted her lips and put her napkin on her plate. "But is it our kind of job?"

"She's not a civilian. She's just another amateur crook who can't go to the police. She sought us out. So ripping her off is fair."

"You believe her reason why?"

"The details? I don't know. It sounds close enough to the truth."

"I got to admit, I feel a little sorry for her."

"Tess, really? She could have filed a lawsuit. She could have changed jobs a long time ago. Instead, she's hiring us to rip them off."

"But she didn't even try to bargain down the hundred thousand."

"But she did negotiate the payment schedule and the job specifics. She's a grown-up making her own decisions."

"What about her company?"

"She's going to rob them, so Lilypad 5—the data-mining program —is already gone." Joe tapped his fingers on the table as their waitress neared. They stopped talking.

The waitress stopped at their booth. "Anything else?"

"No thanks."

She set their check down, collected the pie plates, and turned away. Tess continued. "You're right, Joe. Samantha made her choices. She's just going to get what she's got coming. But what can I say? There's something about her—I don't know."

Joe nodded. "I understand. You've got feelings. There but for the grace of God, etcetera, etcetera. Let me ask you this. You think she'll change her mind if we don't take this job, or do you think she'll just find somebody else?"

"She'll find somebody else."

"Exactly. So it might as well be us. She won't like it, but she'll have nothing to complain about when we leave with all the cash."

***

Thanks for reading this sample. *The Computer Heist: The Travelers Book Two* is available at major book retailers.

FINALLY...

Thanks for reading *The Traveling Man*. If you enjoyed it, please post a review on a review site of your choice. A few words will do. Honest reviews are the number one way I attract new readers. Thanks so much.

I'd love to hear from you. You can reach me at my website: https://michaelpking.org.

The Travelers
The Double Cross: A Travelers Prequel Novella
The Traveling Man: Book One
The Computer Heist: Book Two
The Blackmail Photos: Book Three
The Freeport Robbery: Book Four
The Kidnap Victim: Book Five
The Murder Run: Book Six

Made in the USA
San Bernardino, CA
03 August 2019